A Wish

By Alexander James Copping

This book is a work of fiction. Any resemblance to persons, living or dead, or places, events or locations is purely coincidental. Well, mostly. Alright, some of it is.

Part 1

Chapter 1

There can be no burden heavier than that of a secret.

And of all the times I had imagined telling her, this had to rival the worst. Chained to one another, led down a highway somewhere north of Hội An, the Quang Nam Province of Vietnam. The rain had just picked up and began to swirl and dance. Another rough tug and we were on the move, struggling to push our heavy motorbikes through the mud. One hand on our handlebars, one hand chained.

We were armed with only the clothes on our back, dripping in sweat from the four-hour ride, and a wavering notion of what was going to happen to us next. I had heard stories of bribery and corruption fleetingly throughout my time in Asia, each tale acknowledged in the same way as most travelling anecdotes, with a tip of the hat and the careful selection of a superior story to follow up with. I vowed then to learn, to listen.

We had felt invincible just moments earlier, four backpackers navigating one of the most famous routes in the world, the Hai Van Pass. Myself, my best friend Matty and our two companions, the wonderful Grace, wise beyond her years, and Olivia, the girl I fell in love with the moment I saw her. Luck had dealt us the cards that led to our two companions and we were confident, cocky back then, believing in pushing the boundaries of our luck to breaking point.

'Hurry now,' the police officer leading the four of us ordered. 'You hurry now.' His voice was sharp, high pitched, his patched English cutting through the air.

'Excuse me, sir,' I began, assuming my deepest voice in a futile attempt of intimidation. 'I think there's been some kind of mist...'

'Hey now, you no talk!' another policeman barked as he grabbed my shoulder, his grip tightening by the second. His sharp fingernails pressed into my skin. I spoke no more.

There were five police officers altogether, or so we assumed. How were we to know whether these were coppers or con artists, chancers wearing police uniforms, saying the right things? It wouldn't have mattered either way. We were in their world now and at their mercy. Despite all the potential dangers at the hands of these men, I felt a sickness burning a hole in my stomach as my secret hung delicately in the balance of what was to come.

Everything had been going so well. I had finally found a semblance of what I had been looking for and this would undoubtedly change everything. My secret had the power of change, that's for sure. The power to change circumstances, the power to change scenario, but most importantly, the power to change people.

'You follow me now!' the first police officer said as he dragged Matty, followed by Grace, then myself and Olivia in tow. Matty was a quiet soul at the best of times, but I hadn't heard a word from him since the police pulled us over. It was his lack of helmet that must've alerted them in the first place. He was always more intelligent than I was in situations like this. Now wasn't the time for courage or showmanship. That's what had gotten me a baton to the ribs back when they had searched the bikes. My circumstance had made me a little arrogant in those early months backpacking across Asia, traits developing in my character that hadn't surfaced before.

After what felt like an age, a weary grasp of distance and time as semi-seasoned travellers, we could just make out the outline of a shimmering light in the distance. The battle between day and night was over and darkness had plunged over the roadside. We slowly made our way over to a convenience shack, not uncommon in Vietnam, to serve hot meals, beer and fuel. There was a solitary woman sat out on the pavement, under the

3

cover of a ripped tarpaulin, barely batting an eyelid in our direction despite our peculiar appearance.

The leading police officer muttered something in Vietnamese to the woman, who in turn spoke back, still not looking up from her wicker basket, the contents of which I can't even begin to recall. Indistinguishable to our ignorant English ears, it only became clear what the police officer intended when we were led around the side of the shack to the back entrance, where my worst fears were realised. We had come to a cash point.

'Now you pay,' the police officer said, wiping the rain out of his eyes and taking shelter in the alcove. 'You pay now, four million dong, each!'

We had been in Vietnam a little over a month and had begun to develop a basic grasp of the currency. Four million Vietnamese dong roughly equated to 180 pounds back then, a significant sum for the average backpacker. On the surface, I fitted this stereotype with ease, my tired attire, and overgrown beard masking the secret truth about to be uncovered…

'You two, boys, you first!' prodded the third police officer, who had remained silent thus far, his face more hardened than the rest, a man who I hadn't wanted to cross. Unlocking our chains, he shoved us forward, pulling the girls in tow towards the ATM. The light that shone out looked almost celestial, ghostly as we made our way over. We tried to protest, trying to squirm, barter, and beg but it made no difference. I wasn't getting out of this one.

I pulled my cash belt out from under my shorts, and tentatively unzipped the top pocket. We had always travelled with as little cash as possible since arriving in Asia, always relying on the very ATMs that were now to be our downfall. We had agreed to only carry the one card between us, a seemingly ridiculous idea in hindsight.

I pressed my card into the machine, two police officers' eyes burning over my shoulder, a group of six huddled around the emitted light like cavemen huddled around a fire. I knew the moment had arrived. My secret, my burden, my ace in the pocket was about to be revealed on the dusty screen. It was in this moment, the reactions of each one of this strange collection of people, shackled together in central Vietnam, that would define the story of my life.

Chapter 2

I'd always had a strange relationship with money.

Both my mother and father had come from working-class families, with little to no money to go around. It had been through the grit and hard work that my Dad had put himself through university and climbed the ranks of his accountancy firm, Harold Telfer Limited. In doing so, he and my Mum had developed a strong sense of the value of money, as many working-class success stories do. Throughout our upbringing, my brother and I had been lectured time and time again on these values, so much so that we'd developed a decent understanding by our early teens.

I can't say I'd given the issue more than a cursory thought until my 15th birthday, whereby I was given a place on a Football Association referee training course as a gift. Safe to say I was downbeat at best. Although I loved playing football as a teenager, referees were usually on the receiving end of my most practised and eloquent curse words.

'You'll earn yourself twenty quid a game if you get through that training,' encouraged my Dad, staring keenly over the edge of his morning paper.

I looked over to my Mum who was trying on the new earrings she had received for her birthday, which happened to be that very same morning. I couldn't help but feel cheated, aggrieved that I had been bestowed nothing more than a poisoned chalice, a way and means of making me work for what had, up until this point, come to me unearned.

I believe this was the first trace of a thought, an idea that I would later nurture into an ideology to carry with me for long periods of my adult life. I thought to myself, I don't want to be rich, I'd rather be poor and happy. It was a juvenile, infantile response but one that transcended my youth and fashioned its way into the wider context of my life many years later.

I worked plenty of jobs in the years to follow, from refereeing Sunday league football, to picking and packing merchandise in a local warehouse, all the way to slinging drinks in a cheap student bar during my second year of university. I felt like I'd done it all. A twenty-year-old who'd done it all. One in a million.

These jobs had never paid more than the minimum and they'd never given me anywhere near a true embrace of financial security. That being said, they'd never needed to. My dad had supplemented me with small pockets of cash for as long as I could remember. It'd become commonplace for a twenty-pound note to be slid under the table when my mum wasn't looking, to receive a text saying 'check ur bank balance' in times where I'd begun to struggle at university.

I had what most people strive for their entire lives, a financial safety blanket, unfaltering and dependable. I was poor on the surface, rich behind closed doors. It had created an illusion, a mirage, of existing in the poor and happy bracket I had sought in my young teenage years.

Chapter 3

My life had been nothing if not unremarkable. A happy upbringing in the sleepy suburbs of south Manchester was the backdrop to a loving and fulfilled family life.

My mother, Mandy, had two sons, her first coming in 1992. After being told she could not have children of her own, her eldest, Steven, was a miracle in her eyes. So when another arrived a little later she'd truly hit the jackpot. She delivered her youngest on her own birthday, January 29th, 1994.

Alexander Thomas King, the name given by my father, Andrew. A very happy birthday indeed. I'd spoken to my parents countless times about those early years at our family home, their stories overlapping with flickering fond memories of my own, intertwining like broad brush strokes on a virgin canvas.

This story begins many years after those happy childhood memories, in the same place that it started. Our family home. 23 Jester Street was a traditional Victorian semi-detached house, four floors, two gardens. The house was charming and friendly, like many others on the street it boasted a welcoming pathway, leading up to a heavy wide-framed door. This house was the setting to so many of my best memories, nostalgic and sentimental, but as I walked through the front door that summer's afternoon, I couldn't help but feel a little distant and unfamiliar.

'Nice of you to roll out the welcoming committee!' I shouted with a smirk to whoever would listen.

'They're in the garden,' called my Mum, unpacking the remainder of my bags from the car. We'd just made the journey back from Leeds for the final time, the city where I had spent the last three years at university. My stint in Leeds was rewarding in ways I'd never expected, the making of the man, but at that moment it felt as though all I'd been allowed to take home was a recurring headache and a lingering smell.

Nomadically, I pushed on down the hall, the smell of freshly polished wood and detergent, a stranger to my senses. I made my way out of the back door and into the garden, the May sun prickling against my face.

'Pffffft, nice haircut loser,' my older brother Steve shouted as I strolled out onto the freshly cut grass. Steve didn't look too dissimilar to me, tall, dark, broad shoulders, a constant smirk on his face. I struggled to think back to a time where the first thing out of his mouth wasn't an attempt at humour, always the joker.

He may have had a point though, my hair had lost all the style it once had, the undercut had grown out into thick black hair and its curly top, wild and unruly. Steve and my Dad were lounging out on our rickety old deckchairs, a staple for any day of decent weather in Manchester. Steve was beginning to look more like my dad each time I saw him, I thought to myself.

'How am I supposed to afford a haircut these days, Dad stopped bankrolling me years ago didn't you, Dad?' I exclaimed, trying to appear cool and casual as I always did when I hadn't seen my family in a while.

'I don't think I'll ever get to stop bankrolling you two,' quipped my Dad, 'who do you think paid for the petrol for that journey back from uni?'

'I didn't see you in the car, so I'm guessing Mum paid!'

'Mum…' he laughed, 'now we're talking bankrolling!'

This wasn't an unfamiliar reunion in the King household. My dad was a partner at a local accountancy firm and a very successful one at that. He somehow defied each and every stereotype of what an accountant was supposed to be—larger than life, both funny and charming, he was a very difficult man to find boring. His passion for his work was only surpassed by his love for his wife and children, a love he expressed through sarcasm and jibes as opposed to any real signs of affection. I liked it this way, we all did.

'Are you three talking about money already?' My Mum had just walked out into the garden with four bottles of Budweiser and a tray of what I could only assume was one of her trademark 'different things' dishes as she called it. She had an uncanny ability to hold a million things at once despite her diminutive height. She could always be trusted to provide food and drink in every scenario, always served with a brilliant smile and the kindest of eyes. A caterer in days gone by, she was a lot more tactile than her husband, a true host who loved nothing more than keeping those around her happy.

Mum handed out the beers one by one, the bottle feeling cold and familiar in my hand. At that moment I could see the upcoming summer months playing out in my head like a rolled-out film reel. Family time out in the garden, nourishing meals in front of the TV, a smattering of nights out with school friends, and endless hours spent at the end of my fingertips, swiping through whatever dating app took off next. I enjoyed the comfortable nature of my life in Manchester, its predictability a welcome contrast to those wild nights at university. I was ready to move home.

'I'd like to propose a toast!' sang Mum, once the beers had been handed out. 'To the return of my baby Alex, home again at last.'

'Here, here,' grunted my Dad, already swigging his beer.

'Speech!' Steve heckled, always the joker.

Although this could hardly be considered public speaking, there was something about social expectation that had always thrown me off, made me feel uneasy. I think it had always cast me back to earlier memories of the prickled heat in my ears when

I'd handed in an assignment that I'd half-arsed or not given enough attention to.

Despite these momentary pangs of internal anxiety, I'd always had a knack for outwardly displaying confidence, nights spent on YouTube tutorials about maintaining eye contact, taking mental notes from my more natural, extroverted friends chatting up girls at our local bar.

I cleared my throat, 'Well, well home at last,' I began, looking around into my family's faces. 'It's safe to say I won't be boring you with an "Andy King" special this afternoon, as we only have a couple of hours of sun left in the garden.' I watched my Dad eagerly, his speeches at my brother and I's birthdays infamous for their humour and wit. 'But I will say, after three rambunctious years…'

'Rambunctious!' Steve interrupted, 'Check out the history grad now.'

'Watch out mate, I'm technically on track to be the smartest King of the bunch,' I laughed, trying to get a rise out of my Dad. After no bites, I pressed ahead. 'After my three years at uni, I can safely say I've done my fair share of partying and now I'm ready for a hard-earned rest back in sleepy Sale.' I knew this would please my Mum, who'd been pining for me to come home much more often than had been the case.

'I think we can all drink to that!' she cried, and we all clattered our beers together jovially, maintaining eye contact as was customary in our family.

'Wait, wait, wait. I've got something for you Alex,' my brother laughed, fumbling around in his shorts pocket. He pulled out a small, crumpled card and chucked it over in my direction. It picked up a slight breeze, danced, and landed in my outstretched palm.

11

'Takes!' I yelled, a personal joke between Steve and I whenever a catch was made and we began to laugh even more. It was good to see him again.

I slowly unfurled the card to reveal what appeared to be a euro millions scratch card, untarnished, unrevealed. Noticing my confused reaction, my brother spoke. 'I grabbed a couple on my way home from the pub last night, welcome home little brother.' he chuckled, 'Maybe you can stop scrounging off Dad if you win!'

It was not out of the ordinary for my brother to chance his luck on this type of venture. He fit the typical bloke stereotype pretty comfortably, loving his beers, football, and women, nights spent down the bookies, or at the casino if he was feeling particularly gutsy.

I slid down onto the nearest garden chair, placed my beer on the wooden table, and laughed as I checked my pockets for a coin, unsurprisingly to no avail.

Noticing my struggle, my brother rolled his eyes. 'Honestly, you're unbelievable...' he sighed, passing me a twenty-pence piece. I shrugged, flashing him a grin, and began to scrape away at the corner of the grey wax coating.

'Do I get a better welcome home gift from you two?' I glanced over with a smile to my Mum and Dad. 'I've never won anything on one of these things!'

'You get enough from us Alex you little chancer,' my Dad said. 'You're stuck with that I'm afraid.'

'Let's see how lucky I really am then!'

I scraped around the card in no particular order, my gung ho strategy to cleanse the card of its mystery before checking whatever I'd needed to win. It was beginning to cool down in the garden now, devoid of shade, the time approaching 3 p.m. I was making strong progress across the multiple boxes, each their own mini-game, promising untold riches and prizes.

Thinking back to this moment, I wasn't paying too much attention to the icons and pictures I was revealing one by one, my mind harboured elsewhere, thinking of what I would do with the upcoming evening or who would be around at the weekend, maybe my old flame Sarah May was back from uni? My attention span was short at the best of times, distracted by the typical musings of a 21-year-old.

A sharp gasp snapped my focus back to the present. I looked up to see my brother, who had been watching my progress over my shoulder, his face as serious as I'd ever seen it.

'Alex, mate,' he whispered.

He was glowering down at the little piece of crumpled card in my hand, his glare unwavering. I allowed my gaze to follow. My eyes darted from left to right, bottom to top. And then I saw it. A neat row of euro million-pound signs lined up like an orderly queue, patiently awaiting instruction.

I'd read about moments, fleeting or otherwise, in my favourite novels growing up. Moments that change the course of a person's life, how one simple act can have a ripple effect and alter the destiny of hundreds, thousands even. Never had I felt one of these moments so clearly, so tangibly take place in front of my eyes. I scanned the card to the very top, reading the words that were about to change my life forever.

JACKPOT: £20,000,000.

Chapter 4

The hours that followed passed by in a frenzied blur. Everyone has fantasised about how they'd react if they came into a significant sum of money, be it through the lottery, a winning bet, or even a distant relative passing.

Our reaction was no different to how you would imagine it to pass. Screaming, shouting, hugging, kissing, I think there was Champagne, although it might've been Prosecco?

We'd rang the helpline on the card to double-check this was really happening, and they promptly confirmed the news: twenty million pounds. Someone was having me on, I remember thinking, refusing to accept this new reality. Soon after, rushed words about what to spend, when to spend, and how to spend it. Granted, the main bulk of this incessant speculation was coming from my brother and I, outwardly daydreaming of the holidays, cars, and women we would, in our heads, inevitably come to possess.

I remember looking over to my parents, my mum's head rested on the shoulder of my dad, tears in her eyes. My parents had always been wise, for as long as I can remember. I had always looked to them for advice and reassurance on things I didn't understand. However, at this moment I remember distinctly noticing the unfamiliar look of cautious unknowing, juxtaposed with their usual reassuring smiles.

Hours passed in the same manner, the four of us sat in the garden, eating, drinking, and laughing. From an outside perspective, it would appear we were celebrating nothing more than a regular homecoming, a birthday, or a new job, perhaps with a little more enthusiasm than what was customary. That being said, we had always been a little more enthusiastic than the next family.

'Right then, let's get one thing straight,' my dad said, in a voice uncharacteristic of the mood, 'you are not to tell anyone about this until we have discussed the outcome as a family, understood?'

'Sure, yes, of course,' we chimed, barely listening.

'I'm sure you're both bright enough to understand the impact of broadcasting news of such a sum of money, especially at your ages.'

'Not only to strangers but also friends and family right now!' added my mum, her voice wavering a little.

I immediately thought of my friends, Matty, Turner, and Brown Shoes (don't ask). What they would say, how they would react when I dropped the news upon them. I had been best friends with them since I was 12 years old and we told each other everything.

'I've got to tell the boys though...' I muttered, still not thinking clearly, I remember my voice sounded strange and croaky.

'You absolutely will not,' Dad said, 'not until we've got our heads around it, that's for sure. There will be time for all that later down the line, we need to make sure that we're responsible about this.'

It was clear there were going to be disagreements in the time to follow. How could there not be, with such differing characters in myself, my brother, Mum, and Dad? That being said, the thought never crossed my mind that we wouldn't work things out. These were the people I loved most and who I trusted beyond all others, we were family.

Day had turned to night, with the last corner of sunshine creeping out of sight in our south-facing suburban garden. We carried on talking, navigating through conversational hurdles,

15

spurts of excitement, fear, and awaiting the unknown. The countless times I'd discussed what I would do in this dream scenario, I had always asserted that I'd be straight out on the town, drinks on me, inviting friends from far and wide for an almighty blowout. But now it'd come to it, I already had far too much to drink and it was starting to take its toll. Perhaps tonight was not the night to go big. There would be plenty of time for that.

I remember lying awake long into the night, pondering what may or may not come to pass. I thought again of my friends, who had long been my most dependable source of enjoyment, trust, and who had frequently reminded me over the course of the last year that the upcoming summer would be the best of our lives. I knew I would soon be able to tell them that our empty fantasies of endless possibilities had now transitioned into the realm of absolute certainty.

Chapter 5

The previous summer with my old school friends had delivered so much, jumping from festival to festival, one corner of the country to another, rain or shine we were at it. We'd all dispersed across the UK for university, frequent visitors to my house in Leeds, Matty in Liverpool, Edinburgh for Turner, whilst Brown Shoes (again, don't ask) stayed local at Manchester University.

The relative distance only proved to strengthen the already stable bonds we knew we'd forged through footy in the playground, chasing girls, and ridiculous personal jokes in our adolescent years. We'd been planning the upcoming summer through Facebook messages and disjointed facetime calls for the better part of 2015. The plan was simple, a concoction of four masterminds' ingenuity. We were going travelling.

We'd embarked on the trip of a lifetime, two years prior, traversing what we deemed the unmissable cities of Europe. We flew to Amsterdam, Airbnb'd in Berlin, wandered through Prague, stopped in Krakow, prolonged our stay in Budapest, stumbled to Bratislava and finally collapsed in Vienna, weary and in desperate need of sleep. I still look back on that trip with fondness, a coming of age for all of us.

If I wasn't already desperate to see them all for the first time since Christmas, I certainly was now, dragging along my riches like an overpacked suitcase of my Mum's. I'd just that morning prevailed in a two-day-long skirmish with my parents to let me tell the boys my news, providing they promised to keep it to themselves and their families.

I'd arranged a time and place, at 4 p.m. at our old local boozer, the Steam House, Sale. It felt as though tradition demanded we return to the place we'd formulated so many plans, executed and abandoned, for perhaps a planning session the likes of which we'd never had before.

'I'm off to the pub,' I called quietly, hoping no one would hear. The last thing I wanted was the admission of second thoughts, more factors to consider.

'Wait a sec, I'm coming down!' I heard from upstairs, my Mum with her supersonic hearing. There were muffled voices and the sound of a door slamming shut. She made her way downstairs, not taking her eyes off me for the duration. She looked well, if not a little stressed.

'Don't worry, don't worry, I'm not going to lecture you,' she smiled. She did always have a knack for reading my face I thought, feeling my stance soften. 'I just wanted to wish you luck, I know you've been desperate to tell the boys since we found out about this money malarky.'

'Thanks, Mum, I'm looking forward to it, they'll all be buzzing that even one round is on me, let alone the whole lot,' I said, trying to keep the tone light.

'Just one last word of advice before you shoot off then.' She gave me a hug, a hug only a mother can give. 'Don't get carried away, Alex. And before you say 'I won't Mum' I don't just mean tonight. This is a big change and I know you have a tendency to push your limits at times...'

'I know, I know, Mum. You know I'm not stupid and I won't let this take over my life. I'm happy enough as it is, so being able to buy a few extra things and go on a few more trips is really just a bonus, you know?' I wanted to do better to reassure her, I really did. But the draw of the pub and my best friends proved too strong, so with a kiss on the cheek I pulled away, grabbed my keys, and I was gone.

I lived a fifteen-minute walk from the pub in Sale town centre and spent the duration of the journey rehearsing what I'd say to break the news, whether to lead with a joke or simply show them my bank balance, thoughts churning around my jumbled mind. I wasn't confident in my resolve to not blabber out my news upon immediate arrival, so I'd organised the others to meet half an hour earlier. I wanted to break it to the group together.

I could be quite meticulous like that, arranging things to play out exactly how I wanted them to. I remember a few years prior I was looking for a photo to frame as a mother's day gift, in our attic. I stumbled across some old school reports and one, in particular, jumped out to me, a year three teacher assessment; 'Alex can be quite a manipulative little boy, always trying to impress his peers and get others to follow.' Condemning words to say about a 6-year-old. He sounds like a barrel of laughs to me.

The blazing sun we'd been treated to over the past couple of days had selfishly subsided, relenting to a much more typical Manchester summer's composition, a gentle breeze kissing my face as I pounded the pavement. It was a Saturday evening and a palpable buzz was in the air as I trod the familiar route into the town centre, like a detective retracing his steps.

As I approached, my breathing quickened, unable to stop myself feeling nervous and edgy. I tried to spot my friends through the lightly frosted glass windows, to no avail. Maybe they were late? I looked up at the town hall, only 30 metres from the Steam House, the industrial clock read 4.26 p.m. give or take. They should be here.

I took a breath, composed myself, and pushed open the pub doors.

'Ayyyyy!' A distinct chorus intersected the dull roar of the pub's regular patrons. My eyes were drawn up the stairs, the first table on the left. Perfect spot to observe, to dissect the punters in their natural habitat who never strayed from the norm, all drinking the same drinks year after year. We'd always struggled to not consider ourselves a little better than the typical Sale pub regular. I had shallow tendencies in those years, always valuing those I knew and respected above all others, ignorant to the troubles of those not in my immediate circle.

I locked eyes with my friends and immediately broke into laughter, Brown Shoes first, his grin cheesy and becoming. Tall, slim, short brown hair, by far the funniest guy I knew, he'd gained the nickname for… well, we won't get into that right now. It'd always suited him more than his given name, Connor, and he'd been stuck with it for life.

Harris Turner to his right, two beers in hand, the look in his eye signalling one was for me. A kind face, short frame, and cool fashion sense, Turner had a reserved demeanour, less boisterous than the rest of us, but commanded unsaid respect that I'd always envied a little. He was my oldest friend.

Last but by no means least, was Matty Ford, arm resting on the bannister, a smile curled. We were probably the closest duo, typically the one to spearhead plans by my side. We were similar in so many ways, often mistaken for brothers, although we didn't share much likeness in appearance. He was slight and fair-haired, an aspiring musician, too cool for school. This made up our merry quartet, we were unstoppable, unbreakable, undeniable kindred spirits.

As I made my way up the staircase to join my friends, all the tension slipped away, like a snake shedding skin. What was I worried about?

'Fucking yes lad!' called Brown Shoes, drawing an eye or two from groups nearby. 'The wanderer returns, ey?' Sporting his usual baseball cap and wax jacket, he looked the same as always.

'Evening fellas, how are we?' I leapt the last of the stairs and skidded into an embrace with Matty, first up from the table. 'Long time, long time.'

'Too long mate, you good?' he grinned, loosening his grip and allowing Brown Shoes to take his place, his hug tighter and more natural.

'Always, boys. Turner, get in here you little fucker.' I laughed as Turner rolled his eyes with a smile and joined me for the final embrace.

'Great to see you brother,' he said. I hadn't seen Turner since Christmas, his university life in Edinburgh was busy and too geographically challenging for regular visits.

'Now then, where do we fucking start?!' I chuckled, feeling an optimum three-pint buzz before taking a sip. To be honest, I would've been just as excited to spend time with my old friends had the situation been unremarkable, without any news to share. I held on to this feeling tightly, assuming that it kept me grounded, wanting to keep things as normal as possible given the circumstances.

'Let's start with why you're half an hour late you joker,' pressed Turner. 'If I've ever been five minutes late in the past I get an almighty scolding from you.'

'Not just you mate, the guy's a slave driver, I swear down.' continued Matty, 'He was banging on yesterday about how I *had* to be there at 4.00 p.m. sharp. I was shitting myself arriving at 10 past!' he laughed.

'I dunno, I'm always late.' chuckled Brown Shoes. He had a face that made people laugh, no matter what he said.

'I had things to do, people to see, you know how it is.' I wanted this back and forth to last an age. The last few moments of blissful ignorance before I dropped the bombshell. 'Anyway, I dunno why we're all sat here like idiots without cheersing each other?!' I knitted my eyebrows in a fashion I hoped was disbelief and raised my pint above the table.

'Cheers!' we shouted in disjointed unison, catching each other's eyes, spilling our drinks. I can't imagine there was a notable difference between us and the next group of guys, sitting in their local, drinking cheap lager. But as with anyone immersed in their own story, I truly believed I'd been blessed with the best set of friends in the world.

We spent the next hour catching up on the usual stuff: girls, university, family, friends far and wide. Turner had met a girl, Natalie Freeman, and had been dating her for a few months. She was a Liverpool born scouser living in Edinburgh, an intellect and looked adorable on her Facebook pictures. It was great to see him happy, his dating history inconsistent, he never really took to the sleeping around aspect of uni like the rest of us.

Brown Shoes was a chemistry graduate, categorically the smartest guy I knew. He was bound to get a first, despite his close relationship with the inside of any pub, bar, or watering hole.

As for Matty, I didn't need to catch up with him really, we'd been on the phone every other day, scheming and forecasting the future, whilst simultaneously delving into the ins and outs of our daily lives. If anything, it felt like I'd seen him just yesterday.

'What about you, Kingy?' quizzed Brown Shoes, 'We've been chatting on for over an hour and you've been unusually quiet. What's been going on with you recently?' Perceptive as ever.

They all look up from their beers, expectantly. Time to shine, batter up.

'Let's pop out for a ciggie, ey?' I muse, we'd already drawn a lot of attention to ourselves earlier, boys hugging each other wasn't the most inconspicuous ritual in northern Sale. We all stood, each one of my friends drawing for their lighters and tobacco in unison. 'Oh, can I bump a rollie?' I laughed sheepishly, a sense that irony had loomed its elusive head.

'Typical, shouts a cig break with no cigs to speak of,' sniggered Matty, handing me a set of rolling papers on our way down the stairs.

We push out the backdoors into the makeshift smoking area – a slant of corrugated iron propped over three slabs of concrete paving, just off the side of the car park. There was a chill in the air as dusk began to take hold of the summer's night. We each took a seat in the deserted alcove, a four-person table awaiting us. 'How apt,' I thought to myself.

We rolled in relative silence, I remember my thoughts convulsing, struggling to tuck the paper and butchering the roll. The calm before the storm.

'Well as it so happens fellas, I've got a bit of good news for you.'

Chapter 6

I guess I'd always been lucky with friendships, never struggling to win people over and always seemingly in the right place at the right time. I believed I had the best people in my school year, secured a great flat in my university first-year halls, the green man always did seem to wave at me as I crossed the road. In those days, I toyed with this thought process a lot, whether luck was indeed of my own self-making or whether there was something else, manifesting around those who consciously chose to believe in that kind of stuff.

I think that was always my main internal conflict, never caring much for religion or even science for that matter. It was always the concept of fortune that sparked my interest. Perhaps not in the traditional way however, I was never one to gamble much or to test myself at games of chance. I threw a quid on the occasional football accumulator, but that's just because everyone else was doing it. I was interested in how one perceives luck, with a particular circumstance leaving one person cursing and another thanking the heavens.

I remember the summer of 2014, my Dad had taken us to Las Vegas for Steve's 21st birthday. We'd always been taken on borderline ridiculous family holidays, island hopping the Caribbean or a fortnight in Ibiza and this trip to Vegas was no different. My brother had taken his earnings from the recruitment job he'd been holding down, I think it amounted to around two grand in dollars. It'd been poorly timed from my perspective as I'd just finished my second year of university and spent all my money on the UK festival circuit, Glastonbury, Bestival, and Parklife.

Over the course of the trip, he and my parents had spent frequently on the slots, roulette, even a couple hands at the blackjack table when they'd had a few for dutch courage. Typically, I'd had to borrow a few hundred dollars from my Dad to pay my way. On the final night of the trip, I was left with around $200, spending little and getting lucky. My brother and I were a few beers down, admiring a roulette table in the MGM Grand Hotel when I decided to chance my luck one more time.

I sat down, changed my $200 for chips, and put it all on black. It was the most sizable bet of the week and in this instance, I rode my luck. It came in. My brother clapped his hand on my back in congratulations.

'My turn,' he grinned, his intentions clear. He cashed $400 and put it all on red for the next spin.

The wheel spun.

8 Black.

Curious game, the old chance.

Chapter 7

'Fuck off, what're you on about?'

'Shut the fuck up.'

'Good one, little fucker.'

The smoking area of the Steam House in Sale, my Royal Albert Hall, the expletives of three Mancunians, the orchestra. This had gone on for several minutes since I'd stumbled over my rehearsed delivery and told my best friends I was rich.

I'd always fancied myself as pretty decent at reading people's faces, but at this moment, four pints deep, I was struggling to identify the exact emotions taking over the facial muscles of the boys in front of me.

Brown Shoes, perhaps the least concealed, was displaying some form of queasy disbelief, the sides of his mouth quivering and eyebrows introduced to his hairline. Turner, ever composed and measured, had begun to maniacally laugh, a man possessed, the remnants of lager still bubbling down his chin. Finally, Matty, straight-faced, watery eyes fixated on an insignificant point in the distance, a look I can only describe as inspired madness.

I drank the moment in. It was significant in more ways than one, although I had a blinkered vision at that time. It felt great to uncover the secret, share the load, spill the barrel of beans. We were now in this together, brothers in arms. I saw this as our win, our good fortune and as a means for the four of us to do as we saw fit, no limitations holding us back.

'Well, what are we waiting for?' I finally said, breaking a rare 10 seconds of silence since the last gasping laugh or stifled celebration.

'Yeah… yeah…. What on God's green earth are we going to do?' Brown Shoes exclaimed, seemingly finding his feet in reality again.

'Fucking hell, imagine what this summer is going to be like now…' Turner said. He was gradually regaining composure as well, putting himself back together, wiping his chin.

'We'll get to the summer later, you crazy bastards!' Matty shouted, then immediately lowered his voice. 'Imagine what tonight is going to be like…'

This is why I liked Matty, he had an undeniable grasp on the present, whilst casting an eye to the future. It was never one or the other. It was what we needed right now, with the prospect of losing the night to frenzied planning a real possibility. I was desperate to celebrate.

'Right, let's weigh up the options.' I wanted to help steer this ship in the right direction. 'We're four best mates with unlimited money, it's 6 p.m. Saturday, what do we want to do?' My eyes scanned across the smoking area. My friends' interest had unquestionably been sparked.

So followed a booze-fuelled brainstorm of the ages, a meeting of minds, traversing the tightrope between genius and madness. We started the debate small, what drink would we get next, whether to invite the other boys, Caleb and Sam or better yet if any girls would come to meet us?

As time went on, the rapturous discussion toppled into what nights out or raves were on in the city that night. We flirted with the thought of tickets to London, we talked of grabbing our passports. Each idea receiving slaps on the back and furious fist bumps. We were innovators, of that there was no doubt. The more left-field the shout, the more thunderous support it got as the drinks ebbed and flowed.

'I'm obviously backing all of that stuff!' Turner shouted, his usual eloquence failing him, in exchange for more primal, meat-head dialect.

'It's a good job we all went to uni, otherwise, we'd be wasted by now!' Brown Shoes slurred, as he tried to wipe up his spilled lager.

'No time to be drunk, we've got the whole night for that!' Matty proclaimed, his eyes closed firmly shut.

Someone, a genius, had the idea to move over to the adjacent pub, the JP Joule, Wetherspoons, for a 'swift one' before embarking on our impending, momentous undertaking. Four more pints ordered, my bank card a chariot, we sat down in a four-man booth.

'How apt,' I shout, wondering whether I'd said that earlier.

'Now, now, now. Let's get one thing straight before we hit the road, yes?' I realised that in the midst of all this discussion, I'd forgotten to reveal my master plan. 'Now we've got our golden ticket, I wanted to announce just one thing.' I may have been slurring. 'Now I'm sure you'll agree with me when I say with great power comes great responsibility. So now I've got this lucky ticket, I've decided in my infinite wisdom that you're all coming travelling with me whether you like it or not. We're buying one-way tickets to Thailand tomorrow! Agreed?'

The boys fell silent. I don't remember the exact reaction I wanted or expected. I doubt I'd given it much thought, the big scratch card reveal occupying the lion's share of my headspace in the days approaching. My intoxication aside, I knew it was asking a lot to expect three separate people to up sticks and embark on such an immense trip, requiring each of them to uproot and leave the families they had just returned to. We had discussed the possibility at length in the past, especially Matty and I, countless evenings spent talking route, destination, and endless variables to the finest detail. But none of us were prepared to execute the plan so soon. We had all been devoid of the finances, four university students in their first week back at home. It was a big ask.

Matty was the first to speak. 'Mate, if you're saying what I think you're saying… you're asking us to join you on a trip across the world, recreating the interrailing trip of 2013 to the tune of multi-millions of Her Majesty's English pounds?' He paused for dramatic effect. 'I for one, have only one word for you… *Obviously!*'

He slammed his drink down on the table, so hard in fact that it sent a half-eaten packet of pork scratchings on the end of the table spiralling onto the floor. The action, so primal, had its desired effect. Turner and Brown Shoes sprung into gear, so synchronised it suggested there'd been some kind of prior agreement or rehearsal.

'Try and stop me, fella.' Turner was precise, surgical, to the point. There was no messing about with Turner. He caught my eye, subtle and unnoticed by the others, and expressed his gratitude and confirmation with nothing more than a cursory look. I'd always had an unspoken bond with him, forged through years living so close in proximity, sharing walks to and from school, and putting the world to rights.

'You lot would be clueless without me to be fair, who'd learn the language?' Brown Shoes joked. Whilst interrailing through Berlin, Brown Shoes had successfully talked us into a European techno super-club called the Berghain, using a potent combination of smattered year 10 German class learnings and flamboyant, engaging body language.

'Browners, you'll end up marrying a local within a week, you joker,' I said, unable to wipe the grin off my face.

'Shit, I hadn't even thought about the girls out there...' he whispered, dropping off into a drunken daydream.

My best friends were with me, on what promised to be the best time of our lives. I couldn't shake the feeling of fate, destiny, whatever you want to call it. Maybe it was the eighth pint talking, manipulating the mundane into the extraordinary, but I felt like that night was the start of something truly significant.

From what I remember past this point, the prospects of debauchery in the promised land quickly transitioned to a longing for kebab meat and a place to rest our weary heads. The wild nights weren't going anywhere we assured ourselves as we stumbled to Tastebuds, a chicken shop just a few doors down, a siren song's smell luring many fatigued Saturday night sailors to an early demise.

A double spicy chicken burger, large chips with peri-peri salt and gravy signalled that the first night of our reign as champions of the universe had come to an end. We bid each other fond farewells, the untold promise of what was to come palpable in the air. We embraced as brothers, Matty and Brown Shoes heading towards Northern Sale Moor, Turner and I back towards Ashton on Mersey, a spring in the step of each of us after a night we'd not forget in a hurry. Well, not entirely forget.

I wish I remembered the conversation en route home with more clarity, I can only imagine the pearls of wisdom a misty-eyed Turner would be able to formulate off the back of a night like this. I vaguely remember an attempt at a heart to heart, swiftly dismissed by stifled laughter and a forced hug at the end of his street.

Back again at the end of my road, a two-minute walk to my family home. I took the journey at a stroll, basking in the success of the night and in a state of blissful reflection. I dismissed notions that I'd forgotten something, creeping in and out of my mind. No time to dwell on negativity now, we were really going, my best friends and I, on another adventure.

Chapter 8

Bleurgh.

Those last few days had played host to a whole catalogue of unfamiliar emotions, redefining the scale at which I believed each of my feelings could stretch, accentuating the ordinary to the extraordinary. That morning, however, I was presented with a feeling I knew well. My mouth bitter and barren, the corner of my eyes a crusty habitat, a bass drum in my head. The feeling was one I had endured through plenty of practise, an expert honing his craft. Absolutely worth it, I thought to myself as I grasped for the sacred chalice of water on my bedside table and groaned, head emerging from a dungeon of linen and pillows.

It was Sunday morning, just shy of 9 a.m. I'd never been one to enjoy a lie-in, the benefits alien to me as such an inconsistent sleeper. I had slept soundly up until my teenage years where a combination of late-night videogames and an introduction to heavy boozing had bucked the trend.

I pulled open the heavy blackout blinds, cleansing the room of its darkness. The sun was shining bright in the sky, intense and majestic, a few dotted clouds compromising an otherwise spotless morning vista. I scanned around my childhood bedroom, a room I had called my own for 18 years, nostalgia surrounding each piece of furniture, occupying every space where posters and wall art used to hang.

There wasn't much personality left in there, I thought, the majority of my old belongings buried in the chestnut wardrobe unit or locked away in the attic. I can only imagine the plans I'd have for the room had I been resigned to moving home for the foreseeable future. My room at university had been plastered wall to wall with photos of friends, canvases of my favourite bands and other miscellaneous tat I thought made me look cool.

I could hear the faint sounds of movement emanating from downstairs, likely my mum pottering about with chores, my dad in tow to lend a hand. With one final stretch, wide and exaggerated, I slung my legs from underneath the covers and made for the bedroom door. I had an idea of how I wanted the day to play out, scheming as always – I'd hoped for no curveballs.

My family and I had discussed the big picture of what we'd do with our newfound riches intermittently, but I wanted to clarify some details before pressing ahead with the more exciting chapter of my plan: booking plane tickets for Thailand. I had already assured my parents that they'd be trusted to donate or shrewdly invest the lion's share of the cash, £20 million was an incomprehensible amount of money after all, especially to a broke uni student at the time.

With Dad being a successful accountant, he was the natural council I sought in knowing the best course of action to take with such a large amount of money. My brother Steve, I'd decided, could have as much as he wanted. I mean he'd bought the winning scratch card in the first place. I didn't give too much thought to what he'd do with the money, my mind introspectively focused, too cloudy to dissect his motives.

To my surprise, as I trotted down the carpeted staircase, I heard my brother's voice amongst the conversation in the kitchen. I couldn't think of a time I'd seen him surface before 10 a.m. for the duration of our adult lives. Although we looked and sounded like brothers, we were very different people. He was a creature of comfort, in his element sitting in front of the TV watching football with Dad. I guess that's why I didn't pay much attention to how he'd spend the money, most likely collecting retro football shirts and buying video game add ons.

'Morning all!' I chirped, executing a fool-proof impression of sober Alex as I pushed open the kitchen door.

'You're still drunk, dirty Herbet,' lectured my mum without looking up from the stove. She was tending to an oversized frying pan, overflowing with bacon rashers, sausages sliced length-ways, fried eggs, and what smelled like garlic mushrooms. God, I loved my mum.

'How did last night go, Alex?' Steve called from the conservatory adjacent to the kitchen. His voice sounded guttural, compromised by the preceding night, much like my own.

'Yeah, very good. Ended up staying in stinky Sale though, typical.' I nodded at him and Dad as I took a seat on the empty sofa. 'Did you go out?'

'Yep, we were in Sale as well, Carter's Arms obviously,' Steve said.

'Eurgh, what a dive. We stayed around central, did you end up telling any of your lot?' I asked, hopeful the answer would be no. I had never taken to Steve's friends, all reinforcing the stereotype I'd been fighting against growing up, a typical Sale boy, rough, dimwitted, harbouring little to no ambition outside the confines of our hometown.

'Na, but they probably suspect something's up, I was buying rounds all night.' he laughed, 'I doubt I'll end up telling anyone the extent of it, most likely tell them I got lucky on an accumulator early next season or something.'

I held in a sigh of relief. Not a chance his mates would keep quiet if they found out, unlike my lot.

'Did your friends say they'd keep it to themselves?' Dad interjected, putting the newspaper down and focusing on me.

Shit. Had I told them to keep it quiet? I honestly couldn't remember, I was so caught up in dropping the news and planning ahead, had I forgotten the one condition my parents gave me?

'Yeah, I'm sure... they will do,' I deflected, faltering my delivery.

33

'Well did you tell them to?' Dad asked, sitting up straight, eyes fixed.

'Yeah, I definitely mentioned it, they won't tell anyone anyway they're not stupid,' I said, greeted with a flashback of Brown Shoes attempting to purchase a chicken burger with his library card the night prior.

My dad didn't look impressed. 'Well let's hope not,' he said, reaching for his paper again, having made his point.

'Anyway, what are you doing awake Steve?' Perhaps not the most subtle change of subject. 'I've not seen you at this hour since we were kids.'

'Far too excited to sleep, little brother.' he said, beaming. 'I've started the flat hunt this morning.' He beckoned over to me, holding his phone like a trophy.

Of course. He'd been talking about getting his own place for the better part of a year. We'd discussed it last time he rang me, about a month earlier as I was approaching my last exams in Leeds. He'd moaned that living at home had become a drag since graduating and the job wasn't for him anymore. His plan was to save up as much as he could and then beg Dad to spot him a deposit for a flat in the city centre. How times had changed.

I made my way over and checked his phone, scanning the real estate website he'd had open, '£450,000!' I gasp, 'you're having me on!'

He laughed, a deep belly laugh this time. 'What? Did you think I was gonna get a bungalow in Urmston? Time to start spending our cash, Alex!'

I saw Dad roll his eyes from behind the newspaper. Saying that, my brother had a point. I hadn't grasped the dynamic of this new reality whatsoever. I remembered back to last night, continuing to buy rounds of Fosters, the cheapest pint on offer, even after I'd broken the news. Creatures of habit, set in our ways, it wouldn't be easy to adjust to this new lavish lifestyle.

'Breakfast!' came the call from the kitchen, my mum, as shrill as she was sweet. We each rose from our respective sofas and pottered in, senses stimulated, ready to feast. We always ate well in the King household, beneficiaries of Mum's culinary past. That morning certainly did not disappoint, a full English fry up spread across the table, coffee, juice alongside an army of hotly buttered toast.

We quietly ate, sidestepping the topic of money as much as possible at my mum's request. She claimed the dinner table was no place for that kind of talk and I appreciated her for it. The conversations we'd had previously hadn't all gone smoothly, a progressive edge developing each time. The dynamic in my family had been set in stone our entire lives. My dad the provider, the hunter, my mum the gatherer, my brother and I the grateful recipients. It was a balance that worked. I had a limited concept of this delicate poise back then, believing nothing would change between us, no matter how extraneous the circumstances.

RING-RING… RING-RING…

A succession of short classic rings, intruders in the room. I shrugged my shoulders in protest of my family's disapproving looks, it wasn't great etiquette to take a call at the table.

I shuffled to the left of my chair, pulling my phone out of the pocket of my tracksuit bottoms and without looking, accepted the call.

'Yes, mate! It's Caleb, what's this I hear about you being a millionaire?'

Chapter 9

Each city researched, the route mapped out, tickets booked, nothing to stop us conquering the continent. Interrailing 2013 was one of my greatest memories.

On the one hand, the trip had been easy to organise, Turner taking the predominant lead. He had a sensible head on his shoulders, an aptitude for navigation, and a keen hiker. We'd arranged a weekend to meet up in Liverpool a couple of months earlier to finalise the details, all travelling from our respective universities to Matty's first-year halls.

Matty knocked around with a group of five boys, two from down south, Chris Jenkins and Howard Long, both of whom I got along with well, later becoming some of my closest friends. The remaining two were our school friends from Manchester, Sam Maler and Caleb Anderson. Visits to Liverpool University were frequent because of this, three for the price of one.

As could be expected, there'd been some discussion about who'd be coming on the trip, the social politics that can only be created by an exclusive guest list. Matty and I were a given, the founders of the idea, inciting enough of a buzz to get it off the ground. Turner and Brown Shoes next, our best friends, their invitation never in doubt. We'd need them anyway for where we excelled in formulation, we lacked in execution, prone to getting carried away and led off track. They added a balance to the trip, key ingredients, the salt to our pepper.

We'd certainly entertained the idea of inviting all of our friends – school, university, or otherwise – but we knew a sizable group of guys would potentially deter other backpackers, principally females. That left the quandary of what to do with Sam and Caleb.

At this time, Sam would've been my first choice. We'd been in the same form during school, sharing a number of lessons together, similar in our levels of focus and distraction. We'd always been close. The only reason he wasn't a cert for the trip was through his own volition, distancing himself quite a lot in his first year at university, a boy meets girl story taking up the majority of his time. I remember being happy for him but we were single, nineteen-year-old boys planning a trip around Europe. The last thing we needed was one of our companions to be pining after a girl he'd left at home. So it transpired, he booked a separate trip with her that summer, and the decision was taken out of our hands, a blessing in her best disguise I guess.

That left Caleb, six foot seven, larger than life, quite the character. Youngest of four brothers, he was competitive and brash, harbouring a mild inferiority complex that can only be fostered in such an environment. He had his sense of humour on his side though, undeniably hilarious and gift baskets of gab. I'm pretty sure he was the inventor of the Facebook hack, somehow guessing passwords and setting embarrassing status' across each one of his brothers' accounts. If I had one friend who I could rely on to make a good impression it was him, always capable of immeasurable charm and wit. We each loved him, personality issues aside, he would've been a great addition to the trip.

Unfortunately, there was another variable we had to consider. Caleb, like his brothers before him, had a pretty serious gambling problem. I could never figure out why each of them had fallen into the same trap with it, but it had taken hold of Caleb – a Venus flytrap, unrelenting and fatal. It made him erratic, unpredictable, coming into significant sums one week, begging to borrow money the next. Matty took the brunt of it sharing halls with him, constantly subject to a restless presence, one he wasn't sure would benefit a trip on a shoestring budget as it was.

Breaking the news to Caleb was as difficult as we expected. I was thankful to Matty for taking the lead in such a difficult situation, explaining our arguments well, and handling his objections in a practised manner. There was no getting away from the ruthless nature of his omission, but it was a necessary sacrifice we felt we had to make.

Chapter 10

My history of dealing with problems was substandard at best. At this point in my life, I'd never realised my tendencies of habitual avoidance, assuming I'd always had the rub of the green when it came to facing any issues of substance.

After brushing off Caleb on the phone a couple of days ago, he had subsequently peppered my phone with calls, texts, and Whatsapp messages, not letting me get off the hook. Burying your head in the sand only gets you so far, it seemed.

I knew the issue would not go unresolved. Caleb was the personification of persistence at the best of times, he'd likely be knocking on my front door soon if I didn't face it head-on.

Unfortunately for Caleb, the dye had already been cast. We had booked the flights. We were due to leave in four weeks' time, a straight shot to Phuket, the largest of Thailand's southern islands, according to Wikipedia. From there, who knew? I had left the route planning to the others, my part to play already taken care of.

Well, almost taken care of. The small matter of what I was going to say to the big man still loomed over me like his enormous shadow. The unwelcoming embrace of deja vu convulsed around me as I picked up the phone to call him. It'd been hard enough sitting on the sideline when Matty delivered the news that he couldn't come interrailing and this time I was due to give the decisive blow.

I went over my argument with a fine-tooth comb before tapping "call" on my touchscreen, Caleb's phone contact photo giving me a dirty look.

'Yesss lad, been waiting for your call, is it true then?' Caleb asserted, barely one ring tone playing out on the line.

I forced a laugh. 'Yes mate, long time no speak, how ya getting on?'

'Always good mate, you know me! So, Matty tells me you've had a bit of good news haven't you?' Blabbermouth Matty.

'Pffft, what's he been saying, the joker? But yeah… na… yeah, I've come into a bit of money so it happens!' I stuttered.

'Absolutely unbelievable news mate, you absolutely buzzing?' He boomed the words down the phone, the tonality of a Viking war cry.

'Mate, it's pretty mad yeah, not going to lie to you. All been a bit crazy my end as you can imagine.'

'Yeah, I fucking bet. So gimme the details then, how much you get? When do you get it? You got access to the money now?' he chattered, the excitement tangible in his voice.

'Slow down, mate.' I laughed, authentic this time. 'What was the first question? How much? Fucking shit loads lad.' I said, unsure whether specifics were the right avenue to go down.

Booming laughter. 'Fuckin' hell mate, what I would do to be you right now! So, do you have the money now or what?'

'Yeah, we got it a couple of days ago, pretty mad. My brothers buying a fuckin' flat already the mad guy.' I continued, pretty pleased with how the conversation was going.

'Yeah, obviously!' he shouted. 'I'd be buying absolutely everything I could get my hands on. What are you spending the money on then?'

Truth time.

'To be honest mate, that's what I wanted to talk to you about.' My resolve untested as of yet, I pressed on. 'I think me and the interrailing lot are gonna go to Asia for a few months. I'm gonna lend them a bit of cash to pay their way initially and we're gonna try and travel a bit, then go to Australia maybe. The plan's not exactly all set in stone yet, but we're gonna head there in a few weeks.'

I waited a few seconds to no reply. 'But yeah, I obviously wanted to invite you and Sam as well but Maler's moving in with his girlfriend pretty soon so doubt he'll want to.'

Still no reply.

'And yeah, obviously it's pretty awkward but with that gambling stuff it's obviously more difficult innit?' I'd said obviously way too many times, but I was struggling to find the words.

Still no answer. 'Yo, you still there?'

'Yeah mate, I'm here. Obviously pretty gutted that I can't come, not gonna lie,' he muttered.

'Yeah course man, I wish it was different 'cause I'd obviously want you to come and everything. Just pretty peak innit,' I managed, no conviction present in my voice.

Should I just invite him? I thought, losing sight of why he wasn't invited in the first place. I loved the guy, he'd be fine on the trip, surely?

'To be honest with you mate, I am gutted but I did want to ask you something as well,' Caleb said, a change in intonation indicative of an incoming favour.

'Yeah? Anything mate,' I said, wiping my hands on my jeans, removing the sweat.

'Funny you should mention that gambling stuff 'cause I'm a bit fucked for cash at the moment,' he grunted sheepishly. 'Well, not a bit fucked, I'm fully struggling, big time struggsville to be honest.'

'Jesus mate, what's happened?' I asked, two and two putting themselves together in my head. Clearly, Matty hadn't told him about travelling, he'd just mentioned the money, lighting a fire under Caleb.

He sighed. 'Well, I don't know what you know about how much I owe my parents for bailing me out last year, but I've been having to borrow money off cash lenders online to pay them back.' He paused momentarily. 'But yeah, I've left myself on a shitty wicket because they've all come calling at once and I need to stump up some cash quickly.'

Bloody hell, I thought, my mind hopping between the moral high ground and comforting empathy. 'Oh shit, lad. That's not good at all.' I paused, quandaries like these demanding more time than the split second they're required to make a decision. 'Well, how much is the damage?' I asked, tentatively.

The conversation littered with them, a long pause was left to hang.

'Mate, I'm about £15k in debt.' Regret in his words. 'In total though, £15k in total,' he spluttered, quickly following up.

'Fuck me lad, how have you managed that?' I shouted, probably too loud to avoid a judgemental tone.

He managed a weak laugh. 'God knows mate, not all as lucky as you, are we?'

There are certain points embedded into the story of my life that stand out, some more perceivable than others, jutting out like fragments on a botched building job. Although insignificant to my wider tale, this moment, over the phone with my friend Caleb, was the first time in my life that I used my wealth to solve a problem, with no thought to the repercussions it may have.

I was posed with a two-pronged dilemma. To bail him out and hand him the cash he was asking for, simply leave him to deal with his problems alone, or to spend time with him, talking through the route cause of the problem and formulating a solution that worked best for him in the long run. Spelt out like that the right decision seems an obvious one, but in my head on that particular day, time was a limited commodity, a commodity I didn't feel I had to spare.

'Listen, mate. Send me your bank details and I'll fire over the cash, alright?' I said, a wannabe saviour.

'Oh my god mate, are you actually sure? That would be the best thing in the world mate, I swear down.' he spoke with guttural emotion, the gratitude in his voice unmistakable.

'Yeah mate, course. Can't let you struggle like that can I?' I began to feel a mistaken sense of pride creep through my head.

'You're actually unreal mate, you don't understand how much this will sort me out. Plus I can now save up and come and meet you all travelling. I'll put the gambling behind me lad, I swear to you.'

'Music to my ears brother.' And it really was. I forced myself to believe this was true, through ignorance or just not wanting to know, I believed him.

We carried on talking for a little while, shooting the shit as good friends do. I invited him to the leaving do we were having in our final week in the UK and he wished me good luck with the packing. As I hung up I felt as though the conversation couldn't have gone much better and I made my way downstairs with a smile on my face. Little did I know then, throwing money at a problem would only ever paper the cracks.

Chapter 11

As with any period in time when all eyes are cast towards the future, minutes can turn to hours and hours to days in a moment; blink and they're consigned to the past. In the case of the weeks approaching our flight, it was no different. A flurry of what, where, when, and why queries juggled, taking care to not leave any stone unturned, each member of our travelling quartet had been put through the wringer trying to organise our lives into four manageable rucksacks.

We'd been surprisingly secluded from each other in the three weeks leading up to our departure, opting to spend time with our families, voluntary or otherwise. The summer had continued in the same fashion as it started. Uncharacteristic heatwaves rippled across England, invigorating the country and her inhabitants, the parks awash with people young and old, commutes to the beaches a frantic endeavour.

It would take a phenomenon of extravagant proportions to keep my friends and I from exploiting a summer like this to the full, beer gardens knowing us on first name terms. Fortunately, we had a common goal that united us in resolve, to swap the day trips to the beach for department store rummaging, and trade the day sessions on the booze for deep crawls into travelling forums. We'd certainly taken lessons from our trip around Europe, where each of us had packed almost entirely useless items and sported the same t-shirts three times over. No wonder we got so much action back then.

It was Saturday morning, June 6th, 2015, a mere five days until our departure. With the lion's share of our necessary admin complete, the day of our leaving party had arrived, a welcome treat amongst our tiresome tasks. We'd planned to meet that afternoon at a local pub, The Block & Gasket, the exhaustive guest list far-reaching and comprehensive. We wanted one last hurrah, a chance to showcase our existing persona's for one final time before 'finding ourselves' out in the open, wild world. Essentially, we wanted to show off.

'Alex!' Steve bellowed from his room in the attic.

'What?' I shouted back, rifling through my wardrobe like a man possessed, flinging jumpers and coats out onto my bed.

'Have you seen my denim jacket?'

I dropped my clothes and emerged from the tall, imposing wardrobe and quickly scanned my bedroom, eyes fixing on a washed blue denim jacket hung up on the back of my door.

'No, sorry!' I shouted, tutting as I returned to my hunt. Today was not a day to be wasted with menial sibling squabbles over who wears what, the 3 p.m. meeting time fast approaching. I'd attached a substantial amount of importance to the forthcoming event, desperate to leave a lasting impression on the wider circles who we were leaving behind. We had invited a dynamic ensemble of family and friends, grandparents, cousins young and old. It promised to be a momentous occasion, a ceremonious final farewell, for it would be a yet undetermined period before I saw many of them again.

I pulled out a creased white t-shirt, along with a well-worn checked shirt, and returned to the wall-length mirror that sat up beside my door. I pulled the clothes on quickly, adjusting the lay of the fabric to adhere to my tall frame. My hair wasn't looking it's best at this point, any semblance of style had been abandoned since I'd decided to grow it out from it's usual cropped cut, focus fixed on the new 'man bun' trend sweeping the nation. I pushed it back with a generous scoop of hair wax I'd taken from my brother's room that morning. 'It'll be worth it,' I recited to myself repeatedly. Grabbing the denim jacket hung up on the back of my door, I made it down the landing to the bathroom for some finishing touches.

A cool breeze rolled through the outstretched window as I grabbed my Dad's electric razor and peered into the mirror. My facial hair had grown into something resembling stubble just a few months earlier and the thrill still hadn't worn off. As I began to trim the edges from my makeshift beard, I examined my face closely in my reflection. I looked older, I thought to myself, jaded green eyes focusing on blemishes and intricacies that go unnoticed exclusive of the beholder. A slap of aftershave and a scrub of the teeth, and I was ready for action.

'Let's get this show on the road then!' I called up to my brother as I headed back out onto the landing, dappled sunlight shining through the window at the top of the stairs.

'We're going to meet you around sixish if that's okay?' my Mum shouted from her bedroom, across the hall from my own. She'd already started to get ready herself despite a four-hour cushion before her expected arrival, dress to impress her unspoken mantra.

'No worries, see you there in a bit,' I called, heading downstairs. 'Make sure to tell all the family which bit we've reserved!'

'Okay boss man!' she shouted, poking her head out the door giving me a pretty smirk.

Leaping down the stairs, three at a time, I bounded into the hallway and skidded towards the front room. 'Dad, we're offski!'

Sitting in his usual seat on our king size leather sofa, my dad put down his newspaper and came into the hall.

'Where you going?' he asked, feigning bemusement.

'You know where I'm going.' I retorted, as a back and forth conversation ensued.

'How would I know?' he quipped.

46

'I don't know'

'Neither do I'

'Right then.'

'Right.'

We look at each other, a silly stalemate reached.

'Well then, see you in a bit,' I said, offering a truce.

'Yeah, see you in a bit,' he accepted, digging my arm playfully before retiring to his seat.

Duel settled, a flash of inspiration came to me in the form of road beers, a cold pair of old fellas patiently waiting for selection in the fridge. As though trialling for the Olympic 100m sprint, I jetted down the hall and into the kitchen, time being of the essence. I grabbed twin Stella's from the bottom shelf, generously thinking of my brother. Now I thought of it, where was he? I'd specifically told him to be ready to go for 2.30 p.m. ensuring we'd be first to arrive and not miss a second of the action.

'Steve!' I roared as I ran back into the hallway, elongated the vowels for ultimate effect.

'I'm coming you nutcase!' he shouted, appearing at the top of the stairs, hair quipped into a quiff and clad in a new Ralph Lauren crisp white shirt. 'That's my jacket!'

I laughed at him, 'C'mon, it's the last day I'll be stealing your clothes, have a heart.'

'Pfft you're a millionaire you scruff, buy yourself a new coat,' he laughed, joining me in the hallway. 'In fact, have you even changed your wardrobe at all?'

'Nope.' The only clothes I'd bought were a few pairs of swim shorts and t-shirts for my trip away, hardly sparing a thought for the present. Maybe I should've got myself a new shirt though.

'Don't get bladdered before we get there!' my Dad shouted from the front room as he spotted the beer, sound advice before the impending events.

'Course' we harmonised, heading for the front door. Grabbing my keys, I yanked open the front door and stepped out into the summer's afternoon, breathing in the fresh air, an invigorating elixir.

'Bang on schedule!' I exclaimed, taking the first few steps out at a trot. 'Turner will be at the end of his road I reckon.'

'Cute,' he said, catching me up.

We made our way towards Sale, a pulsating atmosphere in the air, the indescribable momentum that manifests itself at the precipice of a big one. I still to this day struggle to think of a superior combination than the sun, beers, and chats with friends, the intermingling of each individual component transcending the sum of its parts.

The sun, nature's marvel, offering warmth and flattering 'golden hour' lighting, dancing amongst our stories, improving delivery, and conversational reception.

The beers, so cold and irresistible, triggering sensations in touch, smell, and taste, liquid courage intoxicating the mood.

Finally, the chat. The cherry on the cake, cognitive fuel ignited by our closest friends' comedic anecdotes and tall tales. The consolidation of each, amalgamating from exclusive to medley, complementing one another and becoming one. I fucking loved it.

We took the walk at a stride, sipping our drinks, purpose in our path. As we approached the impending cul-de-sac I held my breath, the trivial matter of Turner being on time felt like a vital cog in the afternoon's machine. No sign of him. Whilst silently and viciously berating him, visualising the rest of the evening not adhering to my plan, he popped around the corner, eyes fixed on a make-believe watch on his wrist.

'Time do you call this, fellas?' he asked sternly. 'I've been sitting here for about 20 minutes.' He was dressed sharply, a tan corduroy shirt buttoned up to the top, smart trousers, and a worn-in pair of brogues completing the ensemble. Very Turner.

'We've been waiting here for 40 minutes so dunno how we didn't see you!' I challenged, stretching out my fist in anticipation.

He returned the gesture, perhaps a little too hard and we both winced on connection. 'Nice one then!' he said with a smile. 'What you saying, Ste?'

My brother loved Turner nearly as much as I did, perhaps the only one of my friends who he'd truly taken to by this point. 'Buzzing mate, can't wait to be shot of this one!' He laughed, digging me on the shoulder. 'How're you?'

'Absolutely laughing, ta,' he said, visibly on form, he'd probably had a beer before he left the house. 'Starting already, I like it. Literally can't wait for today, so many fucking people coming, doubt we'll even see each other!'

'Yeah, today isn't about seeing each other.' I said as we pressed on towards the town centre, 'It's about leaving a legacy, a memory of ourselves that will last the test of time. *If* we return I should say! All I'm going to be doing is showing off as much as humanly possible, chirpsing any girl that comes into my path, all whilst keeping a somewhat semblance of decorum in front of my grandparents. A delicate balance indeed.' What bravado.

'Who are you gonna be chirpsing you joker?' Steve interjected, a wry smile on his face. 'You're gonna end up rat arsed before Mum and Dad even arrive!'

'Who is even there to chirpse?' quizzed Turner, 'Can't exactly get with any of the old lot from school can you?'

'Na, obviously not. I'm sure there'll be a friend of a friend of a friend there who wants a new sugar daddy!' I laughed as I slurped down more booze, intending the joke to be self-deprecating but not confident that it hit the mark.

'Yeah actually, you're not wrong,' Turner said, simply. 'None of that for me anyway, I've invited that Nat girl I was seeing at uni, she's gonna get the train down from Liverpool later on.'

My brother and I both looked up, surprised. 'Oh really? I didn't even think about Nat to be fair,' I said, trying to hide my disappointment. 'Are you two like, together then or what?'

'Na, not together, together,' he said, catching my eye and reading my disappointment with ease. 'Just one last hurrah innit.'

'Better make it an almighty hurrah then!' I exclaimed, visibly satisfied with the response. Turner knew better than most that I wanted no ties back to England once we'd set off on our travels, the scenario with Sam and his girlfriend still not sitting right with our group.

We continued our route to Sale with a wind of momentum behind us, breathing in the familiarity and nostalgia we'd soon be leaving behind. We talked through our guestlist, assessing what traits each individual would bring to the table, both with optimism and cynicism in equal measure.

It was chats like these that I was glad I wouldn't be leaving behind, a social comfort blanket wound tightly around my shoulders. One of the things I'd missed most in my three years at university was the commonality and intimacy that was shared between myself and those who I'd grown up with. To me, it was a common ground that couldn't be nurtured through anything other than traversing the test of time with someone, a gradual development of trust and respect gained through shared experiences, both the good and the ugly. Little did I know back then that the amount of time spent with someone was not pivotal in the formulation of real connections, a lesson I would soon come to learn.

Chapter 12

'And that is why you need to avoid Koh Phi Phi at all costs!' cried my cousin Ben, slamming his hand down on the table with a force that echoed around the beer garden.

We burst into a chorus of laughter, six or seven of us perched around the central table in the Block and Gasket's beer garden. The sun was still high in the sky, giving ample light to the terrace around me, a palpable buzz emanating from the crowds of people, drinks, and cigarette smoke that commingled in the air. We had it all, a royal flush.

The day had been executed to perfection thus far, a military operation pulled off with precision. Turner, Steve, and I had arrived at the pub around 3.05 p.m., just shy of on time, to find Brown Shoes, Sam and our friend Joel stood chatting at the bar. The pub was busy, not too much, not too little and surprisingly there were a few free tables out in the sun. How convenient.

Pleasantries exchanged, we'd ordered three of their coldest and took a seat, prime location for the debauchery ahead. The conversations began with misinformed narrations of current events, touching on football, girls, and recent nights out, soon moving onto detailed anecdotes about who slept with whom.

We transitioned from anecdotes to talk of our trip, the other boys vocal about their jealousy and desperation to join us, or so they claimed... As we shot the shit, more and more of our guests arrived to scenes of increasingly wild greetings, hugs, and high fives galore, each adding to the atmosphere like the gradual seasoning of a dish. Matty's arrival was greeted like a last-minute winner as he strolled in with his two friends from university, Howard and Chris, as a surprise. We were getting good at surprises.

Not long had passed before we'd taken over two-thirds of the smoking area, dancing between one-on-one catch-ups and group discussions, a choreographed madness. Only when family members began to arrive were the breaks pumped a little, each taking stock and thankfully slowing down on the booze.

It was around 5.30 p.m. before I managed to exclusively summon Matty and Turner to my side, in a desperate need to talk tactics for the night. I guided them to an inconspicuous vantage point inside where we should've been free of the shackles of small talk and chin-wagging for at least a few minutes.

'Where in God's name is Browners?' I interrogated, scanning the wilderness for signs of him.

'God knows, probably twatted off his head already isn't he?' laughed Matty, pushing his hair behind his ears. He'd also committed to the long hair quest, brothers in arms in most things we did. He had definitely copied me though.

'I've not seen him since he ducked away from Amelia Rice when she arrived!' Turner stated, 'Most likely hiding in the toilets.'

'Wait!' Matty cried, beer overflowing from his pint pot, his mouth curling into a grin. 'Looks like he didn't hide very well!'

We followed his gaze to see our best pal Brown Shoes, hands in his pockets, staring at the ground, every telltale sign you can imagine of intangible awkwardness. His face distorted every five seconds into variations of what I imagined he thought were engagement and interest, but what looked more like the expression a cat makes when tickled under its chin.

He was talking to Amelia Rice. You'd think this level of gracelessness would only be exhibited by someone who was speaking to an ex-girlfriend or someone who had scorned them in the past. You would, of course, be mistaken. Brown Shoes, as charming as he was, was single-handedly the most hilariously

53

awkward guy I knew, making the simplest of interactions appear troublesome through overthinking and overcomplicating the irrelevant. Thankfully, his klutzy approach was one of the most endearing things about him so he pulled off this demeanour exceptionally well. It was one of the things that made him so likeable, such a comedy character to watch and to revel in.

'Shall we go save him?' I asked, through stifled laughter.

'Save him from what?' Matty said. 'They kissed one time in fucking year 11!'

We burst out laughing again. 'That'd never phase Browners, he'd make ordering a drink at the bar a fucking ordeal!' Turner said, gulping his beer.

'Yeah, you're not wrong there. But we need him, I wanna have a little four-man planning!' I said, grabbing their shoulders and making our way to our friend.

We cut across the bar, ducking eye contact and friendly faces, covert in movement. I'd had around six pints by this point so my stealth was partially diluted and with a stumble, I clattered into Brown Shoes and Amelia.

'Yes, lad!' I shouted, throwing my arm around Brown Shoes, knocking him off balance a little and spilling his drink, beer flowing off the edge of the table. 'Shit, shit, sorry mate!'

He looked up from the spillage and met my eyes with a steely gaze, albeit gratitude rather than condemnation. 'Was fuckin' empty anyway!' he lied. 'Let's go to the bar and get another six each, eh?'

I laughed triumphantly as the other two made their way into a perfect half-circle. In unison, we all looked around at Amelia, the outsider. The joker in a pack of cards, ironically enough. I'd already had my stint of pleasantries with her and had moved on to pastures new.

'Oh, I'll make myself scarce shall I?' she sniggered, scanning around our faces, reading the mood. We looked blankly at each other, each waiting for the first to speak, accidentally beginning to laugh. Sometimes you just can't help it.

'Yous are unbelievable!' She swung her hair, rolled her eyes, and went off into the night. With an inaudible cheer, we made our way to the end of the bar and readied ourselves for the chat.

And we were off. 'Thought you needed rescuing there, lad!' I started, clapping a hand on Brown Shoes' back.

'Dunno what you're on about, it was fine,' he protested, unbeknownst to him that his eyes were a giveaway.

'Why did you look like you were in anguish then, mate?' Turner asked, his turn to strike.

'Na, very amicable that, mate!' he carried on, averting everybody's eyes.

'You sure about that lad?' Matty probed, not letting him off the hook.

'Why? Did I look awkward?' he replied, his panic clear behind a plastered smile.

'You? Awkward? Never mate.'

He took a deep breath before a smile betrayed him. 'It was fuckin' well awkward though. Dunno why she wants to come and chat on to me anyway, I may as well just lips her up again later.'

We bellowed with laughter, the theme tune to our lives. I looked around at my friends one by one, my comrades had assembled. 'Look boys, time to make a plan,' I began. 'I reckon it's nearly time to take it up a notch. What do you reckon?'

'What do you mean?' Turner asked. 'I'm already liquored!'

'I reckon we could smack a few tequilas or something? I reckon we could get pretty lairy tonight,' Brown Shoes agreed.

'Yeah, I reckon if we each neck one more pint we'd be at our optimum drunk level,' Matty prophesied, a conviction in his words.

I wasn't usually as fraught with boozing indulgence, typically saving this kind of excess for raves or random house parties. However, tonight was a big one, as I repeated to myself. 'Deffo, what you saying, Turner?'

Turner, the sensible one. Turner, the man who invited his girlfriend. Turner, the voice of reason.

'Obviously boys, I reckon we down two more each?' he said.

Following through with our illogical promise, next thing I remember I'd made my way into a diverse assortment of my nearest and dearest, who were captivated by the enchanted ramblings of my Dad, midway through one of his most rehearsed jokes. I always enjoyed watching him in this kind of mood, coming alive in opportunities to run the room. I watched my family and friends' reactions as he delivered the punchline, met with rapturous delight and laughter. It was only when the merriment began to die down that he addressed me directly.

'Look who it is, the man of the moment,' he said, prompting the others in the group to fix their eyes upon me. 'Surprised you're still standing since you've been here since 7 a.m.!'

I fought to hide a blush. 'Us King men must be made of sterner stuff, eh?' I drunkenly bantered, looking up to my Uncle John, trying to catch his eye.

'Ah, you'd have to be a man to qualify for that I'm afraid,' my Dad replied, to a full house of sniggers.

'Ah well, hopefully, this trip will be the making of me, eh? All those ladyboys in Thailand must build a certain amount of character!' I shot back, preempting his predictable next line of jibes. Self-depreciation always seemed a banker for cheap laughs.

'Alex, you better not end up marrying one of them, you'll lose your claim to the King throne,' interjected my Uncle John, a broad smile plastered across his face.

'Wouldn't dream of it UJ. I hear they're only good for one night anyway.'

Tasteless jokes always went down a treat with my Dad's side of the family, as my Uncle John, his children Edward and Emily, my cousin's boyfriend Matt, and my Auntie Jennifer sounded their amusement with feigned groans and stifled giggles. I'd always got on well with my extended family, but I knew I was in the good books that night specifically, as only a few weeks earlier I'd requested that my winnings be used to clear any family debts and bestow a good sum of money upon each of them. No wonder I was getting a decent reaction to my jokes.

I carried on in a similar fashion for the next hour or so, one foot in, one foot out of conversations. I dove headfirst into one group, seamlessly entering the discussion with what I deduced as a valid and fascinating perspective. Once that crowd had been satisfied, I moved onto the next, harmonizing with Katie Baker on how great working in finance was, offering insights even she had not thought of.

Before I knew it, I had been promoted to the promised land, working my way up through the conversational ranks and through sheer merit had been granted a seat at the social pinnacle of the pub, a chat between two of my friend Caleb's older brothers and their three friends, the immortal "girls in the year above". It was evident that this was my chance to shine, to impress the demi-god status girls who'd been the subject of fancy for all boys in South Manchester post-2008, probably.

'Now then boys and girls,' I said, 'who's having a good time?' Strong start indeed.

The younger of his brothers, Charlie, welcomed me with a shake of the hand. 'Now then indeed, the man of the moment himself gives us a second of his time.' The Anderson brothers all shared the same mannerisms, engaging and entertaining.

'Hi Alex,' purred "girl in the year above" number 1, her intoxicating voice threatening to lure me too close.

'When do you leave?' enticed "girl in the year above" number 2, an enchantress well skilled in seductive leading questions such as this.

Was the air conditioning broken? 'We leave in a couple of days. Don't worry still ple-e-e-enty of time left,' I assured, effortless charm eroding from my lines.

"Girl in the year above" number 3 blushed and giggled, or was that a cough? Maybe the air-con actually had broken?

Sexual tension evident, the eldest Anderson, Chris interjected. 'Yeah, surprised Caleb hasn't managed to convince you to let him come away with you!'

Oh shit, Caleb. Had he told his brothers about my money? Is this why I was being shamelessly seduced by these three otherworldly angels?

My game faltered as I stumbled over a laugh. 'Oh, na not yet. Where is Caleb anyway?' Thinking back, I hadn't seen Caleb all night.

'Fuck knows, said he was going to be here but hasn't showed up,' Charlie said, turning his focus back onto the vixens. 'Shouldn't you be getting back to your party anyway, don't let us waste any more of your time, big shot.'

My fleeting thoughts of Caleb dismissed, I realised that my momentary lapse in concentration had cost me dearly. The spoils had slipped through my fingers and my older, wiser competitors had bested me. Maybe I should've bought them all drinks? Ah well.

Insatiable in my appetite for pastures new, the fear of missing out rife in my head. Each conversation seemed juicier and more fulfilling than the last, a ping pong rally between family and friends, strangers, and bartenders seemed like it would never end. But alas, no amount of money or booze can change the begrudging fact that all good nights must come to an end, and unfortunately so here does my recollection of this one. Talk about a big night.

I prefer to remember the night in this image, the memories untarnished with what was to follow. What was supposed to be a night to remember became one sullied with blanks and partial amnesia. A night that was billed as my final hurrah, my opportunity to leave a lasting impression had choked at the final hurdle, clattering down to its knees. I've heard a number of renditions of what happened post 8 p.m., the sentiments ranging from the lenient "not too bad" to the harsh "an absolute embarrassment". I suppose you never really know when relying on the narrative of other people, the beauty of any night's events in the eye of the beholder.

A man falling down the stairs is hilarious to some but causes shame to another. Getting kicked out of a bar is abhorrent to A and a triumph to B. Slurring to your distant ex-girlfriend Alex Perry that you still loved her in front of her long term boyfriend, well that one may be an exception.

Chapter 13

June 11th, 2015.

This was the big day.

Armed with travelling rucksacks and an appetite for endeavour, the four of us had arrived at Manchester Airport, Terminal 1. The few days preceding had been a blur of emotional goodbyes and last minute admin, one day tumbling into the next ahead of our imminent departure.

I'd wanted to spend every moment with my mum, dad, and brother, drinking in everything they said, committing them to memory. It was these three who were my ties to home, the essence I wish I could take with me exclusive of themselves. My mum was taking it the hardest, her brave smiles never shy of a wobble, determined as she was. She had only just got me back where she wanted and now I was making her say goodbye again, this time without the comfort of periodic visits and a firm date of return. My brother and dad were doing a better job of masking emotions, opting for a macho display of indifferent bravado. I was thankful for this as my own emotions threatened to boil over as it was.

Once the initial greetings of excitement were complete, we each made our way over to the electronic terminals to print off our boarding passes. Our loved ones watched on as we exchanged personal jokes and insulted each other's passport pictures, personifying excitement in our actions and aura. I made my way back over to my family of three and braced myself for the final goodbye.

'Right then boyo,' started my dad, like clockwork throwing his arm around my sobbing mum. 'About time we got rid of you.'

'Too right.' I said, dispelling the rising flushed heat from my face.

'I... I... I'm really going to miss you, Alex, be safe okay?' my mum whispered, breaking free of my dad's embrace and throwing herself around me. My eyes were beginning to sting.

'C'mon Mum, I'm only going on flipping holiday aren't I?' I chuckled through bated breath. No way was I crying in front of my friends.

'True, come back soon okay? Even if it's just for a bit? You've certainly got the bleeding money to do so!' She managed a weak laugh and allowed me out of her arms.

'My turn little bro.' Steve stepped forward, grabbing me and lifting me off the ground in a bear hug. 'Don't come back a hippy, whatever you do.'

I laughed, strained of breath in his grip. 'Get off, ya lump.'

He threw me back on my feet and offered an outstretched hand.

'Right you lot, I'll ring you from Phuket, don't go spending all my money without me!' I laughed and gave my bravest grin as I hoisted the bag up onto my shoulders. 'Love you all!'

'Love... Love You Alex!'

'Love ya kid.'

'Smell ya later.'

I gave them one last look and turned to my friends, my substitute family of three, waiting with eager faces, a new chapter about to begin. If we revisit the notion of moments in your life that you're drawn to, milestones that break up and stick out in the fabric of your story, I'd be hard-pressed to find one more significant than this. The mundane nature of four twenty one-year-old boys getting on a plane to Thailand can be dismissed as

61

nothing more than an ordinary occurrence, nothing to write home about. But as is the case with anyone recounting their own tale, the beginning will always be fiercely celebrated, for without a beginning, there can be no middle and with no middle, there can be no end.

Part 2

Chapter 14

DING DING DING DING!

The bell's chime sliced through the muggy atmosphere, a deck of cards perfectly cut in two. The time for talking was over. There was nothing else I could do but fight this man.

He approached me from the far corner of the ring without a moment's hesitation, each step more confident than the last. My vision was cluttered with the surrounding crowd, a clamour of roars and energy causing a slight vibration to the crimson red ropes that caged us in, the lion's den.

The piercing shine of the overhead floodlights compromised my focus as I looked into the face of my opponent, a young Israeli man around my age, his face unflinching and determined. I tried to sharpen my concentration, shrugging off any effects of the mixed spirit buckets of liquor I'd been bonding with in the hours preceding. I could do this, he wasn't that big...

Shaky confidence regained, it was time to plan my first strike, channelling a predetermined strategy would be key in this duel. Flicking through the archives of my mind, I tried to pinpoint any fighting experience from my past that would come in handy in a hairy situation such as this. I'd been punched on nights out a handful of times, but I wasn't sure that would help me get the better of a man in Muay Thai combat.

Sticking to the classics, I opted to settle for the 'left, right, goodnight' proverb, a proven tactic in most action movies I'd watched growing up, how to beat a bad guy 101. Only, the guy whose downfall I plotted wasn't actually so bad in fairness. In fact, I'd considered him a close friend about twenty minutes prior.

He was my roommate in the Blanco Beach Hostel, a very decent chap as it so happens. But we were friends no longer. He was now my nemesis, my one true enemy in this world. It was he who stood between me and the love of my life, Julietta. Granted, we'd only met her a few hours earlier but our connection was instant and resolute.

Oh Julietta, how wonderful she was, her eyes windows of desire, enticing me into her Scandinavian story like a moth to its flamy demise. I looked out to the crowd one more time, scanning the sea of staring faces to meet her gaze.

She'd assured me she'd be waiting, arms open to the night's possibilities once I'd done the business in the Muay Thai ring. 'It'd be hilarious,' she sang, just before we signed up, my judgement impared by her Norwegian witchery. But where was she? I couldn't see her. She wasn't where I'd left her. Had she gone?

Thud! With an audible whack, my vision was tainted as my head was pummeled by the scarcely padded fist of my friend, a left hook connecting with venom. I stumbled off balance and swung blindly at the air, my aim devoid of a target.

Planting my feet firmly on the mat, I looked up bewildered at my opponent, readying himself for another, possibly decisive blow. Nothing grabs your attention like being hit in the face, a primal fight or flight response triggered within the human psyche. Those options limited by the four-sided enclosure, I was left with a single prerogative.

I plucked up my best combination of courage and strength, whirling a right hand at my target, exercising unexpected speed and power in its flight. My hand whistled in the air before uniting with the left side of his face, a bullseye with my first arrow would surely leave him incapacitated. Feelings of panic matured to bravado, starting to believe I had won the fight in just one shot. I puffed out my chest, tall and triumphant, ready to celebrate.

He hit mc again. Maybe I should've been hitting the gym.

The crowd was entertained, that much was clear as the resounding bellows reverberated around the beach bar's foundations. It felt like something out of a movie, Rocky fought an Israeli man in the fifth film I'm sure?

Each contestant satisfied by the discernible response, we jumped into a second engagement. Jabs were thrown against resulting defences, limbs flying in all directions. What felt to me like a clash of the titans apparently did not translate to the observing masses, later transcribed to me as like two little girls fighting over a doll.

But surely, they were just jealous. I felt like Achilles in the ring, sharp and fast, darting in and out of battle, stinging my adversary with jabs, hooks, and uppercuts to devastating effect. By the end of round one, I was surely on top, undistracted by the ringing in my ears and the thin trickle of blood dripping from my nose. I returned to my corner with an intended swagger, only to be met with the sight of my friends cackling faces.

'What the fuck was that, you absolute whopper?' Matty was bent over from laughing, staring up at me from the ringside stairs. He stood amongst a group of six or seven people who we'd met that day, huddled around a crying Turner in hysterics.

'That was the funniest thing I've ever seen!' he shouted, wiping a tear from his eye, 'I thought you'd been dropped in one shot!'

I couldn't believe what I was hearing, deducing that they must be drunker than I first thought. I swore I had this guy for the taking.

A second's reflection was all it took to realise how much I was panting, devoid of breath in the two minute round.

66

'Shut up, mate. I reckon I'll drop him next round,' I panted, immediately wishing I'd conserved my words, precious breath wasted on this pack of fools.

They burst into new floods of laughter. 'Yeah man, bit more of the same and you're sorted,' Matty yelled with a note of sarcasm falling on deaf ears.

'Where's fuckin' Julietta anyway?' I shouted back, realising there may be a chance I'd missed her in the crowd, the catalyst behind this whole charade.

'She's fucked off mate, went off with another fella I think!' Matty laughed, the drunken messenger of my fate.

For fuck sake. What a waste of time. Why was I fighting this guy if the glory of victory wasn't going to meet me in the form of a girl?

I let my eyes take a survey of the surrounding bar whilst I slowly caught my breath. The deafening beat of electronic music was unrelenting, pumping bizarre remixes of mainstream music to the heaving masses of backpackers, each person caught up in the tale of their own night's adventure. The bar spilled out into the streets of Koh Phi Phi, captivating the attention of all passers-by.

DING DING DING DING!

The soundtrack to hell rang out again, the second and final round upon me. I gingerly approached the centre of the ring, zero motive, no desire. As we were summoned by the in-ring official to touch gloves before the commencement of round two, an intriguing idea knocked on the door of my intoxicated mind.

This guy had fallen for Julietta harder than I had. Did he know she had left? As with all cunning plans, machiavellian musings began to snowball in my mind, creating a dastardly blueprint for his demise. I would use my very own weakness to my advantage.

'I want good clean round, okay?' demanded the diminutive referee, looking around at us fiercely. 'No scratch or bite, okay?'

We nodded, fixing our eyes upon one another, his face frustratingly untarnished. As we touched gloves, I shouted over with a smirk. 'Fucking hilarious this isn't it?'

He grinned back at me. 'Mate! All this over a hot girl! Hopefully, it will be worth it for one of us!'

We broke gloves and moved back to our starting positions, readying ourselves for the impending conflict. I waited with bated breath. The referee's arm swung. The fight was back on. My opponent began to advance, just as he had done at the beginning of round one, a seasoned warrior.

'Oi mate, Julietta has fucked off! Check it out!'

Trap sprung, his eyes lost all focus, his confused face swinging over to the spot where we had left her. Like a coiled snake, I took my shot, throwing all my weight behind my right hand.

Whack! My fist landed flush against his nose and sent him tumbling to the ground. I watched him fall in what felt like slow motion before he hit the mat with a bang.

I knew the fight was over as the referee raised my arm in celebration. A mixed palette of emotions took over, the guilt of knowing full well I'd hit him with a sucker punch, whilst simultaneously revelling in the glory of my victory.

The rapturous drum of the crowd quickly drowned out all my moral doubts. I looked over to my friends, both old and new, cheering loudest of all from the side of the ring. Little did they know the unheroic inceptions of my win.

Why should I tell them? My concentration had been equally compromised earlier in the fight, if anything I was just levelling the playing field, making it a fair fight, perhaps tipping the scales ever so slightly in my favour.

If I'm honest Thailand hadn't exactly lived up to the billing of wild adventures thus far, our comfortable stay in Phuket's most luxurious hotel offered a different experience, providing untold comfort without the need for us to lift a finger. But Koh Phi Phi was different.

Koh Phi Phi was where things would really kick-off.

Chapter 15

There wouldn't be much time for self-reflection on the islands of Thailand, that much was becoming abundantly clear.

If you are looking for solace, for a place to ponder or contemplate the broader nuances of life, a means of finding yourself? I would suggest looking elsewhere, for the only version of oneself that could be found on these shores was one of overindulgence, blinded by temptation, the candle of your soul burning brightly at both ends.

It was apparent in those first few days on Koh Phi Phi Don, the largest of the Phi Phi Islands, that the exotic, untarnished utopia that had been promised in so many books and movies was no longer, its place taken by a different animal. Whilst rolling white beaches, crystal clear waters, and tropical treelines had survived the evolution, it was the essence of each that had been undeniably compromised. The once stainless beaches were now home to countless hostels and dance clubs that spanned the width and breadth of the island, daily morning clean-ups only scratching the surface of prior debauchery.

The ocean remained beautiful and picturesque, lapping the shoreline in the early hours, despite the high tide littered with cheap cigarette butts, vibrant plastic buckets, and an army of used condoms. The trees, perhaps the only natural marvel to resist, stood high out of the reach of their corrupted hands. It wasn't as if we'd expected an unblemished paradise, not exactly pioneers in the decision to go travelling through South East Asia. But I have to say I was surprised by the seemingly one-dimensional nature of the island. It seemed it was almost man-made to party, a carousel of sins.

'Good morning stranger,' came a whisper in my ear.

If heaven had an alarm clock this was it. A whispered greeting, an enchanting foreign accent taking hold of the three simple words, emphasising all that could be good about a morning. I prayed it was Julietta.

I opened my eyes and waited for my vision to adjust to the room's light, pleading with my memories to adjust in turn. The swimming edges of the room began to settle as a vague figure could be made out in bed beside me.

Spoiler—it wasn't Julietta. The name of the girl was a mystery to me but upon quick inspection, she had kind, recognisable eyes, curly brunette hair, and a smile that lit up my unfamiliar surroundings.

'Good morning indeed!' I smiled, holding back a full grin in the fear of any morning breath seeping through. I rubbed my eyes, pushed my hands through my tangled hair, and sat up in the bed, propping my head up against the headboard.

'So, last night was fun! How long will you be staying in Phi Phi, Alex?' she asked, playful and lighthearted in her tone.

Had she showered and got ready? She looked remarkably fresh-faced for someone who'd been out on a crazy night. But to my surprise, I was beginning to feel pretty great myself. The prospects of a morning marred with headaches and visits to the toilet seemed to be dissipating around me, replaced with a clear mind and possibilities endless.

'Much fun. I'm not sure yet actually, I've only got a couple more nights booked in my hostel. Not all as lucky as you to have a private room like this!' I pattered, surprising myself with the apparent sober confidence.

'This isn't my place silly!' she laughed, dropping her head onto my shoulder. 'You booked a five-night stay in this room last night when we were drunk. You said we needed somewhere private to chat if I remember correctly!'

For fuck sake. I'd managed to last all of two nights in a hostel before throwing money at a private room again. Upon arrival in Phi Phi, we'd each made a pact to slum it in hostels to help achieve the *authentic* travelling experience. Our time in Phuket, although luxurious, wasn't entirely different from the resort holidays we'd all been on before.

'How very noble of me!' I sighed, hoping she'd pick up the sarcasm. We chatted over the night preceding in a breezy, carefree fashion. It transpired that she was called Sofie, a 22-year-old dental student from Denmark. She told me stories of her trip to Northern Thailand, emphasising how brilliant a place called 'Pai' was before she had to go meet her friends. They were leaving the island later that day, citing the party atmosphere as too intense for an extended stay. Some people just can't hack it.

Once we'd bid a fond farewell my attention turned to the day ahead, as if encounters like this were commonplace in my life. I lay back down on my bed and read through a couple of messages from the boys, urgently enquiring as to my whereabouts. I quickly arranged to meet them back at the beach, just a short walk away if my hazy memory of the night served me correctly.

A quick rearrange of funky shirt and Adidas swim shorts, a splash of cold water and I was away, back out into the dazzling Asian sunshine. I was greeted with a pleasant breeze as I took to the street, my flip flops scattering pebbles as they pounded the makeshift walkways that intersected the island. It was quiet on the street, only a few local shopkeepers stood a short distance away, their foreign dialect echoing off the wooden fences that surrounded the road.

I breathed in deeply, taking in my surroundings with unclouded clarity. With no particular route in mind, I relied on false intuition and the treacherous stories of my memory to lead me back to the beach, taking each indistinguishable signpost as gospel in my quest. Two wrong turns, three reroutes and a request for directions later I had made my way to a clearing where a winding path opened out to the ocean.

A panoramic vista of the southwestern shoreline massaged my eyes as I strolled out onto the beach. Koh Phi Phi had earned the accolade for the 'Jewel of Asia' in the online forums I'd been researching in the months prior, the dominant green cliffs looming over a tranquil bay. A scattering of fisherman's boats bounced whimsically on the high tide.

'There you are, you joker!' came a familiar voice from the distance.

Sheltering my eyes from the sun, I looked up to see my three best friends running over in my direction, appearing alarmed, in some form of distress.

'Yo! What you lot saying?' I called jovially to the approaching pack. As they came closer, the desperation in their faces became much more apparent.

'Mate, it's like 12 p.m.! We've just copped boat party tickets for us all and it sets off in fuckin' five minutes! Let's go!' Matty shouted .

'What?! We're going right now?! I've not even brushed my teeth!' I protested. Before I could protest further, Brown Shoes had grabbed me by the arm and began to run.

'We need to get there right now you idiot!' he laughed between his strides, 'They just said they're setting off without us if we don't get back. Forget brushin' your teeth lad, you will not wanna miss this!'

We ran past our hostel entrance, a clear purpose in our path, not so carefully avoiding the sprawling bands of backpackers populating the beach. Turner led the charge, making our way over the largest boat ashore, a harem of local men and hostel reps heaving to push it into the water.

'Last call for the booze cruise!'

'Hey mate! We've got tickets!' Turner shouted. 'Matty, you got them?'

'Yeah man, four tickets right here!' he said, pulling the crumpled fluorescent pieces of paper out of his money belt and handing them over to the rep.

'Nice one fellas, welcome to the Blanco Beach Hostel booze cruise!' he sneered, his strong cockney accent pronounced and exaggerated, 'Unfortunately, you're the stragglers today. This first boat is full so you'll be joining them boys over there on the second boat. Tough luck chaps!'

He signalled over to a separate boat, about 20 metres away. It was a sorry sight compared to its rival, little more than an inflatable dinghy. Aboard, there were around seven people, all male, pasty white faces catching glare from the midday blaze.

'Obviously not,' Matty said bluntly.

The hostel rep eyed us up, arrogance plastered across his stupid face. 'Not your day is it son?' he snapped, pointing over to the boat as he turned his back and pulled up the docked rope. 'Off you go!'

Begrudgingly we made our way over to the shitty raft, cursing our rotten luck and a new enemy. I can only speak for myself but it felt as though I hadn't had a moment to think since arriving on the island, each remarkable event spiralling into the next, memory overlapping memory, intersected only by drunken slumber. However, in a rare moment of objective interpretation, I summoned up enough mental clarity to realise I was feeling sorry for myself.

I, the man who'd won a millionaire jackpot, was feeling down on my luck because of this negligible turn of fortune. Hadn't I learned anything yet?

Chapter 16

'Please tell me that's not the actual reason they call you Brown Shoes?' she asked in disbelief, twiddling the ocean through her long blonde hair.

'Tell me about it' he began, 'I'm the one who has to live with the name. One mistake and the rest is history. Speaking of names, by the way, you haven't told me yours…'

I'd found another ingredient to my mantra for life, transformative in its powers of elation and delight, providing crucial buoyancy to the original three components: sun, beers, and chats.

It was so simple, so effective in its primal state, a vast sea of possibilities that engulfed its inhabitants. It was of course, the ocean. What better way to spend an afternoon than bouncing amongst the waves seamlessly kept afloat by overused life jackets, a cold, local beer at your mercy. Banish the notion that too many cooks spoil the broth, for we'd found a hallowed briny deep that welcomed all.

A multinational consolidation of people far and wide, a meeting of nations in every direction. Spanish senorita's laughed with hearty German men, whilst Irish charm fixed on the delicate Dane's. A duo of Columbian travellers had taken charge of the boat's speakers, supplying the backdrop of surrounding limestone cliffs with a unique motif of South American disco music. This was what we were here for.

It is rare to come across a moment that each person you love hits top form at the exact same time. Typically in social situations, you're hard-pressed to find one person that has been blessed by the touch of the gods, reaping the convivial rewards that come with it. There's no exact science, the extraneous variables too many to count.

But on this day, submerged waist-deep in the boat party to Maya Bay, Koh Phi Phi, my friends had somehow achieved it. I'd spotted each of them periodically throughout the day, the epitome of joy and happiness, emanating from their being.

I'd seen Matty, fresh off a boat side backflip, welcomed into a circle of Swedes. His Scandinavian blonde hair and blue eyes made him instantly appreciated. Within minutes he'd successfully instigated a play on the best looking girl. As you may guess, I wasn't jealous at all.

Next on my list of legitness was Brown Shoes, who'd caught my attention less subtly as the catalyst of a booming roar of laughter a few groups away. On closer inspection, I could make out across the watery turf that he was attempting to tell jokes in the local tongue to a group of five Germans. His antics were met with an almighty *'prost!'* followed by a chugging of beer.

That left only Turner, for whom I scanned my crystal clear terrain. For a while, I was unable to spot him but then I heard it. The steady supply of Columbian disco had somehow perfectly mixed into a strangely familiar number, the siren sound of trumpets adding a supplementary layer of music that I didn't know I needed.

My eyes were drawn to the welcome silhouette of Harris P Turner, triumphantly stood on the rig of the boat, hoisted up by his Columbian co-mixers like a three-pronged antenna. He'd naturally put on the carefully selected playlist that we'd concocted together in preparation for the trip, only dreaming of broadcasting it in a setting like this.

Each of my friends' activities was further etched in my memories by the enormous grins on their faces, far-reaching, and well earned. As for myself, I didn't need a grand stage to showcase my feelings, for that was my first meeting with true happiness on the trip, a level of internal satisfaction I'd felt profoundly in the moment.

'What are you doing bobbing about on your own you sad bastard?' called an approaching Turner, two beers in each hand.

'Drinking it all in fella! Not sure I've ever done anything this sick before...' I summarised, kicking my way over in his direction.

'Ever? You do love an exaggeration. But yeah, not bad at all, is it? Those Columbian guys are so fuckin' joke mate, they're gonna come to our hostel later I think.'

'Yeah, hopefully, all this lot will come out. Never met so many safe people.'

He laughed. 'Never? Yeah, I can imagine there's going to be a lot of first's on this trip. Where the fuck were you last night by the way?'

It was my turn to laugh. 'Just went back to this girl's place, absolutely smashed it, you should've seen her!' I didn't feel the need to tell him about my renting of another private room, our promise to try out hostels still enforced.

'Oh really? I swear I saw you and her come into our dorm room at like 3 a.m.?'

'Did you?'

'Yeah definitely, you were clambering around on your bunk for a bit but think I heard you bumbling about, saying you had a plan and then scarpered. I assumed you were just gonna go to the toilet or something. Why did you not just go to hers in the first place?' he asked sipping his beer.

'Ah mate, she didn't want to initially but I managed to convince her didn't I?' I quickly replied. 'What happened to you anyway?'

'Well, after your KO victory we all got split up didn't we? I think you three went off with birds so I ended up with the rest of the group at that Slinky Bar on the beach. Was decent man, the tunes are so fucking shit though.'

'You not see any girls you liked the look of?' I asked, noticing a slight falter in his conviction.

He paused momentarily, 'Na, not really. Bit wet but I was pretty into that Nat girl before I came out so finding it a bit weird to try it with anyone else if you get me?'

Undeterred, I pressed ahead. 'It'll pass mate, it always does. Plus, there are so many options out here I bet you'll be over it in no time.'

'Yeah mate, you're right I reckon' he sighed. 'Anyway, enough of that chat, let's go get involved!'

He signalled over to a fledgling group amassing just a stone's throw away. Matty, Brown Shoes, and a third guy who I didn't recognise were playing catch amongst the waves with a battered tennis ball, zipping pitches at one another at treacherous speed. We'd honed this infantile activity whilst interrailing, the inception of the sport of takes.

'Send it this way!' I shouted, directing my cry at the one unfamiliar face of the trio. Like clockwork, his arm changed trajectory and executed a throw of precise accuracy into my outstretched palm.

With each throw-catch combination, our synergy increased, waves and wavelengths becoming one. Who was this patriarch that Matty and Brown Shoes had recruited? His guile in hand-eye coordination was only bettered by his tendency for occasional drops, finding the perfect middle ground between impressive and intimidating. Once the half time whistle had figuratively blown, we encroached from the far corners of our arena to meet in a group of five.

'Decent little rally that boys,' I said, flicking the salty water out of my tangled hair. Turning to our new companion I introduced myself and slipped in deserved praise for his impressive takes.

He looked up from the group with a smile. He had a welcoming face, the corner of his eyes lined with firm creases, a good indicator of frequent laughter I'd read somewhere.

'Nice to meet you, man. I'm Ryan.' He spoke with a goofy American accent, later confirmed as Canadian. 'Not going to lie to you guys, I'm atrocious with names so don't scold me for forgetting, hey?'

'Never mate, names are overrated anyway,' I laughed, trying to show off. 'Where you from man?'

He looked around at our eager faces, in reality, a group of four Mancunian guys, not the ideal company in a boat party full of attractive girls. He began to speak in a hushed tone.

'Listen, boys, let's skip the whole rigmarole of *where you from, what's your name, and what you on?* We've got plenty of time for all that later on. It's time to make the most of this day party and make sure we claim the best girls before that cunt of a rep gets the chance. Are you with me?'

I was taken aback with awe. Did this mere stranger just suggest bagging the best girls at the party, shitting on the guy we hated most whilst simultaneously quoting the lyrics of one of our favourite bands, The Streets? Could people be carved straight from the heavens? A kindred spirit from half a world away, we had surely made our first true friend.

Despite our romantic intentions, we barely broke ranks in the hours that followed, cultivating friendship's strong bond through a mutual love of music and shared stories of travels, despite all our adventures being infantile. Ryan Choman had set off from Vancouver as a solo traveller, arriving in Bangkok just over two weeks prior. He was allured by the wanderlust that infected most people we met, but what set him apart was his unrelenting desire to see and do everything a place had to offer.

In his two weeks in Asia he had already toured the temples in the capital and browsed the famous floating markets' exotic produce. He had braved the motorbike whilst intersecting the city, dotting out for unmissable hikes in the wild outer provinces. He spoke with such passion of the places he'd visited, a human thesaurus of purely positive turns of phrase.

I'd certainly never met anyone like him before, a conviction in his desires unyielding and bold. I'd go as far as to say that he influenced my core values in those first few hours. I'd always cherished comradery and shared experience above all, but his independent self-assurance was intoxicating enough to add merit to the 'nomad' character he portrayed. I quietly held hopes that we could convince him to stick around.

The bite of the tropical sun had lessened on our sun cream covered shoulders, leaving the murmur of nightfall dropping hints around the party. We'd managed to abandon our second rate vessel for prime seating on the maiden voyage back to shore. Our now party of five, a party within the party, had slowly submerged into smaller pockets of conversation, each unknowingly entering the second phase of the day, leaving behind the untarnished memory of part one.

Unapologetically the scene of the crime, our boat effortlessly traversed its waters with unblinkered ease, skimming only the surface of the deep, leaving behind a trail of bubbles and beer cans. The tarnished nature of the Phi Phi Islands had startled me upon arrival, but as I'd been helplessly sucked into the offerings of the island, so too had my cares for such things. I was oblivious, unaware of any external issues when having this much fun, exercising my ignorance of the negative as habitually as cracking a beer.

Chapter 17

A tiresome week passed before we were ready for departure, fragments of our mind, body, and souls left littered across the overpopulated island.

Our time spent in Koh Phi Phi, tempestuous in nature, did not stray too far from the predetermined path, a binge-drinking tornado swept around pool parties, local fire shows, and beachside dancefloors. Thankfully, the boat party pep talk by our new friend Ryan did not fall completely on deaf ears, our intrepid sides emerging like a blossom in spring.

We'd abandoned our prerequisite morning snoozing and made an effort to approach midday like we did midnight. An exhausting kayak trip to Monkey Island provided a memorable day, whilst hiking to the island's standalone viewpoint was a highlight.

Unfortunately for us, we were once again down to a quartet, for we had lost Ryan to the bottomless chasm of Phi Phi. We'd foolishly forgotten to exchange details with him in the madness of the party and unsurprisingly our last-ditch attempts to type simply 'Ryan' into Facebook were futile. Nevertheless, his impact was made, leaving an imprint on us that he would not be forgotten, as we assured ourselves in the days that followed. Although a brief meeting, he had struck a tone that resonated with each of us individually, a lease of life we didn't know we needed.

Weary heads, heavy eyes, and aching backs made up just a few of our gathered mementos. Thankfully we'd managed to avoid the many makeshift parlours that populated the island, well practised in bamboo tattoos and happy endings. As we lugged the last of our belongings onto the overcrowded passenger boat, the foreboding prospect of a nine-hour journey across sea and land loomed.

We were due to travel overnight across the southern provinces of Krabi and Surat Thani, before an additional boat journey to Koh Phangan, home of the infamous Full Moon Party. Despite the route making little geographical sense, our resolve had been swayed by the incessant recommendations of countless people we'd met, all promising us that the Full Moon was not to be missed. What we hadn't taken into account is the shared sentiment amongst the travellers in Koh Phi Phi. It seemed like almost everyone on the island had been sold the dream, the boat's fixtures beginning to strain under its growing community.

It was apparent we wouldn't be sitting together, although a chance to collect my thoughts wouldn't go amiss. I left my friends and made tracks for the upper deck, rubbing shoulders with international backpackers of all shape, colour, and creed, taking the stairs at a plod before spotting salvation.

An opening had unveiled itself at the end of a well-occupied bench, a crevice of credibility, a nook of noninfringement, a saintly seat of solitude. I might've had to break out my new Muay Thai moves if anyone challenged me for the throne, but fortunately, I was unopposed as I doubled down for the journey.

The upper echelons of our transport were largely unsheltered from the elements, the metal-framed roof held up by posts and beams. A gratifying breeze kissed my face like a dancefloor stranger as I took in my immediate surroundings. The harbourside of the island, named Tonsai Bay, seemed almost unrecognisable to me as I tried to make out any familiar shops or pathways I may have trod in the preceding days.

My attention was drawn to an approaching boat, a transport not dissimilar from our own, tasked with unloading the next hoard of perpetrating party goers. The atmosphere exuding from a ship's arrival compared to that of a ship's departure is paradoxical, a momentum-swing like a pendulum's weight. Catching myself lost in thought, I zoned back into reality and adjusted myself into an agreeable position, pushing my iPod headphones firmly into my ears.

I thought of home for the first time since our departure, melancholic speculation of my family's fortunes back in Manchester, lackadaisical wonderment of what was being made of the fortunes I'd left behind.

Had Steve made inroads for his new flat? Had my parents invested the money into stocks and shares already? I allowed myself to enjoy these moments of reflection, as well as granting passage to less familiar transcendental strings of thought that only derive in hungover heads.

The sound of Alt J's 'An Awesome Wave' album provided a fertile breeding ground for experimental, even psychedelic tangents, before the sudden shuddering underneath me signalled our long-winded journey had begun, a step on the insurmountable ladder of exploration we had embarked upon. I bid a silent farewell to the rolling cliffs of scraggy limestone and dozed into a dreamless slumber.

Perhaps the journey's weren't going to be as bad as people said?

Chapter 18

'Na, you've got it all wrong lads. I'll tell you exactly what happened last night,' objected Matty, pulling himself onto the concrete panels that lined the side of the pool.

'Here we go,' sighed Turner, closing his eyes in the shelter of the midday sun. 'None of you will remember what happened, lost your heads, the lot of you!'

'Trust me! I'm the only one who remembers. Turner, you were completely out of control. I genuinely thought you wouldn't make it home so dunno why you're piping up!' I challenged. 'Only guy worse than you on that entire beach was fuckin' Browners and he only turned up about an hour ago.'

Matty scowled. 'Listen here boys, I'll do you all a favour and recount the night properly since all of you were mentally compromised. So…' he paused, awaiting dramatic development. 'You'll all remember how the night began, the four of us drinking outside the hostel with those girls in our dorm. We got stuck in from the get-go, pounding those mingin' buckets whilst playing that "would you rather" game. Alex, I think you were chatting to the mate of my one, no idea what her name was though.'

'Think it was Amy, dunno I lost her pretty early doors I…'

'First off, you didn't lose her! Do you not remember Brown Shoes fully terrorizing her other mate for her tattoo?'

'Na I don't actually, I was too busy chirpsing to bother with any of that. What did he say?'

'Mate. She had this little tattoo on her wrist with the caption saying something like 'you already have your wings, all you have to do is fly' next to some picture of a bird. Brown Shoes was reading it and then started going off on one like, 'Why have you

86

got a quote about flying next to a picture of a penguin. Aren't they flightless?' He wouldn't let it drop and ended up literally laughing in her face. Anyway, she ends up like crying her eyes out because the tattoo had some deeper meaning about her relative who'd passed away. Mate, it was so brutal.'

'Yeah, I remember him getting unbelievably awkward and protesting his innocence, claiming it wasn't exactly his fault that they'd passed away. It was genuinely like that scene from the Inbetweeners,' laughed Turner.

'Yeah, so after that, those girls fully sacked us off and we ended up finishing their buckets. Brown Shoes genuinely had like three before we even set off for Full Moon.' He took a lasting breath as he grabbed his sunglasses from beside him, carefully placing them on. 'So anyway, from there we were on our way to the party when that fucking Toby guy showed up.'

'Toby!' I shouted, a memory triggered in my head like the striking of a match, a perspective shift on the preceding night taking place. 'What an absolute dickhead he was.'

'You were literally buzzing off him so I dunno why you're chatting on like you hated him straight away. I immediately said we should sack him off but you two kept chewing his ear off.'

'Us two?' Turner said. 'I spoke to the guy once and I'm pretty sure I told him I hated him so I've got no idea where you've got that from.'

'Na, this is way before you started acting like the biggest bastard in Koh Phangan, don't worry.'

'Pardon?'

'Oh I'll get to that mate, don't you worry. Back to the story, once us four and fuckin' Toby got to Full Moon, he told us that fuckin' stupid story about Lucky Chang's. He was saying that they don't regulate the alcohol content in the beer, so each bottle has different strengths. He honestly believed it as well… Anyway, we ended up completely ignoring him and getting those little energy drinks from a local on the beach. Biggest mistake of the night right there, I swear down they were laced with something because after that point you lot completely went insane.'

'Us lot?! You obviously don't remember when you…'

'Erm, let me finish Kingy, we can get to your flawed version of events afterwards lad.'

When Matty was in this kind of mood it was better to just let him get on with it, determination in his eyes. 'Anyway, Browners started skanking out with the most ridiculous dance moves I've ever seen, he was genuinely gyrating around the floor, fully banging into people and shit. I tried to chill him out but he fuckin' asked this girl for a dance-off and she actually did it. Only she had professional battle dance moves in the locker. She was shouting for a dance-off and loadsa people started chanting and making a circle around them.'

He certainly set the scene well, I thought as I submerged my head under the clear water. He'd conveniently missed out the fact that it wasn't only Brown Shoes who'd got us excommunicated by those girls at the beginning of his story, but he himself who'd come on way too strong with the aforementioned lady. But I'd let it slide, I thought generously.

Once I'd emerged, he continued his tale. 'You should've seen Browners' attempts at dancing, he tried the fucking worm and ended up with his face shoved fully into the sand, everyone was dying laughing. Such a fuckin' idiot mate. After that point I barely saw him again, he was off his barnet!'

Matty paused, his eyes following two bikini-clad girls who had walked past our prime pool position, before snapping back to reality a couple of seconds later.

'I'll continue my story with you Turner, or should I say, Harris, your complete alter ego. Do you remember partaking in a certain jump rope activity?'

There was a momentary pause, Turner's usually unflappable demeanour faltered ever so slightly before he spoke. 'Yeah, fucking too right' he said with growing confidence. 'I absolutely smashed it, not a burn on me.'

It took me a little too long to realise what they were talking about before the proverbial penny eventually dropped. Strewn haphazardly across the entirety of the Hat Rin beach were enormous ropes coated in gasoline and ignited into blazing flames, wielded by groups of local entertainers who offered party-goers the chance to test their luck within. But surely Turner wasn't stupid enough to do that?

'Yeah you did amazingly well, I couldn't believe what I was seeing! But that's not what I'm on about. Your part to play in this tale is not the man who went into the fiery ropes, it was the man who came out, a man who went by his given name of Harris. You abandoned all sense of self and humility when you emerged from the fire and started acting like a complete ego-maniac!' he shouted, enthusiasm increasing with every sentence.

'Shut up, no I didn't!' deflected Turner, a grin creeping up one side of his face.

'Oh, but you did. I thought you were going to go on a mad chirps' but you were saying you didn't want to because of Nat I think, so instead you challenged fucking Toby to an arm wrestle in the sand. That was when we all started to hate him, do you not remember? He was blabbering on to every girl we met that he was well strong and shit. Was honestly tragic. He only shut up when Alex challenged him to a Muay Thai fight later on and we all convinced him he was actually trained in it.'

'Oh shit, I remember that,' I lied.

'No you don't,' said Matty simply. 'You surely can't remember anything?!'

My friends turned towards me, expecting my inevitable protests to ensue, a counter-story to be told. I'd have to think on my feet for this one, that much was certain. The shabby patchwork of my recollection was torn in numerous places, gaping holes of the night left abdicated by memory. But that didn't mean I would be going down without a fight. I drew in my deepest breath and braced myself to begin my account, a raconteur without a story.

'Wait a second! I think you'll find it's my turn to tell you what actually happened, now that Matty's finished with that collection of lies. Buckle your seatbelts fellas,' asserted Turner. 'In fact, let's grab some beers first?'

Good old Turner.

Chapter 19

'Now then, let's get down to the hard facts. Matty, I don't blame you for having a hazy account of the night's events considering the state you were in, but at least you got the Brown Shoes bit right,' Turner began, wading his way over from the poolside bar of the hostel. 'So, I'll pick up from the supposed egomaniacal escapades of this so-called Harris character.'

I loved it when Turner was in this kind of mood, typically a man of few words but had a knack of emerging victorious in verbal jousts due to his rare combination of brash eloquence.

He continued. 'So before you start painting me as some kind of narcissistic renegade, it was you who first tried to back yourself in that jump rope game!'

He signalled at Matty with a pointed finger, whose face had twisted into a crafty grin. 'You were chatting in Toby-esque fashion saying you could beat anyone at jump rope and all I was doing was trying to drag you back from the centre of the circle. At that point, the fuckin' locals spotted us and demanded that we had to participate. Shockingly, your bravado failed you and you fuckin' scarpered leaving me to pick up the pieces!'

Matty had doubled over in laughter, nearly knocking over his bottle of Chang in the process. 'That absolutely did not happen!'

'Oh, but it did my friend. Thankfully, I came out unscathed and made my way back over to you two who were both trying to claim you could do better. Very typical, I'd say. Anyway, the key aspect you're missing from your story of the night is the enigma that was Alexander Thomas King.'

Oh shit. I was hoping to avoid the limelight in this story, making every effort to piece together what had actually happened.

The only faded fragments I could manage to identify were that of a mystery girl. Shock.

But who could harbour hope of completing a jigsaw without the pivotal corner pieces? I resigned myself to the inevitability of a full, comprehensive recap and laid my head to rest on the side of the pool, signalling for him to continue unopposed.

'So after you'd scared off wanky Toby, Matty, you stole that crutch from one of those Brummy guys who were with the girl Alex got with. It was that muppet who'd fallen off a moped whilst drunk driving, he had scars all over his back!'

'Oh shit yeah, what an idiot, who the fuck would drunk drive out here? And I fully forgot about that, did I give it back to him?'

'Did you fuck! Think you gave it a girl as a chat-up line at the end of the night. She wasn't your best conquest if I remember correctly,' Turner laughed.

'What happened with my girl then?' I interjected, suddenly very interested in the outcome of the story now a possible love interest had been introduced. 'Was she hot?'

'She wasn't bad actually, you were chatting to her for ages before you did it.'

'Did what?!' I shouted, perhaps a little too loudly as another collection of Full Mooners looked over from the adjacent side of the pool.

'Made a fucking dart for the sea! It seemed to happen in slow motion, you were just blabbering away at her then all of a sudden you both turned and pelted it through the crowds. We almost lost sight of you 'cause there were so many fuckin' people but we could just about make you out sprinting for the water!'

Like a flash, the memory emerged from the murky depths of my mind, the intricacies of the night knitting together, an unravelled yarn being spun. I'd propositioned this girl to swim out to the taxi boats anchored a little way out from the shore, opportunistic in my intentions.

It seemed like a foolproof plan at the time, a simple means of obtaining the one commodity not on offer on the Full Moon beach, a bit of privacy. But something wasn't right about the story, something didn't fit. A plan so flawless in its conception did not yield the triumphant result it had deserved, I just couldn't figure out why.

'What happened then?' I queried, trying to work out from Turner's face if I was destined to be the tale's champion or dunce. 'I remember going into the sea with her and trying to get on one of those taxi boats, but can't remember if I pulled it off?'

Turner's face put any doubt in my mind to rest. 'Did you fuck pull it off! You made it to the boat and tried to hoist yourself up. Little did you know that the boat's fucking owner was in there. He jumped out at you and sent you spiralling back into the water. Me and Matty had run out to try and stop you at this point and we saw the whole thing!'

Matty and Turner were in floods of laughter, any trace of hangovers left in merriment's stead. I couldn't help but accept the amusing nature of Turner's version of events, despite the depreciating bottom line. 'Ah well, happens to the best of us I suppose,' I relented, plastering on a face of acceptance.

'Oh it doesn't end there brother, that's not even the funny bit,' Turner continued, a merciless scoundrel adding insult to injury. 'When you'd managed to get out of the sea, you and the girl made your way over to me and Matty. We spotted it straight away, a horrible little condom stuck to your arm. The sea around Full Moon was absolutely dreadful, full of piss and shit, a proper mix of all the crap people have dumped over the island. You dove head fuckin' first into the thick of it. You both absolutely stank!'

'Brilliant. Typical of me to end up being the only guy in history to get an STI without getting laid.' My one-liner was met with its desired response, granting me a limited moment of breathing room, a welcome reward.

Without warning, a chorus of barbarian shouts emanating from the boys beside me, a bridge of ineligible greetings being cast into the distance. I allowed my eyes to follow the direction of their calls, to see a triumphant Brown Shoes striding out of the hostel entrance.

Chapter 20

The man. The myth. The Brown Shoes.

It is here that his name should reside in tales of folklore and myth. The story of his Full Moon experience had to be seen to be believed, the twists and turns of an impossible maze, dwarfing our petty discussions under an overarching umbrella of implausible fantasy. He swears by his fable to this very day, but I'll let you be the final judge on whether to take him at his word.

'Wait? You lot didn't make it to Eden?' asked Brown Shoes, a quizzical look taking hold of his face.

'What the fuck is Eden?' asked Matty, still in a state of disbelief at the ramblings of Brown Shoes thus far.

We had been sat with our friend for over twenty minutes before any of us had interrupted his monologue, aside from the occasional gasp or exhale of scepticism. He'd recounted his steps from the time he'd lost us with a matter-of-fact aloofness that suggested they were true.

He began his tale of wonderment in the same place we each had faltered, the dance-off. In contrast, he claimed to have easily come out on top, suggesting he'd used comedy value as a strategy to eclipse his foe. He continued by narrating a detailed description of a mystery girl who he'd met as a result of his victory, how she'd invited him into her fold of friends, all exclusively beautiful of course, who'd each taken turns to enchant him with promises of a great night ahead.

Allegedly, they had told him of a secret "Eden" where one could leave behind the excessive mainstream clamour of the Full Moon party and journey to an authentic alternate event, the upper class of Koh Phangan's offerings that were held secret by those on the exclusive guest list and only discussed in hushed tones with those outside the elite circle.

'Trust me, fellas, I didn't believe them either but we all ended up getting into one of those little taxi boats at the edge of the beach. He charged us all like 50 baht each to take us there. That's only like a quid innit?'

'Yeah like ninety pence,' Turner said.

'Yeah so well fuckin' cheap. So I thought fuck it why not? Well anyway, we were travelling for like 15 minutes in this boat until he took us to this secluded little beach around the side of the island with like a rock walkway leading up a cliff. It was absolutely sick to be fair, for some reason I just assumed yous would follow me there, I had no idea I was there on my own!'

'So what was it like? What was going on there?' I interrupted, eager for more.

'Hold on, hold on. Let me think a second. I'm not sure if it was a separate island or still on Koh Phangan, I think it might've been the same…'

'No, obviously I don't care about *where* it was you doofus, what was the bar like?!'

He sheepishly laughed. '*Oh*. Oh yeah, it was pretty sick mate. Was just loads of people on like bean bags listening to reggae and stuff. Loads of people were smoking bud and that but we all just went to this bar and had like beers and fruit shakes and stuff, it was pretty chilled.'

'You didn't do the magic mushroom shakes did you?' asked Matty, astonishment personified.

'I dunno, I don't think so.'

'Obviously, you would've known if you'd done them!' Turner laughed.

'Oh. Well, I dunno. The girls did all start acting pretty west. Oh yeah, and there was this wedding on the beach that we all went and watched!'

'What?!' we cried in unison, aghast at his nonchalance.

He jumped a little at our uproar and started to laugh. 'Yeah was mad, this couple was getting everyone at the bar to come and join them on the beach and people were handing out scran and shit. I ended up going down there with that initial girl I'd met at the Full Moon party, we just sat on the beach and ate and watched them get married. Like a full ceremony. Was pretty sick to be fair.'

'That absolutely can't be real, you sure you weren't tripping out?' Matty asked.

'Pretty sure yeah, remember it all pretty clearly, to be honest.'

'What happened with the girl then? Here was me thinking you'd gone off bladdered and broken your leg or something and you're off galavanting with a mystery girl at fuckin' Eden!' I exclaimed.

'Oh, fuck knows. Obviously, we slept together on the beach but then I lost her by the time the sun started coming up. Felt like I was at Eden for a long fucking time so just jumped on the taxi boat back with a couple of random heads.'

'You slept with her?!'

'Yeah obviously, have you not been listening to the story? I was at a beach wedding in Thailand with an unbelievably fit girl, we didn't talk about Man City's starting 11 next season mate.'

None of us knew what to say next. If it was true, Brown Shoes had without a doubt pulled off the best story of the trip, most likely of his entire life. We each looked at him in a poorly hidden expression of admiration and astonishment, coupled with jealousy and slight suspicion.

We were quite fortunate as four twenty-one-year-old guys to not allow much of a competitive edge to develop in our friendship, preferring to encourage and support one another instead of belittling and discrediting, aside from the occasional parody argument. However, speaking for myself at that moment, I did feel a tiny hint of resentment creep in by the end of his story.

'Oh yeah, I forgot to say I saw that fucking Toby guy passed out on the beach on my way back to the hostel. There was loads of neon paint leftover on the beach, so I drew a massive dick on his head for good measure,' summarised Brown Shoes as he stood up and made his way to the bar. 'Anyway, Lucky Chang anyone?'

Any flickers of selfish bitterness were swept away with his final rhetoric. I felt ashamed for my jealous thoughts and quickly dispelled them from my mind. This was the first time on the trip I'd felt anything negative towards my companions and it felt alien and unwelcome, a mistaken emotion in its inception and target.

I dismissed the trespassing thought process as a mere product of poor sleep and alcohol ingestion, my mental alignment an insight into the belly of the beast. We were about to enter our third week of the trip and were yet to press the pause button on proceedings. It felt almost futile to resist the urge of a night out or a day party when the concept of finances no longer had a part to play.

Any time spent washed ashore of the wave of momentum was heckled as boring and an insipid waste of 'the time of our lives.' It didn't look like we were due to slow down any time soon, the next in the collection of Koh's would be soon upon us.

We'd been promised a more laid back experience on the island of Koh Tao, but if what I'd seen of Thailand so far was anything to go by, I wasn't sure I trusted the notion. I looked up from the pool to see a grinning Brown Shoes returning with four probably very Lucky Chang's and took a deep, lasting breath.

Chapter 21

Stepping out onto our far-reaching veranda and absorbing the panoramic views of beach, jungle, and ocean, it was clear we had made the right choice.

The time on Koh Phangan had been lavish in letting loose, feasting on the island's manufactured gifts like the spoils of war, a knees-up of epic proportions.

But as the age-old saying goes, what goes up must come down and we were a living testament to that as we tentatively boarded the outgoing ferry from the island, sore heads our badge of unison. The boat between Koh Phangan and Koh Tao was only a short four-hour journey, much to the delight of my friends who didn't seem to enjoy the pleasures of long-haul travelling stints as I did. To our surprise, the transport wasn't as crowded as we'd come to expect and we'd managed to find ourselves a generous space sprawled out across the top deck.

It didn't take long for discussions to begin as to where we'd be residing in Koh Tao. In a decision that mirrored our rare spot of comfort, we opted to hire a 4-person villa for the duration of our stay, a villa that sat pretty along the top row of booking.com when sorting the price high to low.

The adage that money can't buy you happiness faced fierce competition on the tour of our new place of residence, an architectural man-made marvel in its own right, the villa was built to delight. The marble white exterior shone, poised and elegant, protruding from the vibrant jungle backdrop like a spot of dew on a mid-morning lawn. The cosy thatched roof offered security and authenticity to an otherwise modern design, the western-influenced architecture a strange sight to our South East Asia accustomed eyes.

The rooms were spacious and grand, white linen and immaculate bathrooms a stark contrast to the cluttered dorm rooms we had been calling home for the past couple of weeks. The enormous living space was punctuated with huge sofas and grand dining tables, each piece of furniture more exaggerated than the last. But the crème de la crème, the pièce de résistance was the boundless tiled terrace that opened up from the centre of the villa, an overhanging infinity pool its crown jewel.

Breathtaking views of the island's delights could be found in every direction. It was all ours. I couldn't believe it. If we weren't sold on the dream already, it proved difficult to find fault in the service provided by the friendly landlord who welcomed us in with such agreeableness you'd think we were close relations.

This was the side of Asia that our fellow backpackers were not able to access, an exclusive taste of the island's elite tier that only the rich would ever experience. Granted, even the highest prices in Thailand were still relatively affordable to those who saved up year-round to holiday here, but for the majority of those we were brushing shoulders with on our travels, this degree of luxury was left consigned to the imagination.

This austere differentiation in atmosphere, surroundings, and, frankly, cleanliness had left me at a juncture in which it felt appropriate to try to call home. I hadn't spoken directly to my family since leaving Manchester, aside from the occasional WhatsApp message to confirm my safety. I knew my Mum had been pining after me ever since my departure so I took sanctuary on one of the many sun loungers out on the decking and fired up the FaceTime app.

The camera exposed my tired features in ultra high definition as the dial tone rang out, the bags under my eyes etched deeply into my face. Thankfully, the makings of a strong tan helped mask my olive complexion, the remedy of sun-kissed skin superseding any sleep-deprived blemishes. I pushed my hair out of my face and plastered on my most endearing smile as the connection was made with my distant home.

'Alex? Oh, Alex! Hello! How are you? I miss you, I miss you!' rambled my mum, her face pushed far too close to the screen. She appeared to be in our conservatory, enjoying a mid-morning cuppa I assumed. The UK was around six hours behind the local time in Thailand, making it about 11 a.m. back home.

'Hi, Mum! I'm alive and well thank you very much, how are you?' I asked, suddenly missing her a lot more than I realised. She adjusted the camera to an appropriate angle and revealed her full and elated face.

'Oh Alex, it's amazing to see your face! We've all been missing you so much, even Dad has said it a couple of times if you can believe that... Tell me all about it, where are you? Where have you been? Who are you with?' She spoke with such excitement it put me a little on edge, the prospect of cramming all that had happened on our trip so far into one account was a daunting one on its own, never mind when trying to apply a PG filter.

'Great to see you too Mum! I'm missing you all loads. It's been amazing though, everything I imagined it would be and more if I'm honest! Do you want the long version or just want me to pick out some highlights?'

'Oh I don't want the gory details thank you very much, just tell me how you are and how your friends are, I really hope you're being safe!'

'Oh perfect. We're being very safe, you'll be happy to hear there's been no motorbikes, tattoos, or sharks as of yet!'

'I should think not! Do they have sharks in Thailand? You better not go in the sea then, Alex!'

'Yeah they do, but they're quite rare I think. Don't worry you won't catch me doing any scuba diving, I'm way too scared!'

'I was going to say, you can't have changed that much already! So how many places have you been so far? Is it all mud huts and no toilets?'

I laughed at her cute ignorance, although it wasn't dissimilar to my own just a few weeks prior. 'No, no, it's nothing like that Mum. It's actually quite westernised from what I've seen so far. For every pad thai you see, there's a full English fry up on offer across the road! But yeah, this is our fourth island so far, not bad for two and a bit weeks I'd say.'

'How interesting. Well, I'm very glad you're enjoying it and you look like you've got yourself a tan as well! How are the boys getting on?' She had settled down a little now, or at least her demeanour had. Her eyes still welled with intense emotion, a maternal fire lit within.

'They're all fine yeah, we're all loving it. How's everything at home?'

'Oh fine, nothing to report from back here really. Everyone said they really enjoyed your leaving party though, you've had a lot of well-wishers and thank you cards for all that money as well. I think you've become a minor celebrity in our family! I suppose there's no point asking about how your money's getting on is there?'

'I guess not, no. We're not spending that much really, to be honest. We've been staying in hostels mostly so we can meet people and experience the normal backpacker stuff.'

'Oh well, that's very mature of you, Alex. I assumed you'd be staying in swanky villas and posh hotels the entire time!'

'Well...' I laughed with a sheepish grin. 'We have actually just splashed out on a little treat for ourselves. Shall I show you around?'

'Oh have you now? Yes please, I could do with a bit of excitement myself, show me your world!'

I stood up from the comfort of my lounger and began my virtual tour. I took her around the inner workings of the villa, showing her the rainfall shower and beautiful Thai artwork that hung in the hall. I talked through the island's features, describing the tropical paradise in an idealistic manner, omitting any mention of the plastic littered oceans and overcrowded beaches. We spoke for a long time, covering all topics a mother and son can cover, half the world away.

It was great to see her and hear that things at home were going well. Steve had found a flat he wanted and was due for viewings in the coming fortnight. My dad was my dad, the same as always, a man of simple pleasures. I enjoyed listening to her run of the mill stories about my grandparents and the local town fair from the previous weekend. It provided me with a gravitating sense of normality that I'd been missing. I was pleased to find that any emotional chat had been kept mostly in check as we approached the end of the call.

'Right then Mum, I better get cracking anyway. We've got dinner plans down near the beach and I haven't even used that swanky new shower yet,' I said, still keeping the tone light.

'Okay Alex, okay. Just try to give us a ring again soon, try and wait for your dad to be here as well, I know he'll want to hear from you,' she rushed, squeezing in her last parental instructions before the end of the call.

'I will do. I love you and miss you! Speak soon.'

'Alex, one more thing…'

'Yep?'

'Please don't get eaten by sharks.'

Chapter 22

Of the many acts and endeavours that made up my bucket list, scuba diving could be considered an outsider at best.

Growing up in suburban Manchester doesn't exactly open your eyes to the vast mystery of the ocean, your first worldly associations instead coming in the form of a favourite football team or your dad's CD collection. If I'm honest, deep water had always freaked me out a little, the unknown, murky depths seemingly full of threat and danger, a notion fortified by the countless Hollywood blockbusters that depicted shark-infested oceans as watery graves.

That being said, I'm not ashamed to admit that all the logic and reason in the world goes out the window when following the assurances of a girl like Freya. The Swedish Afrodite had lured us to our fate during a game of beer pong on our first night in Koh Tao, citing her terms of victory as the four of us signing up to the diving course that she helped run on the island.

False bravado only gets you so far with a girl who surely played professional beer pong, so the rest of the story tells itself. Four reluctant signatures later we were onto our next adventure, cursing our luck.

To my secret delight, the first day of the open water diving course was strictly orientation and theory, running through the basic procedures and know-how of what to expect over the upcoming four day period. It was a surprisingly welcome change of pace from the island's preceding, the need to channel our studious sides required an application of mental prowess that had not been required when tasked with simply chatting shit and binge drinking.

I'll admit my intrigue was nurtured over those first two days, helped by Freya's passion for the beauty she'd seen in the ocean, the feeling she got every time she entered the waves. It was difficult to resist her enthusiasm as she spoke candidly about the various species we may encounter, citing sightings of whale sharks as the holy grail, as well as the customary run-through of the basic hand signals and safety checks that would keep us under her wing when out in the sea.

Our confined water training was efficient and comprehensive, familiarising ourselves with the gauges of pressure and depth, getting used to the weight of a tank above and below the surface. Once we had sized up our neoprene wetsuits and selected our masks, all of a sudden we were ready for our maiden voyage to the deep.

We sailed out after lunch on our third day of the course, dressed to the hilt in scuba apparatus after passing our knowledge development final exam. Despite only a short two day period, my feelings of anxiety had significantly lessened, diluted with the intrepid need to know what all the fuss was about. I wouldn't go as far as to say I was excited, but I was making progressive baby steps the further we journeyed out from shore, a loading screen of giddiness slowly edging closer to completion.

The scuba tank felt heavy on my shoulders as I peered over the edge of our boat, my reflection unsteady amidst the rippled surface. Inner feelings seemed to mirror that of the virgin group, each member of our team very much focused on the task at hand, silent rituals internally repeated.

As much as we were in this together, Freya very much by our side throughout, we each knew that once we were underwater it was just us vs the ocean, tasked with finding a careful stalemate between the two. As we slowed to an eventual halt, small murmurs of good luck and well wishes were exchanged between us, feigned confident grins from my friends. It was time to descend.

'Alex, you're up first buddy!' came the call from Freya. 'I'll drop in first and give you the signal when it's your turn, okay?'

Cursing my luck that I'd been called upon, I let my shaky hands form a dramatic "ok" sign in response, the scuba symbol that all was well. My cheeky response got the laugh it sought out, providing me with much less comfort than I desired. I fastened on the mouthpiece, triple-checking every piece of equipment I could reach, ensuring everything was in fact "ok".

Yanking myself onto unsteady legs, I began my waddle to the south-facing side of the boat, passing each of my comrades in the process. Their partially steamed up masks could not disguise the looks of relief that I had to go first, each bidding a silent farewell as I struggled to traverse the slippy deck. The act of hoisting myself onto the side of the boat was executed with as much grace as the fabled Humpty Dumpty, and we all know how that ended up. With my back to the ocean, I arched my neck to see Freya giving her final signal, and with an almighty gulp of oxygen, I let myself plunge backwards into the unknown.

I was an astronaut the moment I entered the water, heavy equipment becoming weightless all around me. As my eyes adjusted to the alien surroundings, I was shocked at my ability to draw in a breath. As I quickly inhaled my impossible elixir, faded instructions began to resonate around my mind. Faint inaudible chants of "stabilise your breathing, stabilise your breathing, stabilise your breathing" plagued me in an incessant internal monologue before I suddenly realised they were talking to me. I like to think I adjusted quite quickly after this as I frog-kicked forward, propelling me an inordinate distance across the water.

The clear ocean vista was vast and endless, a perfect silence interrupted by steady breathing through my regulator, creating noisy bubbles of air. My biggest worry was the pressure on my ears proving too much to bear, but I found it more manageable than anticipated. Perhaps it was my steely focus on buoyancy control that provided the necessary distraction from any negatives I was experiencing, channelling the learnings from the two days prior.

My only concept of time stared up at me from the decompression computer attached to my wrist, a constant reminder of the depth and minutes passed. In a limitless world, we were set a maximum of 12-metre depths on our first day, with a promise of 18 as tomorrow's reward.

I'd never thought about the nuances of the word 'breathtaking' in such a literal manner as I did in those two days of diving. The simple freedom I felt in being invited to an underwater world, it's magical nature no longer a stranger to me. I felt a profound sense of peace when observing the wild, unaltered habitat of so many beautiful species of plants and creatures.

The cynicism inside of me washed away with the gentle currents that taught us how to dance, gently guiding us around new-fangled coral forests, each more dazzling than the last. The solace I'd sought in those early days in Thailand had been waiting for me all along, just a stone's throw away in this immeasurable, unlimited nirvana.

The trials and tribulations of what lay above gradually became irrelevant as I temporarily traded beers for boxfish, exchanging girls for the grin of a greyface moray eel who came out to say hello. All the riches in the world had no bearing on life underwater, transiently free from the shackles of wealth and fortune.

The longer I spent in this transcendent world, the more I grew to appreciate how precious underwater life could be. Minutes became hours at the mercy of the watery paradise, the determination to spot something before anyone else surprised me, my competitive edge not easily triggered.

Towards the end of the final scheduled dive, I plucked up the courage to venture further afield, allowing myself to drift off from the main bulk of the group towards the edges of the dive site. Turner had claimed to have spotted a baby shark yesterday, so I needed something to rival the story.

My eyes strained as I surveyed the coral formations, urging all sea life to give me a wave. On closer inspection, this side of the coral didn't want to oblige, a spooky underworld compared to the main reef we had enjoyed. Fishing nets choked the dull lifeless rocks in an unbreakable stranglehold, patrolled by guarding bottles of beer. The pollution saddened me much more than what I'd seen wash up on the beaches in Koh Phi Phi or the Full Moon, and I wasn't sure why.

But I couldn't allow myself to be bothered. Pride and this strange sense of sadness tussled across the forefront of my mind as we climbed aboard for the final time.

On the one hand, I'd done what I never believed I would do, earning an open water diving qualification in the process, conquering predetermined fears, and proving to myself I could do it. However, in an unanticipated twist, my desire to dive again no longer rested with Freya, but developed into an actual ambition to do so. At that moment, I felt a brief inclination to abandon reason, an appetite for diving becoming an itch that I didn't expect to want to scratch.

Knowing when to walk away is the key to any chancer of fortune, but in the face of moving on, I found it more difficult than it seemed. The profound nature of that first dive felt intense in the days that followed, but as time went on, my memories warped in the realities of the world, trading once gushing memoirs of beauty and nature for references to the first time I pissed in a rental wetsuit.

Anything for a cheap laugh, I guess.

Chapter 23

How had we let them corner us like this?

The crumbled stone walls of deserted convenience stores seemed to be closing in on us as we slowly backed away from the crossroads, our footsteps echoing as we gingerly retreated in a tightly packed unit of four.

A distant car alarm disrupted the eerie silence, causing a unanimous flinch from each one of my friends, an evident build-up of tension with every passing second. I desperately looked around for routes of escape. The dusty pavement was lined with fragments of the ongoing battle. We had only stepped off the plane a couple of days earlier in Chiang Mai and had little time to accustom ourselves to the lay of the land, mice trapped in a hopeless maze, desperate to find a way out.

The sudden descent to madness had been impossible to predict, taking each of us in the winds of chaos and spitting us back out. Where had it all gone wrong?

A mere twenty minutes ago we'd sat jovially discussing the menu at a local Thai restaurant, weighing up the curry vs fried rice dilemma whenever Turner stopped blabbering on about Nat. Our first dabble off the beaten track had been at the recommendation of a fellow dorm room resident, imploring us to visit the most authentic Thai eatery that we'd ever be lucky enough to dine in. We'd hit the road with endeavour in our steps and rumbles in our stomachs, keen to showcase our ability in identifying the intricate differences between the southern island's delicacies and whatever northern Thailand had to offer.

Upon arrival, all had seemed fine, if not exceeding expectations when the restaurant's owner had welcomed us in with the enthusiasm of a whimsical character in a child's fairytale. He danced around us with mischievous glee as we were shown to our table, fussing over the cushion placements and condiment assortment he had provided. We were the only people in the cramped dining room, surely indicating the foregone conclusion that we'd been had for fools.

Nevertheless, when in Thailand, one may as well do as the Thai restaurant owners do. We allowed his infectious energy to take hold of the conversation, encouraging him to sit down and give us his best recommendations for the meal. If his demeanor was exaggerated before our invitation to join us, his performance soon afterward was akin to an Academy Award winner, dramatic gratitude, and inordinately wide smiles his brandished trophies.

He sat down at the head of the table and began to enchant us with stories of his background and culture, for every tale told, a question was posed back to us. He wanted to know who was better, Manchester United or Manchester City, encouraging a lively debate, his genuine interest in our lives making him instantly endearing. He listened happily and in turn spoke with candid grace about the city of Chiang Mai, its history rich and fascinating, especially when recited in such romantic terms.

But all that was now an otherworldly memory, the strife of battle an abstract diversion from any normal patterns of thought. I wiped a mix of sweat and what seemed to be the remnants of a prior laceration from my forehead, droplets beginning to obscure my eyeline. A Sophie's Choice of possible routes lay in front of us; the first coming in the form of a return to engagement with our previous foes, a skirmish we had lost just moments earlier. The second option lay back towards the main road, rendering the term 'sitting ducks' as an understatement. I knew only one thing for certain, if we stayed there we were done for.

'Fuck it. Let's go back the way we came,' hissed Turner, his hushed voice was urgent, impelling someone to make a decision.

'Fuck that! We just got absolutely nailed!' protested Matty, who had come off worst in the most recent clash, still tentatively nursing where he had been hit.

'We can't stay here! Browners? What do you think? I'm saying let's go the other way. I can't face those guys again,' I grabbed him by the shoulder, snapping him back into focus.

'Oh I dunno. Yeah, whatever. Let's go the other way!'

With silent acceptance he'd been overruled, Turner led the way as we made a dart for the closest opening out onto the main road, skidding to a halt at the corner. We took up animated semi-crouched positions, years spent playing Call of Duty on our Xbox's finally coming up trumps.

The deserted side streets we had been traversing were dwarfed by the multi-lane highway that spread out in front of us. It was still quiet, no signs of life substantial enough to draw the eye. *Too* quiet. The highway was lined with imposing trees along the outer lanes, reminding me of an entrance to a palace I'd seen in a Disney movie somewhere.

Out of nowhere, a tuk-tuk taxi hurtled past us with a dramatic honk of its horn and a sudden swerve, quickly becoming a distant figure in the form of a wobbling mirage across the tarmac surface. The rumble of the engine lessened to almost silence before it happened. Before we had a chance.

There they were! The momentary distraction of the tuk-tuk had cost us dear as we spotted new enemies just a few roads away, menacing weapons wielded high above their heads.

'Fuck it. Let's get em,' Turner shouted, breaking into a canter, leading the charge.

'Fuck sake!' Matty cried as he spilled some precious ammunition onto the floor, creating an audible scene.

We approached in what we hoped was an arrow-shaped formation, a strategy we'd decided on amid the last clash. With

112

each step, we advanced towards a roadside no man's land in which the impending carnage would leave only one winner.

I peeled left, as Turner went right, Brown Shoes taking shelter behind an overflowing skip in the centre of our makeshift arena. A wild warcry came from behind me as Matty charged forward, no thought of safety in his mind, a kamikaze entering the theatre of war. I watched on as my best friend was gunned down in front of my eyes, his steps faltering under the barrage of shots. I groaned out in anguish as Turner stepped in to assist, only to be met with a clear, decisive impact to the side of his head, his weapon clattering to the ground with a sickening thud.

In an instant, our group had been sliced in half, leaving just Brown Shoes and I to fight for our honour. All hope was beginning to fade until a precise shot from my partner took down one of our cackling enemies, his laughter turning to dismay in front of my eyes, a futile attempt to cover his face failing as he crumpled to the floor.

But to my sorrow, revenge was a dish best served cold as Brown Shoes was brutally taken down by a close-range blanket dose of munitions. That left only I remaining. A solitary soldier to avenge my fallen foes.

I heaved my dual canister goliath from over my shoulder and dropped the handguns to the floor. It was do-or-die time.

I charged forward into the melee and fired in every direction, barely differentiating between friend or foe, a grand last stand as I sprinted into the madness. I took a shot to the leg, then another to the shoulder, stinging skin beginning to take its toll. I felt fire all over my body. It was over.

As I lay there defeated, staring up at the cloudless sky, I thought back to the words of our welcoming host, his eccentric broken English echoing around my head.

'I will tell you one of the greatest things about Chiang Mai, yes? It is beautiful city, very peaceful, very quiet. But once a year, we have Thai New Year Festival in the city! We call it the Songkran Festival, the festival of water. The celebration is a huge crazy city-wide water fight, everyone stop work and go on the streets to shoot each other with water guns, super soakers, water balloons, buckets of ice-cold water! It is a big party for backpackers and local people like me! It is amazing! The water washes away all sins and bad luck. We love it here at my restaurant and have big super soaker and water balloon store in back. But I tell you what, okay? Since you lovely English boys be so nice to me and my family, I don't want you to miss the party! Songkran is April, 13 April every year, but because you miss it, we do a mini Songkran right now, okay? Me and my little kids vs you four big strong man?'

An outstretched arm appeared in my line of sight as Turner's laughing face came into view. He dragged me to my feet as I steadied myself in the deep, icy puddle that had formed around me.

The fluorescent colours of the assorted water guns mirrored the joyous faces of our foes, the host's children, and their neighbourhood friends. They swarmed around us continuing to shoot jets of water at every target, a sing-song of laughter, and chattering music to my ears.

We continued this jovial water fight with the local kids long into the afternoon, popping back to the restaurant for periodic breaks, drinking delicious fruit juice, and making our way through an impressive assortment of Thai delicacies that our host had rustled up.

In the end, the experience in that restaurant far exceeded the recommendation of simply great food, providing us our first true encounter with authentic Thai culture, a snapshot of how the locals celebrated their new year.

Although falling short of the "right place, right time" ideology, considering we did in fact miss the festival by three months, we had been lucky enough to be introduced to its wonder by our host that afternoon, an experience I wouldn't want to trade, even for the real thing. He had shared with us not only his stories but a living expression of the new year's celebrations, a private front-row seat to the festivities.

As we bid a fond farewell to the family who had welcomed us in, it was hard to not feel overwhelmed. It felt to me at that moment as though we were growing with each passing day, each place we visited offering up a spread that outdid the last. Beach parties and buckets of liquor had felt like the pinnacle of the mountain in those early days until scuba-diving served up something completely different. Now a sneak peek into the culture of the country had offered such a scintillating afternoon it felt like the doors of possibility were open wider than ever, each day bestowing precious gifts of opportunity.

We stayed in Chiang Mai for several days, a carpe diem attitude putting the wind in our sails, spurring us on to explore the complexities of the city. We thought of our distant friend Ryan as we trod the paths of ancient temples, diversified our palettes in the bustling food markets, and took a day trip to the Chiang Mai canyon.

Our adventure into Northern Thailand had begun in such enigmatical fashion, it was difficult to predict what would happen next in the mountain town of Pai, a place widely celebrated in tales past. But if our new friend at his little Thai restaurant was to be believed, we had cleansed ourselves of any chance of bad fate or fortune with the ceremonious washing of water on that wet and wonderful afternoon.

Chapter 24

Over time, memories tend to organise themselves in the busy subconscious archives of the mind, establishing somewhat of a hierarchy when choosing which anecdotes to call upon in times of recollection. All that being considered, the library of my life thoroughly sorted through, grand sweeping statement incoming— the town of Pai, Northern Thailand was the greatest place I had ever been in my life, hands down, no questions asked.

What made it so great could make up a novel in itself, the charming town seemingly without fault according to most adulatory tales. I'd be lying to suggest we had even heard of Pai before setting off on our travels, assuming people were speaking about Greggs bakery when it was brought up the first few times.

Our ignorance was soon put right by the countless renditions of backpackers who had ventured north before us, spinning fanciful tales of the transcendental town that did not abide by the laws of time, disobedient to the ways of the wider world. It was easy to dismiss stories like these—exaggeration was a string to many a backpacker's bow—but the coherent nature of these collected accounts proved too much to ignore, leading to the administrative decision to journey north of Chiang Mai into the delights of the mountains.

We were met with a postcard-perfect panorama as we ascended the winding roads leading up to Pai, traversing over a million sharp turns before the green walls of the surrounding mountains seemingly parted ways, allowing the picturesque town to remove its cloak of invisibility.

On the surface, the town itself was no different to many we had passed through, souvenir shops rubbing shoulders with simple restaurant exteriors, dusty paths leading out to quiet bars, and trusty 7-Eleven supermarkets. But as we journeyed further into the valley, it seemed the standout differentiator from places

116

we'd been before was the uncompromising nature that surrounded us. Mountainous jungle backdrops had never looked so impressive, only to be complemented by sprawling fields and rice paddies, not a bucket of liquor in sight.

Natural beauty aside, we soon became privy to the real secret. The town had another offering that could not be uncovered by the naked eye. The quaint, simple village on the surface had a vast shrouded array of mysteries to explore, a trick deck full of hand-winning aces.

The first taste of this enigma came as we checked into the hostel we had booked a couple of days prior—the Spicy Pai Hostel—a short drive away from the central town. The hostel was unlike anything I'd seen before, dorm rooms made up of entwined branches of trees that propped up hammock-like beds, multiple decked layers making use of space in a genius architectural assortment. The hostel opened out into its own valley of rice paddies flirting with the horizon that led back down the mountain.

We spoke to several people in the 24-person dorm room, a few of whom suggested we should head to reception to find out what we could squeeze into the three days we'd planned to stay. Despite the many purring recommendations we'd been subject to, it was hard to believe the musings of the laid back hippy-looking local who manned the front desk as he nonchalantly mapped out our options.

Jungle treks, cookery classes, and temple tours made up some of the basic options, whilst white water rafting, elephant sanctuaries, and reggae music festivals were declared a must. He explained how a row of natural hot springs lined the outer reaches of Pai, as well as a delicate cave ecosystem that could be explored for a few hundred baht.

Live jazz nights, artsy coffee shops, Burmese temples, waterfall hikes, the list went on and on, each activity more enticing than the last. Our heads spun with the prospect of trying to squeeze in the town's delights in our allocated time, rendering the plan to leave in three days as obsolete. As we'd not decided on our next destination it felt silly to leave so prematurely.

'Boys, you no need taxi in Pai, you rent motorbike from me. Only way to see Pai is on motorbike, okay?'

We looked around at each other, silently weighing up what to say. Thus far on the trip, we'd avoided the noisy temptation of the engine's roar. It wasn't until now that they had been deemed necessary, relying on tuk-tuks and buses to get around. I didn't have a driver's licence at that point so the idea of riding a motorbike was alien to me, not ever having much of a grease-monkey passion.

But on the assurances of the Spicy Pai hostel worker, as well as the inopportune sight of a few young girls zipping off from the garage nearby, we reluctantly accepted the inevitable. Crumpled waivers signed and copies of our passports made, we were led over to the rental bike shed that stood outside of our hostel.

'Okay, any of you boys ride motorbike before?' queried the laid-back hostel rep, padding over to a group of multi-coloured scooters that were chained together at the front of the garage. As he turned to us I noticed his longline vest had a pronounced motorbike graphic headed up by the slogan 'Ride or Die.' I wished I was confident that the two were mutually exclusive.

We shook our heads, trying to hide ashamed faces behind our sunglasses, for riding motorbikes was evidently the done thing for young men in Asia. The rep shook his head and kissed his teeth, clearly reluctant to hand over the keys to such a risky investment.

'Okay, you no ride bike before, you watch me very careful okay? If bike comes back dirty or broken in crash, you pay me damage, okay?'

He signalled over to the first bike and handed Brown Shoes the key. We all huddled around as he began to lay out what would surely be comprehensive instructions and all the bike 101 necessary to learn how to ride.

'Here is throttle, here is break, here is ignition, you ride now.' Not the most informative chap I'd ever met.

We lined up our new vehicles outside the garage, each turning the key to the rumble of the engine. My pulse had a false start as we prepared to embark on our debut ride on the back of our now most trusted companions, the Honda Win scooters.

I'd barely had time to kick away the bike stand when a blasting Matty went throttling forward, the handlebars of his bike evidently not obeying his whimpered commands, a crafty mind of its own trying to escape him. His scooter veered off into a sharp left, then right, then back again until he managed to wrestle the brake to a stop, just shy of the wooden wall of the garage.

In literature, the people who ride motorcycles are often depicted as icons of danger, sex, and outlaw spirit. The image of my friends and I gingerly learning the ropes probably didn't add much merit, our fluorescent scooters in pastel colours not exactly the archetype of a bad boy image.

But that's not to say we didn't feel like it. Once we had traversed the tricky path leading away from the hostel, we turned out onto our first stretch of the open road. There's a certain poetry behind the prospect of a wide-open road presenting itself to you, a dusty stretch of possibilities that at any moment could veer off in a thousand different directions.

The solace of freedom is something everyone who travels is chasing in some capacity, finding it in many different walks of life, through people, riches, and circumstance. I think for me personally, not being a driver back in the UK, I felt a palpable sense of freedom at the edge of my fingertips on that first day in Pai.

I was no longer bound by the busy bus schedules or taxi driver's charge. I was free of the shackles that chained me with predetermined routes, mapped out by people before me. I could go grab a supermarket toastie whenever I wanted. I had a new license, a license to do as I pleased.

Chapter 25

'No freakin' way! You won 20 mil on a scratch card?!' Kori exclaimed, raising a well-groomed eyebrow from the comfort of her hammock. The rest of the group fell silent, bat-like eyes and ears alert to our conversation.

I felt the familiar rush of blood as all eyes fixed upon me.

'Ah, yeah I did, I mean, I didn't want to broadcast it or anything but just before we came away I won it…' I trailed off as some other friends began to shuffle across the wooden floor to hear my story. Soon, a small group had gathered around the two adjacent hammocks where Kori and I were situated.

'Did I hear that right? You won 20 big ones on a scratch card?' Chase asked, taking his enormous aviators from the edge of his nose.

'What's that now?' Marie added, taking her arm from around Matty's neck as she joined the conversation. 'When were you going to tell us, Alex?'

Had I made a mistake in mentioning it? Should I have just kept it a secret like my dad had made me promise not long ago? A sinking feeling of regret took over my mind.

Over the past four days, we had reached the promised land of travelling, immersing ourselves in the delights of Pai. The fable merchants who had promised us that Pai would be our travels pinnacle had massively undersold its riches. Not only had we been able to explore the natural treasures that the town had to offer, but we had also finally succeeded in creating a ten-person strong group in which to share it.

I guess one of the limitations of travelling with such close friends was the inability to create new relationships that rivalled those bonds. A group of four is already strong in number and doesn't quite catch the eye of potential hostel friends as a solo traveller does, or so we had found thus far.

But Pai was different. It seemed the usual backpacking rules didn't apply in this cool mountain air. Things just seemed to go your way.

Our starting ten was made up of myself, of course, Turner, Brown Shoes, and Matty making up the foundations. We'd first added Thaddea and Lina, a duo of attractive girls from Düsseldorf who had invited us for dinner. The numbers grew further over some hostel cooked pad thai as a couple of American guys, Chase and Robbie, sat down to join us.

A boisterous buzz raised the thatched roof as we dined, explaining Brown Shoes' Full Moon party antics in vivid detail. The sound of laughter proved too enticing for some as Marie and Kori shortly added themselves to the mix, an English rose and a marine biologist from Hawaii I think?

There seemed to be something in the air that night, a conversational lifeblood that kept on giving. We laughed and joked, sang and danced, played games from all corners of the globe. We flip-flopped off into two's and three's, inscribing our names into the trusty bark of the night.

The precedent had been set for the following few days, as we remained as tight-knit as that first night's blessing. We journeyed to the cave system, a biker gang in tally, living the experience through each other's eyes as well as our own. Personal jokes were harboured about eating sweets with bats, nonsensical ramblings defining our new language.

By day four we had earned our stripes as Pai perfectionists, having ticked off nearly every activity on the map. In such a short time I was beginning to feel closer to these people than many of the friends I had left back in England, a shared common ground felt underfoot.

'I'm telling ya now aren't I?' I managed, opening my sitting position out to the group, a body language "welcome". 'Come on, gather round you lot,' I signalled to the outer reaches of our posse, beckoning Brown Shoes, Lina, and Thaddea over to join.

'That's actually crazy you lucky fucker! I bet you can buy an awful lot of Chang for that kinda green!' Robbie said, swigging his beer.

'You're not wrong my friend,' Matty said, patting him on the shoulder. 'What do you think we've been doing for the last month? Most of his fortunes have been left at the bottom of the Lucky Chang bottles!'

'I need a Lucky Chang myself...' Brown Shoes laughed, getting himself up from the floor. 'What time are we heading to these hot springs?'

'I think we should head pretty soon, we want to catch the sunset if possible!' Lina squeaked, her German accent both high-pitched and adorable.

We were due to journey to the last natural wonder that Pai had to offer us, an eight-kilometre ride to the fabled hot springs. The hot springs were due to close at sunset but we had been informed by our hostel rep that once nightfall had passed, the beauty of the springs was transformed by the tapestry of the stars. Who were we to argue with such whimsical assurances?

We shot off from the dusty confines of our hostel, an excited convoy, ready for the next facet of Pai's bounty. I had become competent at riding my trusty scooter over the course of those four boundless days, spending more time on the bike than off it. Chase and Robbie typically led the charge, elder statesman roles established in their late twenties, but as we took to the open road they dropped back from the group and steadied their speed to ride level with me. I jokingly swigged at my empty bottle of Chang that I'd left in the drinks holder of my bike, throwing the bottle to the side of the road.

'Yo! Alex!' Robbie shouted, his voice nearly drowned out by the drum of the engines whistling in the wind.

'What you sayin' bro?' I called, taking my eyes off the road to look at him, his long wispy hair flying out the back of his helmet like a sputtering exhaust plume.

His eyes displayed a steely glint. 'What you think about putting that fortune of yours to good use? We can run in and get shit loads of beers for the hot springs?!'

Thinking back, I don't know if it was the distraction of our high-speed dynamics, the feelings of trust I had for my new friend, or the simple carefree state of mind I had at the time. I answered with absentminded certainty as I called across to Robbie.

'Obviously!'

Chapter 26

'Oh shit, was it my turn?'

I wished I could stop being so ignorant, as yet another drinking game round passed me by, the hot steamy water washing over my sins. I struggled to regain focus on my surroundings, a collection of friends old and new engaged in a knees-up like no other, the hot springs mural swirling around us. We were four or five Chang's deep into the incandescent night, the cold beer, hot water contrast offering up an inspiring sensation to the touch and taste. The moonlight winked at us from the sky, stars kissing every corner of the water.

I feared my lack of attention would soon be noticed if I didn't get more involved in the antics. Typically I'd be hard-pressed to not seize a piece of the action on a night like this. But tonight was different. The winds of change had offered me something not strictly on the menu, a true uncharted delight had caught my eye and was not letting go.

My momentary intention to dive back into the action was washed away as she flicked the droplets of water from her dark midnight hair, creating a page-turning story with each ripple on the surface. I felt my mouth agape on my face, misty eyes shrouded with wonderment and awe, consciously thinking that if I had been wearing socks, they would've been knocked off. I needed to pull it together. Each time I tried to snap out of it, she would perform some new fascinating act, a virtuous splash of water in her face, a laugh that infected the world.

I toyed between the reality around me and the improvised fiction I had foolishly concocted, where we had met by chance, an organic and fortuitous meeting, a boy meets girl story, and lived happily ever after.

I gave up in my quest to stop staring, imploring my other senses to come to sight's aid. My ears strained to block out the tomfoolery around me, the commingled voices of England, Germany, and the USA proving a difficult adversary. Vision and sound working in unison, I could just make out a few words from her righteous, beautiful lips.

'I can't wait for Vietnam…'

'Alex!'

I momentarily made the daydreamer's mistake of assuming she was calling my name before I turned to see all eyes upon me for the second time that night. The candles of expectation flickered, lighting up the hot spring water like a thousand-eyed idol. I had no idea what had been asked of me, or even what game we had moved onto for that matter. All I could think about was that angel sitting at the entrance to the water, a distant beauty, unlike anything I had seen.

'Alex? Are you still with us?' Thaddea asked, swimming over to me from the rest of the group. Thaddea and I had been getting close over the last couple of days with what I hoped was innocent flirtation, but probably meant a little more to her.

I looked at her and then around at my friends. 'Yes, yes sorry I was away with the fairies for a second there. What game are we playing?'

'They're playing "never have I ever" and it's your turn, silly! I wondered why you weren't drinking for any of the rounds. I didn't have you pegged as a stick in the mud…' She winked, flashing a pretty smile up at me.

'Oh, shit. Are you guys all wasted? Fuck it, I'll start playing properly now. Never have I ever… Erm… Never have I ever been in love!' I blurted out, putting my arm around Thaddea without thinking.

126

Catcalls whistled round the group as I realised how that mindless action must have looked. I shrugged with a smirk and urged them to hurry up and drink. We swam back into the makeshift circle of our friends and joined them in laughing at Chase's story of falling in love with a delicious bacon sandwich.

I allowed myself to get invested in the game, questions of sex, drugs, and passion inciting flustered responses accompanied by heavy swigging of drinks. I was drunk soon enough, conversations merged into one as the entangled trees surrounding the water became blurred at the edges, misty darkness overtaking the moonlight bounty.

I eventually looked up to see that my mystery girl had vanished, leaving behind a sorry landscape without its dazzling focal point. But I was too drunk to care, intoxication playing tricks with my mind, disguising love as lust, dulling the heart's sense of longing.

My haphazard swamp of thoughts raged like the remote beach parties of Southern Thailand as the night came to a booze enforced end. Chase, Robbie, and Brown Shoes made me look saintlike in their demeanour, stumbling to find the exit to the hot spring basin, laughs forced through diaphragm spasms as they steadied themselves on the forest floor.

The misleading heat of the water abandoned us as we shivered in the night's cool air, shoulder wrapped t-shirts our only defence against the breeze. We trudged over to our army of bikes, parked a short squelching walk away.

I signalled over to Turner and Matty who were collecting their helmets with an 'ok' symbol, who both grinned through chattering teeth, returning the favour. I tried to get Brown Shoes' attention but he was already on his bike, helmet-clad, and ready for the road. I struggled to pull on my trainers whilst wringing out the last of the now cold spring water from my vest. Freezing, wet and murky minded I shoved my helmet over my ears and led my bike back out into the jungle clearing.

High-speed riding has a habit of wiping the slate clean, or so I felt on our journey back to the hostel. The rush of wind and rumble of the engine replaced any shivering feelings and jaded senses from the booze.

Negotiating our way out of the jungle pathways required ultimate concentration, that was for sure, individual focus overtaking bike to bike conversation for the duration of the winding roads. We each went at our own pace, a one-man mission to navigate the tricky terrain with the promise of a quiet, open road at the finish line.

We waited as a troop for the last of us to complete the course, discussing the trickiest turns and treacherous tangles at the bottom. Kori and Marie were sharing a bike and naturally were much slower than the rest, but eventually tiptoed their way down with apologetic smiles. The highway back to the hostel was sugar-coated with a blemishless tarmac, a motorcyclists dream following the jungle track we had just conquered, especially with the heavy burden of Chang beer as our goggles.

We set off with tipsy happiness in our hearts, the reward of a well earned hostel nightcap within touching distance. Robbie and Chase led the pack, followed by Brown Shoes, Turner, and Matty behind. The Kori-Marie combo crept behind, sandwiched by Thaddea and Lina on either side. I let myself drift to the rear of the group, taking the night in through surprisingly emotional eyes. I thought of the trip so far, the highs of partying and exploration, seeing things that most people could only dream of. I contemplated the friendships I had made, feeling as though they could last forever and a day, strong bonds not made to be broken.

My mind wandered introspectively, wondering if the evolution I felt inside was reflected on the surface in my character or if it was just the beer doing the talking. It had only been a month since leaving home but I had started to feel differently, not just emotionally but mentally more open to pastures new, the irons of familiarity and comfort that I'd missed so much at university felt distant and out of mind for the first time in my life.

I looked up to the sky and silently thanked my lucky stars for my fortune, not only the wealth but the journey's blessings I'd gained thus far. It's always the case however, any luck that lasts is always suspected, it can be loaned but never owned. Reminiscing on the back of my motorbike in the hills of Pai, I felt it was my tool to wield, to manipulate as I deemed fit. Oh boy, was I was wrong.

I'd always been told that light travels faster than sound but it was the sickening crash that hit my eardrums before the burning headlights pierced my eyes.

A couple of hundred yards in the distance something had happened. A dust-fuelled commotion enforced through the deafening skid of tires against asphalt and beckoned cries of anguish.

I slammed on my brakes instinctively, my mind taking too long to catch up with this sudden turbulent scenario. What was going on?

Clueless thoughts soon switched as I tentatively approached the group of stationary bikes ahead of me, praying with urgent single-minded hope that nobody had been hurt. The eerie pattern of the confused headlights spread out across the edge of the highway's tarmac, intersected by a roadside cocktail of rock and mud. Black tire tracks marked the devil's pathway off the road and into the dense undergrowth of tropical bushes that lined the edge of the adjacent dirt track.

The rumble of my engine halted as I removed my key from the ignition, expecting a sudden silence to hang in the air. The sound I was met with was quite the opposite, similar to a prime time street food market in the streets of Chiang Mai, screaming and yells from every direction, unorganised madness descending upon the roadside.

129

I strained my eyes to try to recognise the faces of my friends, Matty, Turner and Brown Shoes, amongst the dust cloud that kicked up from the ground. I could make out Matty, struggling to prop up his bike with the kickstand, frantic in his demeanor. I clambered over to him, the rocks spraying up from my heavy steps across the track.

'Yo, you alright man?' I yelled, helping steady the frame of his vehicle.

'Yeah mate, all good... What happened?! Is everyone okay?' he shouted, turning his head to the rest of the group.

'Is everyone okay?!' came an American voice beside us, female in origin.

A chorus of yeah's, all good's and confirmations thankfully responded in turn as the dust slowly began to settle and unshroud the scene. The vague silhouettes of each member of our group steadily took shape, as everyone recovered from the shock of the apparent crash.

I saw Turner, helping Lina from her bike further afield from the road, a hearty cough echoing from him. He looked scared, the crease lines on his forehead etched with woe.

'Fuck! Where's Brown Shoes?!' Matty called from beside me, scampering off in a frenzy from bike to bike, a shadow of suffering.

A deep onset of panic took over me at his words, a rush of blood and adrenaline surging through my veins. I felt delirious. As if the whole world had stood still around me. Turner broke the torturous trance, his voice breaking as he spoke.

'Shit, please God, no. Look over there...'

I fastened my gaze upon him and unwillingly followed his signal, my vision rushing over the natural habitat around us; dirt, leaves, mud, and air, a moving blend of insignificance. That's when I saw it.

Locking in on the wretched picture sticking out of the side of the road, unmoving and motionless.

Jutting out of the overturned motorbike stood two contorted legs, splashes of dark brown mud splattered over two broken shoes.

Chapter 27

I didn't like Bangkok.

I knew I didn't like it the night we stopped over on our way to Chiang Mai, the bustling sweaty streets were suffocating to navigate, municipal wastewater overflowing, creating man-made rivers of sewage everywhere you looked.

Perhaps I'd dismissed it too early, judging a book by it's cover was a tendency I was trying to avoid now that I'd embarked on my travels. Although I was no stranger to big cities, there was something about Bangkok that intimidated me, the vast turnstile of human life that passed through the capital felt callous, hostile even. However, if I didn't like it before, I certainly didn't like it now.

The week since the crash in Pai had been nothing short of a disaster. Foreign hospitals and disgruntled hostel reps aside, the accident involving my best friend Brown Shoes had taken the wind out of the travelling sails immeasurably.

Adversely, whichever way you looked at it we had been extremely lucky to still count our friend as alive. A drunken crash at high speed had claimed the lives of many travellers before him and there will undoubtedly be countless more to follow, but thankfully Brown Shoes had gotten away with a few broken bones, the worst being a fracture of the fibula.

At the time of the crash, we had managed to summon roadside assistance from a couple of local men who hastily called in an ambulance. They resuscitated our friend on the side of the road, putting our worst fears to rest, although struggling to calm us completely. We were shaken to our bones by the experience, the false memory that we'd lost our best friend a brutal and visceral warning.

The slow-moving pace of our short-lived stay in Pai had come to an abrupt halt as we stressed about what to do in the days that followed. We were forced to bid farewell to the people we'd come to see as a family unit, promising to keep in touch and meet up again later along the road, although we weren't sure how long that road was going to be anymore.

After an exasperated number of translated conversations, we somehow managed to negotiate a taxi back to Chiang Mai hospital, where a more extensive examination would be done and a probable flight home would be organised for Brown Shoes.

What added further heartbreak was the conversation we shared with Turner on the flight across to Bangkok that followed. He informed us that he too would be journeying home, presenting us his argument in true Turner fashion, brilliantly thought out and reasonable. He missed Nat, the girl he had mentioned fleetingly over the course of the last month, briefing us that he wanted to go home to make a go of it, as well as holding a noble desire to accompany a devastated Brown Shoes on his melancholic journey home.

I found it extremely difficult to vocalise my emotions to any of my friends in that short span of days, the date of their impromptu flight back to England looming large over our heads. There was little that Matty and I could do or say to make Turner change his mind, for his reasons were absolute.

Consoling Brown Shoes proved troublesome as well, the ghost of his buffoonery scarce in his eyes. And it was his departure that plagued and played tricks on my mind. At the scene of the crash, I remember a bottle of Chang crunched into the tarmac where he had fallen, the image remaining so vivid in my mind.

Although the likelihood of that bottle being my own was a million to one, guilt forced me to accept that I had tossed a bottle into the street earlier that night. I was part of the problem. The acknowledgement of this supposed karmic justice was a bitter pill to swallow, an itch that could not be scratched.

A solemn scene was set on their day of departure, a crossroad of a thousand souls mingling around us in a concoction of sound, smells, and sights one could only find in a foreign hospital. Like the party beaches of the south, privacy was an unyielded commodity in Bangkok, the shared ward of bike injuries, Dengue fever and drunken misdemeanours littered our final goodbye.

'Fuckin' hell then boys… Looks like this is it…' Brown Shoes began, wincing a little as he shuffled in his hospital wheelchair.

'Yeah man, suppose it is,' Turner said. 'The car is waiting outside now so we better get going…'

I looked from their faces to Matty beside me, who looked like he was about to say goodbye forever. I needed to lift the mood, despite my crippling sadness.

'C'mon fellas, chin up eh? Once Browners is back on his crocked feet you can both just jet out to see us again. No big deal right?' I looked around hopefully in an attempt to catch Turner's eye.

He smiled, the first real smile I'd seen in what felt like forever. 'Yeah brother. It's just the end of chapter one this, you boys need to go on and smash chapter two for us!'

'How are these two boneheads gonna cope without me and you sorting them out?' Brown Shoes said, clapping Turner on the back. 'Do yous even know where you're going next?'

'No bloody idea, we've got no chance…' Matty said, through bated breath. He turned to me, my now only companion. 'Where you reckon lad?'

I paused, trying to block out the foreign, crazy surroundings of the hospital ward to achieve a bit of mental clarity. I weighed up my limited knowledge of the best routes available, whether to opt for geographical sense or the badgering recommendations of travellers past. This was usually Turner's area of expertise but surely I could come up with something. The shuffled deck of my mind picked cards at random until it landed on the answer to my question. A magic whisper floated to the forefront of my memory, a hope, a whim, an untold possibility.

'I can't wait for Vietnam…' she had said.

The musings of a crazy person perhaps, to peg our entire trip on an eavesdrop of a complete beautiful stranger, but at that moment, the answer felt like the easiest in the world.

'I reckon we go to Vietnam, I've heard a lot of good things…' I said, firm but fair, a conviction in my sentiment, disguising the foolish undertones of my plan.

'Yeah, sounds good to me,' laughed Matty, who was probably not listening as we embraced our friends goodbye.

Something happens in the world when opportunity knocks and you answer the door, no matter how subtle that knock may be. Things have a habit of falling into place when an offhand decision is made off the back of the faintest indication, wheels set in motion that cannot be undone.

Little did I know at the time that the choice I'd made in the capital of Thailand would lead on to the things that followed. In a week of sorrow, I had lost two of my best friends to chance's cruel circumstance, the very beers that brought about the end of their trip were a direct result of me bragging about my fortune. Had I kept quiet, they would likely have continued on in our quest of self and external exploration.

But as is the case in any tale, there are two sides to the story's coin. On the one side, I felt a burning regret that my boastful carelessness had a part to play in the end of my friend's adventure, a regret I could easily let derail my own path.

But on the other, the righteous, uncharted side of that same coin, those actions triggered an auspicious series of events that sent Matty and I to Vietnam. And Vietnam well, where to fucking start…

Part 3

Chapter 28

'What about you, mate? It's your turn to tell us about your love life. And don't spare on the gruesome details!'

The iridescent spotlights of the makeshift bar inside the downtown Hanoi Backpacker Hostel stopped their erratic hop, skip and jump sequence in favour of what felt like a solitary beam of expectation resting upon me. The scattered lyrics from the repeated psytrance remix of Calvin Harris' "How Deep Is Your Love?" suddenly seemed to be asking me the question directly, as opposed to its intended rhetoric of seducing unsuspecting backpackers into buying another Head Fucker shot from the commissioned hostel reps.

I can't say I wasn't expecting some form of grand inquisition. The group we'd found ourselves sharing drinks with weren't exactly the live and let live type, encapsulating the Brit abroad stereotype almost impeccably. Pint downing, football chanting, and high fiving aside, we were hesitant to call a spade a spade too early. Tonight was our first spin on the wheel of friendship since Turner and Brown Shoes had unceremoniously left us.

'Yeah c'mon Al, you must've dusted through your fair share of skirt on your travels!'

Rolling eyes and shrugging shoulders didn't seem to be working as I'd hoped, perhaps too subtle a deterrent for this particular group of neanderthals. I was left with no option but to relent, to fashion some kind of pompous yarn to appease the assembled masses.

I cast my thoughts back to the out of sight, out of mind memories of girlfriends past to arrive at an appropriate anecdote, apprehensive about my chances.

How about my first girlfriend? Alex Perry, my namesake. We had tentatively tiptoed our way through the rookie boyfriend girlfriend milestones with amateurish grace, scraping the surface of serious feelings in between petty teenage arguments over whose house would be free at the weekend. The beauty of those naive feelings we shared over a six-month romance were marred by a regrettable end, a will-they-won't-they, on and off, back and forth break up that left only animosity in its wake. The truth of it is, she'd arrived in my life far too prematurely and we weren't ready for a serious relationship.

The lamentable final dumping by text would probably be a story heralded by the drunken blockheads who continued to probe me, but even I drew the line at showing off about something I wasn't at all proud of.

I felt the blood rise to my face as I stalled for time trying to think of something compelling to say. I had no idea why I was so intent on impressing these people but if my trip had taught me anything so far it was that pressure only came in the shadow of great opportunity.

I persisted with riding the train of my thoughts, stopping off at each relationship terminal. I recalled a short time after my unfortunate separation with Alex, wasting no time before jumping heart-first into a new relationship.

I fell for a girl called Georgie Ransworth, two years of idealized happiness scuppered when tasting love's cruel potion for the first time. Falling head over heels was an idiom I'd always taken figuratively, not anticipating the agonizing outcome as you inevitably crash to the ground. We spent years convincing each other that we could buck the trend of being too young to go the distance, trust and reassurance becoming the magnetising agent that kept us so strong.

But alas, a frisk and a fumble with a stranger in her first-year university halls was enough to burst the blissful bubble in my life. My world had crumbled all around me in the months following this indiscretion, yoyo-ing back and forth between obsession and revulsion in a crippling loop.

Looking around me, I couldn't imagine the tales of regret from a failed relationship would do anything to lighten the mood, let alone wet the beak of this 'who's shagged the most birds' brigade.

A change in strategy required, I reflected back to the more cavalier escapades of my life, reminiscing on the infamous post-relationship pillaging of hearts during my final year at university. Although I never claimed to be an expert in talking to women, I knew I had a fair bit in the locker. I thought back to the plethora of girls I'd been with, most of which I couldn't remember the faces of, never mind what their names were. I tricked myself into enjoying the camaraderie of counting conquests with the boys, the lack of feelings I had for anyone was celebrated as a good thing, a hit it and quit it golden ticket.

I could pick any one of these stories to tell my new acquaintances: bragging about the people I'd wrapped around my finger, lying about the chance of a threesome, the time I slept with five girls in a week. They would all suffice and let me off the hook. I paused, allowing a tale to rest on the tip of my tongue, uncertain of myself.

A second wave of inspiration soaked over me as I gulped my fifth Bia Hội, unable to shake the hypnosis of a hostel free-beer hour despite not exactly needing to save the cash. These boys weren't here for talk of university, they wanted the juicy stuff, the travelling grand slams. I picked the lock of my recent memories for the most risque examples of what Alex the backpacker had been up to on his trip so far.

I'd come away with what I'd defined as a laissez-faire attitude when it came to women. I believed I'd left behind the traces of lad culture in my days at university, trading it in for a more mature "let's see what happens" mantra that I'd made sure my friends were aware of. But unsurprisingly this had been left in the sand amongst the cigarettes and condoms on the island of Koh Phi Phi, where a combination of weak will and unregulated beer had left me defenceless to the allures of arrogance and boastfulness, constantly finding myself bragging about how unreal that Swedish girl was that I hooked up with last night.

If I was honest with myself, by the time I'd arrived in northern Vietnam I had no idea where my love life was going, whether I actually enjoyed the free reign of countless one night stands or if I was truly after something more. I found myself trapped somewhere in between the two hands of love, not belonging to one more than the other, the shadow of my failed relationships banishing me from the realms of true affection and the lukewarm embrace of meaningless sex not offering much more than a peek at solace in its place.

As I said, I had no idea. In less morbid, good old fashioned layman's terms? I missed being in love but also didn't mind the odd fling with a hot Swedish girl, finding myself stuck somewhere in between the two. Maybe edging a little more towards the latter spelled out like that...

'C'mon lad, spit it out...'

I swilled the options around my mind for the final time, a fine whiskey getting better with age. Taking in a deep breath, assessing the sweetness, earthy delivery, and full-bodied content, I delivered my well thought out response to the awaiting throng of red-blooded berks.

'My love life? Oh you know, a bit of this, a bit of that, nothing to write home about.

Chapter 29

I'll be honest, I'd not seen the 1987 cult classic, 'Good Morning, Vietnam' but I imagined the opening credits must be based around a morning similar to my own, the day of July 16th, 2015. Although, on second thought the title would have to be revised a little. Perhaps, 'Marvelous Morning, Vietnam' would be more appropriate, or 'Best Morning Of All Time, Vietnam' certainly rolled off the tongue.

Admittedly, a cursory introduction to my old friend context would likely help bring that particular morning to life.

Matty and I had spent the first few days in Hanoi earning our city stripes, schmoozing from one egg coffee (delicious) to the next, one step forward two steps back being a necessary mantra to live our lives by when trying to traverse the impossibly busy streets of the metropolis, a humdrum of absurdity leaving any notion of the rules of the road as obsolete.

Under the supervision of irony, we referred to thebrokebackpacker.com as a travel guide when deciding which direction to head, weighing up a tour of Hoan Kiem Lake vs a third bowl of Pho at a street vendor we had fallen for, a sensory overload at the hands of the city. Each option we chose had a secret to tell, uncovering the mystery of a whole new country with every encounter, patched conversation with locals bearing foreign fruit and always adding something else to tick off the list.

We assured ourselves that we would not let the departure of our two closest friends hinder our progress in any way, formulating newfound intrepidity in the face of apprehension, at the height of which a 'Matty and Alex's Adventure Journal' was embarrassingly purchased for 80,000 Vietnamese dong. You'd be forgiven to think we were stark raving mad for spending my wealth so lavishly, but the accolade of millionaire did not travel far in Vietnamese dong, equating to roughly 30 pounds of English currency.

As lady luck would have it, it was our inability to grasp the currency that would lead on so fortuitously to the morning in question, a scene of imbecilic rationalisation at the hostel front desk had caught the attention of a passing party of Mademoiselles who'd thought it best to put an end to our misery.

'No, no, no they're talking in dong silly, you're not in Thailand anymore!' interrupted a vixen, breaking off from her skulk of nearby friends.

'Yeah, we know! They're saying it's 400 quids worth of dong to go on this mountain excursion to Sapa, which seems a little steep to me. No pun intended!' I managed, regretting it immediately.

She laughed ashamedly, taking the leaflet I had shown her. 'No, it's not £400! Take a zero off and you're in business. Guessing it's your first time in Vietnam?'

Before I could speak, Matty answered with assuredness. 'Yeah, we've just arrived from a month in Thailand. Still stuck in the baht mindset.' Too much emphasis on the baht for my tastes but I let his delivery slide.

'Ah, very cool. We started at the south of Vietnam in Ho Chi Minh City, we've just done a couple of months riding up the country. It's very beautiful, I'm jealous you have it all to come!' She spoke in a casual, playful southern English accent, eyes flicking between the two of us, saving a little extra eye time for me, I thought.

Matty, beating me to the punch again, continued. 'Ah, very cool indeed. What're your plans in Hanoi? Do you not fancy Sapa?' He was annoyingly on form that morning, the extra egg coffee must've done the trick.

'Not right away. We've been doing a lot of cultural excursions on our way up and we fancy a bit of a party, blow off some steam you know?' She was definitely directing her rhetoric at me this time.

'Yes!' I rushed, prompting her to jump a little, a puzzled look still suiting her face. 'Yes, I know what you mean. We're probably going to save Sapa till a little later I think.' I recovered slowly, feeling Matty's silent head-shaking next to me.

'Oh cool. Well, I'm sure you've heard but there's the trip to Ha Long Bay leaving pretty soon on the Castaways Tour! It's meant to be a great party plus you get to kayak around one of the natural wonders of the world, you guys should see if there's any space left.'

Hello? Is that destiny speaking? Sorry, I'm busy talking kayak dates with the love of my life, I'll give you a buzz later, mate!

'Yep, sounds good, we'll check it out,' finished Matty. His internal monologue always did shut up before mine.

Like the bustling amalgamation of motorbike, car, and wagon on the roads of the city, we flung our dorm room contents back into our backpacks in a haphazard frenzy. The clamour and excitement of Vietnam's first major milestone was enough to fast forward through the necessary admin of buying tickets, settling money, and checking out of the hostel, conscious thinking castaway to the future.

The indistinguishable method to the madness of the downtown streets did not subside until we were well out of the city, urban landscape transitioning to the more familiar jungle backdrop as we journeyed on. A short three-hour journey was all that stood between us and deliverance, a two night stay on an exclusive, private island in Ha Long Bay.

A three hundred metre stretch of beach to call our own, the only trace of man coming in the form of a regulation size volleyball net, five open-air bungalows, and a wooden dining hall/dancefloor hybrid. If the brochure was anything to go by we were in for a mad one.

Trading bus for boat was becoming second nature by this point in our travels, barely batting an eyelid at the exaggerated safety instructions ahead of our voyage. Instead, we opted to scrawl a weary account of adventures thus far into the newly purchased travel journal, whilst tucking into a bounty we'd acquired from a roadside convenience store. With the absence of our go-to 7-Eleven treats, we were treading carefully with a new selection of snacks, alien brands across the crisps, sweets, and beer. In a move of what I deemed celestial intervention, my first bite of an enormous muffin signalled the go-ahead for the girl from the hostel to come and say hello.

'Glad to see you made it boys,' she purred, flashing a brilliant white smile. 'And I see you're already getting stuck into what Vietnam has to offer!' She pointed at my half-eaten muffin and swelling cheeks as I strained to swallow the godforsaken cake.

'Can't get enough, this one!' Matty joked, nudging me in mockery, casting bait to catch a nibble. 'I actually wanted to thank you for steering us in the right direction with this trip, it should be an interesting few days…'

'It certainly will. My name's Rose by the way. I'm here with a couple of people I met in Hội An. You should definitely check it out on your way down, it's amazing.'

'We'll make sure to add it to the list!' I said, as I finally conquered my spongy Everest, swallowing hard. 'I'm Alex, this is Matty.'

'Nice to meet you both. We'll all get properly acquainted later I'm sure…' she winked and pranced off back to her party, a wink that sealed its place in history as the beginning of the battle of the Rose.

***

To the victor go the spoils.

An age-old proverb drilled home whilst studying for my modern history degree, concluding any conflict, competition, or head to head challenge between friends, enemies, or strangers. You'd be forgiven in thinking that the morning of July 16th was a mere celebration of these spoils, that the reason I was so flush with jubilation was in the face of victory over my friend in the quest for a girl's affection, a hyperbolic account of triumph spelled out one chat-up line at a time. But alas, you'd be mistaken.

Mumbled musings of who had the better shot with Rose were cut short by the strange and wonderful scene that revealed itself as the boat pressed on with its journey. We were accustomed to the bustling nature of the big city, so the stark contrast was undeniable as we peered out of the dusty ship windows into a different world.

Like the floating markets of Bangkok, an ocean top community had been manufactured onto the surface of the water, a sprawling village made from wood, reed, and rope floated effortlessly, suspended atop the lapping waves. Its many inhabitants went about their daily routines in what seemed like almost complete serenity, a peaceful collected aura settled over the village like a blanket, leaving them undisturbed by our presence.

It was clear almost immediately why the scene seemed so impressive, for not only was the floating village so tranquil and absorbing, it also sat on the cusp of the stunning Ha Long Bay. The limestone karsts seemed to number in their thousands as we skipped along the surface of the water, fumbling around with our camera phones like the excited tourists we were consciously trying to differentiate ourselves from on every step of our journey.

Our first gawp at Ha Long Bay that afternoon left any Instagram photo filter as redundant, at the mercy of true wild beauty.

By the time we arrived on our private island home, there was little time to appreciate the extravagant nature of it all, the afternoon playing out in a rapturous back and forth dynamic, similar to that of the battle of subtleties when negotiating with a Hanoi shopkeeper for their local produce. Once allocated open-air dorm rooms, we were left to our own devices on this hallowed haven of hope, a peninsula of potential. If the evening's promise wasn't tantalizing enough already, it was certainly spiked over the net when we got chatting to a couple of German guys who had arrived two days earlier.

'Wait, so you're saying we're not just here with the people on our boat? We cross over with two different groups whilst we're here?' asked Matty incredulously.

'Yeah man! We couldn't believe it either. So many people to meet here and the parties are crazy, just wait until tonight…' he assured us, his English as flawless as all of the other German people we'd met.

'Plenty of other girls for you then, eh Matty?' I sniggered, explaining our predicament to our new friends, a scenario they enjoyed and described as 'typische' in exaggerated tones.

Once we'd shared a couple of drinks and gotten to know a few more people, we felt settled enough to head over to the beautiful Rose and her friends, who were sitting out on the main body of the beach enjoying a volleyball game between some other island revellers. She smiled that great smile at us as we approached and beckoned us to sit down beside her in the sand.

'You two are inseparable aren't you?' she cooed, her windswept blonde hair making the golden sand seem dull and lifeless.

'We're eagerly awaiting your recommendations for the rest of Vietnam you see, we don't trust anyone else with that responsibility. You should feel privileged…' I said.

Trap sprung, she bounced into action, turning away from her friends and began a doe-eyed monologue of Hội's, Phong's, and Lat's that I can barely remember listening to. I was distracted by Matty's early manoeuvre, breaking a barrier we both knew would prove important in this dual.

He feigned laughter at an inconsequential point in her story and placed his hand on her shoulder, instigating the vital physical contact. She continued on and to the untrained eye, it seemed like nothing was made of it. But, I knew better than that. The touch barrier to chirpsing was the catalyst to the flame, the butter to the bread, the egg to the coffee.

'Anyway, you cannot miss Dalat either, it's such an amazing place, you have to stay at the family hostel! Oh and go to the crazy house as well, you'll both love it…' Her eyes flicked between us in an indistinguishable pattern that I couldn't unriddle. 'I was supposed to be going canyoning there but I had a big fight with my boyfriend so we didn't go in the end.'

Boyfriend. Boy friend. BF. Big fucking stupid boyfriend.

'Ah, what's your boyfriend's name?' asked Matty, his face curdled into a smile with too many sweeteners.

'Oh, he's not my boyfriend anymore. I don't know how anyone can have a relationship over here, there's too much temptation!' she giggled, brushing the sand off her long tanned legs.

I watched as the trumpets of celebration erupted in my best friend's eyes, as he probed further into her life, unshackled by her relationship status revelation. We sat like this for a long while, the sun relenting as the conversations became more natural, more flirty under the countless beers we had at our beck and call. I deduced from the comings and goings of the scattered groups along the beach that there were around 80 people on the island, a figure that doubled our expected tally.

After we'd been summoned for a bite to eat inside, the mood on the island descended into the evening's seductive embrace, pleasantries and introductions were swept out of the way in place of heavy flirting, drinking games, and a gradual but expected coupling off of the guests. Matty and I found ourselves sat opposite one another in a group of around ten people on a makeshift wooden table in the converted dining room. We were locked into a game of "Who's most likely?" and the culmination of our bids for Rose's affection seemed like they would soon be settled.

'Okay, my turn, my turn. Who's most likely to get laid tonight?!' shouted Bas, one of the German guys from earlier, who'd perhaps had a little too much of the old das bier.

'Not you fella…' laughed Matty, as everyone looked around the table, assessing who they would cast their finger-pointing vote for. I mulled over my options slowly, deliberating how best to play my hand. I could've always voted for Rose, sitting just to the left of me, but that may have been a little presumptuous for the charming pillar to post rapport I had carefully cultivated so far.

Opting for the neutrality angle, I cast a casual finger at one of Rose's friends who had removed her clothes earlier in the evening as a dare. To my satisfaction, the rest of the group adhered to my strategy in a clean sweep.

'You guys! I'm not like that! It was a dare!' she feigned, pretending not to be loving it. 'Okay, okay, who around this table is Rose most likely to sleep with tonight?!' she asked, arching a poorly cropped eyebrow.

My face was as crimson as the Ha Long Bay sunset as the eyes around the table darted and scurried from person to person, weighing up the eventualities of such a decision. I quickly looked

149

over to Matty, who was smirking with a nonchalant disposition that I'm sure he must've practised in the mirror. The possibilities of this juvenile vote could be pivotal and I couldn't think of how to play it.

'Three… Two… One… Point!'

I looked around at the limbs of fate, each pointed finger a string to my bow or a nail in my coffin. I saw Bas the bastard pointing firmly at Matty, along with the two girls sitting next to him, all laughing and trying to catch their champions eye. But Bas and his cronies weren't key in this dual.

Casting a hopeful glance to Rose's friends, I prayed for their vote of confidence, something, anything that may tip the tide. It didn't take long for my glimmer of hope to be crushed by the wink nudge whisperings emanating from behind their Matty-targeted votes. Like the high pitched fruit bats we'd discovered in the cave systems of Pai, a unanimous squeal of laughter cascaded from the girls in the group as he shrugged his shoulders in reluctant acceptance, pursing his lips in a wordless "what can I say?"

But all of a sudden, the bats fell silent as the laughter abruptly stopped and the attention of the group seemed to fixate on me. What had I done? Had I let something slip? I can't remember voicing my displeasure, but then again it wouldn't be the first time my face had said the words for me.

I peered around sheepishly, looking for some explanation, someone to put me out of my misery. And then I saw it. To my left, a beautifully manicured finger seemed to levitate in the warm island air, a finger that was pointing directly at me. I followed the line of the finger, up the tanned arm of an angel, to see smiling eyes reflecting my own. It was Rose.

Everybody loves an underdog story. Snatching victory in the jaws of defeat is usually the sporting accolade that receives the loudest cheer and demands the biggest praise. But in this case, the events to follow were the absolute antithesis of that. Snatching defeat from the jaws of victory is arguably more difficult a task but I somehow managed it with aplomb in the hour that followed.

Be it clumsy absentmindedness on my part, crafty double-crossing on Matty's, or just plain old fashioned dumb luck, the brutal and uncomplicated truth was made clear when I spotted Matty and Rose hooking up behind the dorms a long time before the final buzzer went off.

Cursing my fortunes, I drunkenly stumbled down the cracked wooden steps that led down to the moonlit beach, the winds of destiny whistling a sorry tune amongst the blaring disco music emanating from the distant dancefloor. I kicked out at the sand like spilled grains of salt as I slumped down onto a half-broken sunbed and double-checked my phone that it wasn't Friday the 13th in Vietnam.

Scowling at the world, I pushed the hair out of my eyes and in a last stand, do or die attempt at salvaging the night, attempted to finally tie it up into a bun at the back, desperate to put an end to the "in between stage" of its growth. I strained and pulled to no avail, before eventually giving up, allowing the curly strands to fall limp, surrendering to my dismal destiny.

I tried to focus on the good, the positive, but it stung to lose out to my best friend. It served me right for treating this girl like she was a prize to be won. I knew I deserved the comeuppance but it didn't make it any easier to accept. The thought process strangely reminded me of the last prize I'd won, the scratchcard jackpot in the garden of my childhood home, feeling like a besmirched memory that had been dragged with me across the world, sullied by the extraordinary twists and turns of my life since it happened.

I toyed with the memory, weighing up whether my fortunes had in fact turned for the better since being bestowed with such a reward, whether the money had made me happier, luckier, or just simply filled up my bank balance. I collapsed back onto the sunbed and looked up to the sky, giving each star the third degree for answers to an impossible question.

I closed my eyes, breathing in the salty air, accepting the lack of answer as a sign of fate that the night was about to be over. Breathing in, I was no stranger to the scent of the sea, sand, and sky combination so I was surprised to find another mysterious aura tickling my senses. It was sweet and fresh, a promise of something new in the air.

'Hey, chin up Manchester!'

I looked up, from the depths of self-doubt on the luminescent sand, I looked up and it was her.

Of course, it was her.

***

Every moment of my trip felt like it had been leading up to this.

Endless laughter shared with friends in the countless towns and cities we'd made our homes, every grain of rice and slurp of noodle that had dribbled down my chin over delicious plates of local delights, each kiss I placed had been nothing more than mere practise for what was about to come.

I looked at her through karmic filtered eyes, taking in every detail that I could see. Her eyes were the moonlight's bounty, giving light and life to everything they fixed on. Her dark hair acted as the strings that puppeteered my every move. Her lips held the secret of the fifth and final addition to my mantra to life, tempting me to venture on and find the treasure of her kiss. She was fit. Very fit indeed.

Channelling the courage from when I'd first told the boys about my scratchcard winnings, I swung my legs around and sat up straight on the sunbed, broadened my shoulders to their full and most approachable width, cleared my throat of the burden of cheap cigarette phlegm and opened my mouth.

CRACK!

Like my dreams of a charming first impression, the sunbed collapsed beneath me as I plummeted arse first through the godforsaken slats and onto the beach floor, my legs rising to become the highest part of my body, just above my cursing head, folded like a losing hand.

As terrible a first impression as it was, it may just have been worth it for the inevitable result. She doubled over in full heart laughter, a joke book bounty, a comedian's full house. When she laughed, it sounded like the whole beach was laughing, an inclusive "come and join in" kind of laugh.

'See I'm making you laugh already! We're off to a flyer,' I said, struggling to find my way out of the sunbed's maze without exerting too much of a physical strain.

'I hear a good first impression can work wonders…' she said, fluttered with a northern English accent not dissimilar to my own. 'Here, let me help you, you big goof.'

'Thanks, but I think I've got it!'

'Clearly…'

She strolled over, her playful steps barely making imprints in the sand as she grabbed hold of my arm. Her touch was pleasantly cool across my sweating skin, causing the hairs on my arm to almost give the game away. To my surprise, she hauled me out of the plastic prison and back up to my feet with relative ease, exercising unexpected strength for her small, petite frame.

'Well, I suppose a thank you is in order,' I said, brushing the sand from my vest and shorts.

'Only if you mean it, Manchester.'

'Oh, I very much appreciate the assistance.' I kept my voice steady, trying to keep the cards relatively close to my chest. 'Hey, how do you know I'm from Manchester?'

'Oh I don't know, maybe it's the rock and roll, footy mad, industrial vibe you're giving off! Or I guess your accent might be a bit of a giveaway?' As she tilted her head up to look at me, I saw the fire of her eyes up close for the first time, a gaslight blue, flickering with intensity.

'Eh, none of that. You called me Manchester way before I opened my mouth. Unless of course, you've been following me around?'

She paused momentarily, her gaze unbreaking upon my face. 'You got me Mr. Manchester, I do know you from somewhere. And you know me.'

'I do?' I asked, weighing up whether to play it cool and feign aloofness.

'Yes. You do. Care to admit it?' The steely fix of her gaze was difficult to avoid, holding my eyes in place and making lying an implausible mission.

'Well, I may recognise you from somewhere, yes!' I laughed, shuffling my feet a little in the sand.

'Ah, well at least you're honest. I just want to check, you haven't been following me have you? Because it'd be quite impressive a feat chasing someone from Pai all the way to Ha Long Bay!'

'Sounds like you've given it some thought! I didn't realise you'd spotted me in those hot springs if I'm honest, let alone been able to hear me…'

'Oh you and your friends aren't the quietest bunch, I think you'd be surprised how many people know you're from Manchester.'

'What about you then? You sound like you're from my neck of the woods?' I asked, trying to gain back a little ground in the conversation.

'Oh no, you're way posher than me. I'm from Wazza Warrington. I'm guessing you're a South Manchester boy?' She didn't strike me as less posh than me, far from it. In fact, I hadn't assumed much about her background at all as it would've required an ability to see past her unbelievable face, an ability I hadn't yet mastered.

'Got it in one.'

'Well, instead of calling you Manchester all night, are you going to tell me your name?'

'Only if you tell me yours first?' Christ, did I really say that?

The roll of her eyes was a dice needing an easy eight, anything else and I was bust. 'It's Olivia, you little trickster.'

'I'm Alex. Well, Olivia, it is actually quite nice to finally meet you after all these weeks stalking...'

'You're weird aren't ya?'

'I'll tell you what I find weird. I find it weird how we're the only two people down on the beach on a night like this! Do you fancy checking out that cave at the end of the beach that everyone's been going on about all day?' I asked. Not the most agile transition of my life.

'That sounds absolutely petrifying. I have a better idea, come with me.' She took my arm with her bizarrely powerful grip and we walked together, the moonlight behind us casting a his and hers, little and large shadow across the paradise island sand.

Around half an hour passed as we talked, yet I found myself unable to take my eyes off the way she moved, a carefree skip when placing one foot after another, as if each step had its own individual purpose, leaving a footprint that the beach hoped would last.

'What are you staring at, Alex?'

'I'm not staring, this is just my face.'

'I see. Any reason in particular why you keep stumbling over then?'

'I'm quite agile as a matter of fact.' We were developing quite the rapport, I thought to myself, smugly.

'We both know that isn't true. I'm the nimble one, you're the oaf.'

'I'm afraid I'm yet to see this nimble side of you, Olivia…'

She stopped very suddenly and cut across my path, turning to face me in her perfect gloriousness.

'Well now is my time to prove it. Alex, I'm not sure how clued up you are on your sciences, but I wanted to know if you've ever heard of bioluminescence?'

I paused, taken aback a little by the sudden break in back and forth. I scanned my mind for any references to the term I may have watched on an Attenborough documentary, cursing myself for not arriving at a quick enough quip.

'Can't say I'd choose it for my Mastermind subject. Although I'm a quick learner if you'd like to enlighten me.' Pretty decent, I thought.

'Very honest, I like it. Funny you should say enlighten actually, as it's essentially when living organisms give off their own light. How cool is that?'

Literally, anything she said would've been cool to me. 'You're not wrong, it's very cool.' I paused, waiting for her to continue. When she didn't oblige and instead stared back at me expectantly, I went on. 'Although the one thing I'm struggling to see is how the self-lighting ability of living organisms has anything to do with how nimble the adorable Olivia from Warrington is?'

She shrugged off the compliment. 'But that's the very thing! I'm about to show you how they're linked!'

'I can't wait to see this.'

She stared up at me for a few seconds and for a second I thought she was going to kiss me. The limited time we'd spent talking thus far suggested to me that we had a real connection, each moment passing by felt like an hour spent together, defying the elasticity of time in a way only possible when truly captivated.

Wishful thinking aside, she took off at a gallop, proving to be as fast as she was strong, pelting towards the quietly lapping tide. I quickly set off after her like a puppy to it's loving new owner. Thankfully the dry sand suited my cumbersome running style and I managed to keep up, eventually skidding to a halt once we'd reached the pitch-black ocean.

'You see that over there?' she asked, signalling over to an inconspicuous spot around one hundred metres from shore.

'The sea? Yeah it's pretty big isn't it?'

'Alex! I'm being serious, look!' She grabbed my shoulder and made me peer intently into the distance. The number of beers

I'd consumed earlier in the evening made themselves known whilst peeling my eyes, hazy outlines of nothingness greeting my gaze.

'I can't see anything!'

'Well then, I'm going to have to show you aren't I?' She grabbed me, looking me up and down with a puzzled and impatient expression. 'C'mon, we haven't got all night!'

'What?' I asked, taking the opportunity to look at her in return. Pfffft.

'Well you're not going in with your phone are you? Get your kit off you wuss.' The stars gave me an "ok" symbol in the sky as she pulled off her grey striped top and yanked down washed denim shorts, kicking them into a heap in the sand.

When life gives you lemons, do the fucking lemon dance, I always say. I pulled off my vest faster than a kamikaze tuk-tuk driver, throwing my phone and money belt to the floor with such venom it may have started a minor earthquake. When I looked up from the pile of now meaningless items, I was shocked to see Olivia already waist-deep in her missile-like invasion of the sea.

Her gravitational pull meant that it didn't take me long to follow suit, the warm ocean touch feeling as welcoming as it ever had before. I plunged ambition first into the dark water, attempting to execute an Olympic standard regulation front crawl to my adoring crowd of one. Barely three strokes into my performance I noticed Olivia had stopped right in front of me, causing me to veer off course in fear of crashing into her. I splashed to the side and gradually found my feet on the ocean floor, soft sand greeting my soles, standing chest-deep in the water.

'Alright Phelps, steady on,' she laughed, giving me a playful punch in the arm.

'Not as oafish as I look, eh?'

'If you say so!' She turned away and allowed herself to completely submerge, holding her head underwater whilst the ocean settled to our presence. When the mermaid emerged, my heart had to slap itself to stop from making its presence known. She was beautiful. So so beautiful.

'Okay, you ready Alex?'

This was it. She had lured me into the sea as an elaborate ploy to seal a romantic first kiss. You've got to love the classics.

'I certainly am, Olivia.'

'Look! Look!' she whispered, increasing the volume of her hushed tone. She was frantically pointing all around us, a strange build-up to a kiss in my opinion, but I'd roll with it.

But as she pointed, I slowly began to realise what the hell she was doing. The water all around us began to come alive, shimmering in colours of iridescent white and blue. The impossible luminescence settled on the water's surface almost instantly, but with each and every movement, a million speckles of light danced around in excitement.

I found myself momentarily forgetting where I was, who I was with, bewildered at this natural phenomenon, rueing the day I'd not listened in that particular science lesson at school.

'Alex.'

I turned to see Olivia stood directly in front of me, the silhouette of her body foreshadowed by the dazzling shine of the flickering waves. I wished I could have lived that moment forever, capturing the image securely in my mind. I drew closer, pushing myself through the warm, tropical water, lapping against my skin like a lover's touch. We stood just inches apart.

159

'Alex?'

'Olivia.'

'I just want you to know…'

'Yeah?'

'Don't get too excited but I'm really happy I met you. I've had real trouble meeting genuinely nice people on my trip so far, especially boys.'

'I'm really happy I met you too, Liv.'

She paused, and for the first time, let her gaze break from my eyes. 'I really mean it though. I mean, it's hard enough being away from my boyfriend as it is, without every guy out here treating me differently just because I won't sleep with them!' She looked up again, I assumed to try and gauge my reaction.

What's the word for gut-wrenching devastation and heartbreak coupled with an intense need to bottle it up otherwise you risk coming across like a single-minded dickhead just like the rest of them?

'Oh!' I said, stupidly.

'Alex, I know I should've said something but I was having too much fun with you and I didn't want to risk you freaking out and running away! Take it as a compliment, I obviously like you don't I?' She stared at me with those misleading beautiful eyes.

I paused for a little too long before finally speaking. 'Liv. Look I'm not going to change how I am with you just because you have a boyfriend. Yes, perhaps you should've told me before luring me into the most romantic setting of my entire life, but other than that, no harm no foul, eh?'

She laughed her amazing laugh. 'Yes, perhaps you're right. Note to self, no luring attractive boys into the bioluminescence before letting them know you are taken.'

I laughed with her, unable to resist the allure of it. 'Who says I wanted anything to happen anyway…'

'Very true. We're just two half Mancunians, sharing a few laughs, having a few cuddles in the sea of Ha Long Bay. I like it. Friends?'

Friends.

'Friends.'

Chapter 30

There you have it. A contextual cross-reference of each and every contributing variable that all point to one simple explanation for why that morning was so great. I had found her.

I wish I could say I knew that it would happen. That somewhere deep down inside of me I believed I'd see her again. That fate and destiny were working in tandem, desperate to reunite star crossed lovers, and that the moonlit beach of an island in Ha Long Bay would be the predetermined grand stage for our adorable, humorous, and sensational meet-cute.

But that would be a lie. In reality, I'd drunkenly overheard a girl say she was heading to Vietnam as the next stop in her travels, proceeded to blindly follow her, and ended up taking the same north to south route she had, striking lucky on a 50/50 chance. Hardly beating the odds. I guess you could call it a serendipitous encounter. The occurrence and development of events by chance in a happy or beneficial way sounds about right. And way less creepy.

Anyhow, the morning in question clearly did not have the spring in its step inception one would assume. In fact, the morning itself wasn't as exceptional as perhaps first implied, considering I'd woken up at the crack of dawn to the snotty snores of bloody Bas Bovlender on the bunk above me, his nasal turbulence similar to the sound made if you tried to eat a bratwurst in one mouthful.

Thankfully, nothing could derail the simple fact that I'd found her. Granted, it wasn't the love story I'd fantasized about but those few hours in the ocean had been some of the best hours spent on my journey so far. We'd talked about life in a way that pierced through the typical travellers tittle-tattle, challenging one another about morals and perspectives, delving into topics of both profound and hilarious categorizations, yet somehow still managing to keep one another at an emotional and unfortunately physical arm's length.

It was decided that we'd try and remain friends despite her imminent departure the following morning, a promise I held plenty of reservations about. We'd yet to successfully coordinate a meeting point with any one of the promise laden friends we'd assured to the contrary, so why would Olivia be any different?

If I'm honest, I almost wanted the night to remain untarnished, a pure, uncomplicated memory where I'd found the girl I was secretly searching for amongst the bioluminescent waves. I could close the storybook chapter on it, without putting myself through the painful unrequited tragedy of trying to be just friends with her.

And close the chapter I did, in emphatic fashion. As well documented, I'd woken that morning with the vigour and vitality of a super-soaker-wielding child in the height of Songkran Festival, wanting to rally the troops for another day on the sauce. Thankfully, my wish was the Castaway Tour operators' command as they wielded a weapon of their own to rouse everyone from their respective slumbers, a weapon that even the hunchback of Notre Dame would be proud of. The repetitive clang of brass on brass meant only one thing to those studious enough to have read the tour's brochure cover to cover. The Castaway's Booze Cruise.

Despite the surprisingly well-curated music that blared out of the boat's speakers at an inordinate volume, the copious Bier Hội's that seemed to flow freely from bow to stern, as well as the awe-inspiring kayak tours around some of nature's most amazing landscapes, the thing that impressed me most on the booze cruise was my best friend's humility towards the night prior. Never usually one to hold his hands up to anything, Matty surprised me with a forthright apology for stealing my Rose, perhaps fearing the effect it may have on our duo dynamic going forward. Little did he know that I'd long forgotten about that sprouting romance and moved onto pastures not so new.

'Shut up mate. As if you've hinged our entire trip on following a girl and you actually found her!?' he said, following my come clean routine.

'Trust me mate, I was more surprised than you. Thankfully I nailed the first impressions as per usual...'

'Course you did, stumble over your words and blush bright red?'

'Oh yeah, big time.'

'Nice. True to form then.'

'So nice. Had a legit little night though, despite the fact she of course had a boyfriend. Couldn't write it, mate.' I said, waiting for his inevitable snort of laughter.

He snorted with laughter. 'Boyfriend?! For fuck sake man, you certainly know how to pick them, don't you? So did you end up trying it anyway or what?'

'Did I fuck. She was literally the most switched-on girl ever, plus she brought up her boyfriend in the same sentence as claiming every guy she's met has tried it on with her, couldn't exactly prove her right.'

'She's absolutely done you there, good on her I say,' he said.

'Yep, she certainly did.'

'So, do you like her then?'

'Like her? I *like* Pad Thai, Matty. She was something else, I swear down.'

'Just like Julietta, Freya and Rose all were?' He laughed, finishing the last of his beer with a noisy gulp. 'You need to relax with these girls lad, no need to get so invested...'

164

'Na, this one is different mate.'

'Course it is. Now enough of that, we're at a fuckin boat party, no point doing a Turner and obsessing over girls who aren't here, cause we both know how that turned out!'

He had a point. His point was one I fiercely championed myself when it came to my friends, arguing the case that anchoring oneself to a girl at our age was foolhardy and ended up with the perpetrator missing out on the best of times. But it was easier said than done.

I returned to the action side by side with Matty and resumed the regular narrative of our travels, forcing myself to shrug off the perplexing feelings I'd developed for Olivia in such a short amount of time. Fortunately for me, distractions don't come any better than those packaged within a travellers boat party and before I knew it I was free again, albeit temporarily.

Thoughts of her eyes were replaced with the free liquor shots in the repetitive drinking games hosted aboard. I replaced the twists and turns of her long dark hair with the intertwined ramblings of a story being told to new friends. But the one thing I couldn't replace, no matter how many jokes landed, no matter what I tried, nothing could live up to it.

I could not be free of her laugh.

Chapter 31

I awoke from my heavy slumber in an instant, her laugh reverberating around the bottom bunk of my bed, trapped in a prison of my memory with nothing to greet my groggy eyes but the dusty slats of the bunk above, creaking with every slight movement that a sleeping Matty made.

I groaned in frustration and pulled the scarcely padded pillow over my head to block out the world. We had journeyed ten hours from Hanoi to Phong Nha, a township residing on the north-central coast region of Vietnam, heralded by a few of our Castaway colleagues as an adventurers paradise, home to some of the world's largest caves. We had agreed that after the debauchery and emotional taxation that had been collected in full during the Castaway's tour, that a change in tact was required in the days that followed. We assumed they wouldn't sell beer in the cave systems of Phong Nha, so it seemed to be the perfect fit.

But the sins had caught up with me by the time we'd arrived, despite the valiant attempts of our deranged bus driver who must've taken all speed limit signs as the bare minimum requirement to pass. This particular night was supposed to be a rare night off, a chance to replenish our minds, bodies, and souls with a long and fulfilling sleep. While the inescapable sound of her laughter had plagued my thoughts on more than a few occasions, the fact that it had woken me up from much-needed rest was bordering on ridiculous.

Rubbing my eyes in a weary daze, I grabbed my phone from the charger beside my bed and checked the time. The digital clock read 11 p.m. I scrolled through my messages without paying too much attention to their contents, flicking past something from my mum, a couple of missed calls from Caleb, and a message from Turner saying my ex girlfriend Alex Perry had finally split up with her loser of a boyfriend. About fucking time. Nothing excited me enough to probe any further so I threw the phone back onto the bed and turned over to return to sleep. Her laughter seemed to have stopped at least, replaced by the comings and goings of the Easy Tiger hostel nightlife, the faint murmur of distant music emanating from the bar downstairs drowned out by a bustling corridor activity just outside of our dorm.

I dozed off for what felt like a second before she haunted me again with that definitive laugh, this time seeming to shake the very foundations of the bunk bed. But something was different. The tantalizing chorus wasn't echoing around my head like it usually did but instead seemed to be coming from outside, like the sound of a gig when standing outside in a queue in the rain. Before I had the chance to register what was going on, the door of our room burst open and in fell two very drunk girls, bringing a marketplace full of noise, light, and smells in their wake.

I sat up with a start, feeling the movement above me indicate Matty had done the same, bewildered by the sudden bizarre hysteria that had bundled its way into our two-person dorm. I let my eyes adjust to the light that shone brightly onto the giggling heap writhing on the floor, but my ears adjusted faster as it became clear who one of the girls was. It was Olivia. An extremely drunk version of Olivia.

'Liv?' I called, assuming a tentative tone of voice in case my obsession had reached an all-time high, severe enough to hallucinate her appearance as well as her beautiful laugh.

'Alex!' came the rasping call, breaking all reasonable decibel scales. The two figures slowly unfurled themselves from the pretzel-like mass on the floor, rising up into shaky stances. Strangely, the screeching voice was not recognisable as Olivia, it was a southern English accent manipulating my name.

'Alex? Alex!' shouted Olivia, her excited voice as wobbly as her legs seemed to be as she tottered over to my bunk.

'Olivia! What are you doing here?'

'I owed you a stalk I seem to recall, so now we're even!' She grabbed hold of the bed frame and stood over me, dipping her head towards where I was sitting upright in bed. 'Oh, how rude of me! This is my new friend Grace!' She signalled over to the girl standing a little way behind her, who in turn began to giggle infectiously.

'Oh, hi Alex!' she began, barely able to get words out through her laughter. 'You don't know me but Olivia has told me everything and I'm really glad to finally meet you!'

If the sudden presence of Olivia in my dorm room wasn't overwhelming enough, the eager face of the expectant Grace certainly made up for it, her pretty features clearly under the influence of a shed load of booze. Before I had a chance to reply, Matty hopped down from the bunk above, causing all three of us to jump.

'You not going to introduce me then, Alex?' he quipped, pushing his hair out of his eyes and looking frustratingly fresh-faced compared to what I felt.

'Oh shit yeah, sorry,' I mumbled, suddenly very aware of my own bedraggled appearance and trying to adjust my hair. 'This is my best mate, Matty!'

'Hi Matty!' the girls cried in unison, their timing of the shout causing each of them to double over laughing again.

'Hi girls, Olivia and Grace yes? Now then Liv, Alex has told me all about your little Ha Long Bay date!'

'Shut up!' I feigned a laugh to cover my outrage with Matty and tried to quickly change the subject. 'How on earth did you find me... us... I mean?'

The pair of hyenas carried on as they started, barely registering Matty and I as they tried to catch their breath in between fits of giggles. Olivia eventually managed to calm down enough to respond.

'Well, Grace and I have been on a little mission you see… Funnily enough, we met earlier today on our cave tour and obviously became the best of friends, she's literally the greatest person I've ever met.' I could smell the liquor on her breath and she sat down on the end of my bed, using her arms to prop herself up in a slouched manner.

'Olivia, you are the nicest person in the world. But yes, yes, we met earlier and Olivia was telling me all about you Alex, she said you had the best time on Castaways and you were the nicest guy ever!' She spoke with such charming giddiness that her smiles quickly became your own—contagious energy almost glowed around her.

'Yes!' Olivia shouted, causing Grace to burst out again in a new eruption of laughter. 'Yes, sorry am I being loud? But it's just so exciting because we had a mission to find you and we have completed it!'

I found myself laughing as well, despite not really knowing what the two girls were talking about. 'Liv, you're supposed to be telling us how you found me!'

'Oh yes! Oh, but you see that's the best bit! We were talking about you and Grace asked me what you looked like. So when I was describing how goofy and tall you are, your curly black hair and telling her about your loud Manny accents, she said she had spotted a couple of people on the way back to her dorm earlier that might've been you!'

'Yes, oh my gosh Alex, I saw you and Matty get off your bus earlier after our cave tour and when she was describing you something just clicked in my head that it may have been you!'

Matty, sensing a rare opportunity to interject, threw his hat in the ring. 'Hold on, hold on. So you're telling us that you spotted two people you didn't recognise earlier, then when Olivia described Alex you somehow knew it was one of those people? You two should be detectives!'

'Yes, Matty! I like you already!' cooed Olivia, adjusting the buttons on her white linen shirt, effortless in her delivery. 'Oh but that's not even the best bit! We waited downstairs for a while to see if you would turn up but accidentally got blind drunk on cocktails.'

'Matty, Alex…' Grace whispered. 'We got so drunk. I mean really really drunk boys.'

'You could've fooled us,' I said.

'Cheeky! Anyway, when you didn't show up downstairs we decided to start our mission to hopefully hunt you down. Grace and I tried a few dorm rooms but people were starting to get mad at us so you'll never guess what we did…'

'What?' asked Matty and I at the same time, causing us all to laugh.

'Well… Don't be creeped out but we went to reception and told them I was your girlfriend and needed to know if you were staying here. They believed it anyway and said you had checked into this dorm, so hey presto, we came and found you!'

It was a lot to process. The serendipity of our first encounter still hadn't worn off completely and yet again, here I was I face to face with the girl from the hot springs of Pai, this time after she'd tracked me down on the off chance her description had been detailed enough to trigger her friend Grace to recognise a stranger. I looked around at their drunk, happy faces and couldn't believe it was really happening.

We invited them to stay and spoke for a long while, sitting in a circle on the floor of our dorm. A strange feeling of familiarity settled over the conversations, suggesting we'd already known the

170

two girls for a very long time, personal jokes developing quickly as the clock ticked on. They teased us about calling it a night early, while we tried to match their energy with sober minds. It was decided that they would go on a beer run whilst we got changed to hit the town. After they'd left, Matty turned to me with a widespread grin across his face.

'So that was *the* Olivia, eh?'

'I guess so, the drunkest girl in North Vietnam by the looks of things.'

'I think Grace would give her a run for her money. You're lucky I like them, I'm still absolutely knackered.'

'Mate, I'm fucked, had literally no sleep.' I said.

'Nothing a few brewskis won't solve though, eh? I bet you're absolutely buzzing she's come to find you though?'

I laughed sheepishly and stretched out on my bed. 'Dunno mate, seems like she just wants to be friends, do you not think?'

'Yeah, so what? We need friends more than you need a girlfriend man, and these two actually seem fully safe. They're going on a beer run for us for Christ's sake!'

He wasn't wrong. We'd been on the lookout for some travelling companions since Turner and Brown Shoes had unceremoniously left our sides, with little to no luck thus far. If I could get past my crippling crush on Olivia, there was no reason at all we couldn't employ her and the giggling Grace as part of a new quartet.

By the time the girls returned, Matty and I had devised a concrete plan to seduce them into friendship, a plan that was executed with military precision. The evening passed by one beer, laugh, and story at a time, each one of us taking turns to contribute the perfect layer of conversation. Our plans to hit the town of

171

Phong Nha were scuppered by the constraints of time as we rambled on long into the night. It was around 4.30 a.m. before our incoherence was interrupted by a disgruntled member of the hostel staff who firmly suggested we call it a night.

Thankfully, the dye had been cast and the bonds had been forged, a circle of friendship formed on the dorm room floor. Although my feelings for Olivia had not at all subsided, I had to admit having her as a friend was a lot better than not having her at all. I clung on to a secretly harbored ulterior motive as we bid goodnight to our new friends, arranging to tackle the town together the following day.

And when the time came to leave Phong Nha after a crazy three days, as beautiful and awe-inspiring as the multiple-day treks to the cave systems were, it was this night of detective work, rude awakenings, and new friendships that commemorates the town. Matty and I had journeyed to Phong Nha in search of a different type of adventure and frankly a little bit of rest, but instead were greeted with something entirely different. People spend their entire lives seeking out nature's greatest marvels, crawling the globe for the next discovery, but some may never find what we found on the hostel floor that night, the treasure of real friendship.

Chapter 32

'I think we should do it,' announced Grace, dropping her backpack to the roadside with a cushioned thud.

'I agree with Grace, it might be a little expensive for our shoestring budgets but I think we probably have enough to rent until we get to Hội An?' Olivia said.

Matty and I looked at each other, trying to communicate our mutual concern without alerting the two girls. A burrow of the eyebrow, turn of the lip, and a slight shrug of the shoulder indicated to me that he would be willing to give it a second chance.

'Ale-e-e-ex...' Olivia implored, elongating the vowel sounds in an adorable fashion. 'I know it's horrible that your friend Brown Shoes crashed in Thailand, but look on the bright side, you've got me and Grace to look after you now!'

How could I resist that? 'Okay, let me speak to the guy and see if I can sort out a deal,' I said, subtly checking my money belt for its contents.

'Alex, taking charge! I like it!' She placed her hand on the underside of my arm, sending cool shivers to my shoulder and neck. Pull it together, I thought.

I left my three companions sitting expectantly on a wall outside of the warehouse sized garage we had just popped our heads in to enquire about the possibility of renting motorbikes to drive from Hue, a charming riverside town that we'd been residing in for the past couple of days, to Hội An, a 125km drive across the infamous Hai Van Pass. The route was widely celebrated because of a Top Gear special that detailed the beauty and breathtaking views that came with it, a 'must-do' activity when travelling in Vietnam.

But Matty and I were a little unsure as to whether we wanted to get straight back on the horse, so to speak. Thoughts of Brown Shoes' crash proved stubborn to dislodge from my mind as I approached the motorbike dealer that we had previously spoken to, his shabby appearance left redundant by the salesman's glint in his weathered eyes.

'Oh hey, my friend. You want rent motorbikes, yes? You and friend have two pretty ladies who want to share bike with you? Lucky man my friend, very lucky man!' He spoke with a wicked grin, revealing a gold tooth in place of his incisor.

'Hey, my friend. Yes, I think we do. Although, the girls want bikes of their own. They don't trust me to drive!' I laughed to signify my joke and he seemed to understand, patting me on the shoulder and bellowing out a throaty laugh.

'Yes, yes, strong woman I like as well!'

'I have a question for you,' I began, weighing up how to pose my query using simple enough English for him to understand. 'I had an accident in Thailand on a bike so I want to make sure we only drive the safest, best bikes available? Would you be able to sort that out for me?'

He looked me up and down, his smile faltering very briefly. 'Oh, you have accident? Okay, okay. Let me show you what I can do.' He grabbed me by the arm and dragged me deeper into the garage, the sunlight-filled entrance becoming darker and darker as we progressed, the rows of heavy machinery and vehicles becoming dustier and less appealing in turn.

I started to believe he had misinterpreted the question before he turned behind a small alcove jutting out from the wall and rested his hands on a tarpaulin-covered mound that lay dormant in its depths.

'These are my best bikes, yes? I only show these bikes to special customer, very rare in Vietnam so you are lucky boy!' He turned his attention from the tarpaulin to me, the glint in his eye brighter than it was before despite the lack of light this far into the garage. With an almighty heave, he pulled the cover off and as the dust settled I laid eyes on the bikes, gleaming bright and seemingly unused.

'Okay, how much to rent?'

'Oh no, these bikes are Honda SH automatic, best in the business, you cannot rent! You will never come back! You have to buy them from me, my friend.'

I quickly deliberated his proposition. On the one hand, to the untrained eye, these bikes looked top of the range and were likely our safest option. But on the other, there was no way the girls would be able to afford to buy the bikes outright.

'How much we talking, buddy?'

'In dollar? These are $3000 each. In dong? 70 million.' He smiled a sickly smile up at me, a smile that spread across his entire face. I don't know how, but he knew that he had me.

'Okay my friend, I'll tell you what. We can make a deal but you have to do exactly as I say…'

I returned to my friends with a good samaritan's smile plastered across my face, assuming that my noble actions would secure some sort of positive karma. I had carefully explained to the salesman that I would purchase the bikes, providing he would pretend we had made a cut-price rental deal. I was keen to avoid any questions about money. Matty and I had agreed that after the events in Pai, we would be keeping our financial situation very much to ourselves for the remainder of the trip so as not to complicate any future relationships, an agreement I intended to stick by.

'So, how did we get on?' Matty asked, holding an iced water against his forehead to combat the relentless heat of the sun.

'Look at that smile, he must've found us a deal,' Olivia said, standing up from the washed stone wall and skipping to join my side.

'Alex, you superstar!' Grace giggled.

'Yep, we're all sorted, ladies and gentlemen. You each owe me about 500,000 dong but we can sort that when we arrive!'

'500k? Isn't that only like 20 pounds?' Grace asked, her grasp of the currency much stronger than the rest of us.

I caught Matty's eye as he smirked at me. 'Something like that yes, I told you I'd cut us a deal. The guy was very... reasonable.'

'I bet you've got us the biggest bangers in the garage you...' Olivia began but was cut off by the sight of the salesman and his fellow Vietnamese mechanics emerging from the cave-like entrance, rolling out our new noble steeds that appeared even more triumphant in the midday blaze.

'Hey, my friends! Here are your *rental* bikes, okay? Only for *rent* remember! No sale for me today!' he shouted over, winking and laughing as he strolled.

I rolled my eyes and put a finger sharply to my lips, thankfully universal in all languages to put a sock in it. He talked us through the operational aspects of the bikes with a gleeful tone, clearly still revelling in his new unexpected fortune, but the girls didn't seem to notice as they playfully fought over which of them would get the turquoise shade stallion.

It had been a while since my staggering wealth had really come into play as a decisive factor in our trip, the affordability of Asia not really necessitating any significant outlays of cash. At that moment, it felt good to be able to take care of the fee, leaving my new friends none the wiser, a selfless act that felt less conceited than bragging about it as I had in the Spicy Pai hostel about a month prior.

The cumulative chorus of the engines behind me sounded pronounced and distinctive, echoing across the cheery rice field that bordered the road. We had decided to begin the roughly 6-hour journey at the earliest opportunity, leaving ourselves plenty of time to drink in the rumored natural delights of the drive. Bags packed, helmets on and fee settled, we set off to embark on our next adventure, feeling the smooth acceleration, ample power, and pump of the brakes that actually seemed to work.

Isn't it amazing what money can buy?

Chapter 33

I felt the police officer's hand on my shoulder tighten as I waited for my secret to be exposed, the dusty ATM screen flickering slightly like a lightbulb on its last legs before plunging into darkness.

I gingerly entered my four-digit password into the steel keypad, feeling a chorus of panting breath from the collection of people around me, friends and foe, cherished and strangers, amalgamating into a nightmares harmony around the back of the roadside convenience shack in central Vietnam.

My story began with the turn of fate that brought us here. From one hairpin turn to the next we had crashed from the highs of a winding roads bounty blessed with misty mountains, deserted sandy beaches, and the distant illuminated promise of towns and cities to come, to the lows of corruption, bribery, and the imminent haunting revelation of my secret.

The chaotic storm that raged on outside of the sheltered back entrance paled in comparison to the tornado of possibilities that plagued my mind. What would the police do when they saw so much money? Would they try and take it all? Would I be taken to a Vietnamese prison to get around the ATM withdrawal limits? The prospect of losing my fortune and going to jail was incomprehensible, but irrationally the main focus of my inner panic came at the mercy of a softer, bluer pair of eyes than those of the policeman around me. What would happen when she found out?

It was only a couple of days prior that she'd told me again how much she respected my honesty, a compliment I was only too happy to accept, fanning the flame that I was, in fact quite the catch. I had convinced myself that as long as I didn't directly lie to her about the money, then I wasn't technically doing anything dishonest and could continue to champion myself as virtuous and true. But that rouse was about to come crashing down.

I stared down at the "Confirm" button that invited me in menacingly from the right-hand side of the keypad, a final word that separated me from judgement. I had hit the "Confirm" button plenty of times since winning my fortune, booking tickets to Asia, finalising hefty transactions to loved ones, the satisfying closure of my overdraft ridden student account, but this time was different. This time, I was confirming my worst fears.

But there was nothing else for it. It was time to consent to the inevitable hopelessness that I found myself unable to escape. I pressed the button. Like the long-distance journeys I'd become familiar with over the past month, the ATM took its time in processing my sentence, a gradual whirr of ventilated air upping the ante, second by second, passing by with an agonising tempo.

Any minute now my bank balance would appear on screen in English pounds and Vietnamese dong, as if they needed more than one piece of evidence to prove me guilty. Any minute now. Surely? Why wasn't it working? I prayed for a technical fault. But then something appeared. Something that wasn't expected.

ACCOUNT SUSPENDED
FRAUDULENT ACTIVITY SUSPECTED
PLEASE CONTACT BANK FOR DETAILS

I blinked, small splashes of rain dripping from my eyelashes like a dysfunctional gutter, not understanding what was happening. Account suspended? There had to be some sort of mistake. I'd used the card only a few hours earlier?

But then it hit me. The penny dropped in resounding fashion, the gold-toothed smile of a salesman in Hue flooding my mind. Suspected fraudulent activity. Hadn't I just transferred a significant sum of money to his personal Vietnamese account? The transaction must've been flagged at my bank back in

England, fucking vigilant bankers. I vaguely remembered the warnings that this sort of thing did happen. It did make sense.

The downpour of emotions was difficult to explain, relief, happiness, gratitude making up the initial shower, followed by worry, uncertainty, and dread in equal measure at the prospect of what on earth I was going to do next.

'Hey! Where is money?' The policeman who held me barked in a sharp tone, spinning me round to face the gathered troupe of people all looking at me with equally puzzled faces.

'I don't know! My account has been suspended!'

'What?'

'I can't get your money!' I signalled at the ATM and shook my head, trying to convey my quandary with frantic hand gestures and facial expressions.

'You no pay, you come with us! Big fine at police station for no license, no helmet!'

I looked to Matty for help, but he merely shrugged, the sodden t-shirt on his back sticking to his skin helplessly. My eyes then turned to Grace and Olivia, who stood huddled together next to me, visibly struggling under the weight of their backpacks that were still clinging to their straining shoulders. There was no way they could afford the bribe, 16 million dong was too big a hit. I couldn't let them do that.

I had to think fast. On the plus side, the policemen hadn't seen the extent of my fortune. They would have no way of distinguishing us from the next backpacker, aside from the flashy motorbikes that were propped up against the side of the convenience shack. Four very expensive, very *fast* motorbikes.

I'd admit that the best ideas aren't made when your back is against the wall, figuratively and literally, scrambling for a way out. But acting out of instinct can serve up some solutions that would never cross your mind in the real world, solutions that just might work.

'Okay, can you take us to the police station?' I asked, looking the police officer directly in the eye. His face darkened, although a slight flicker in his vision seemed to suggest he was surprised with my sudden request.

'Police station will give even bigger fine!' he said. 'You no pay, you go jail.'

I briefly imagined the idea of going to Vietnamese prison. I'd seen Prison Break season three enough times to know that I wouldn't cope well in a foreign jail. And I couldn't imagine I'd be very well equipped to break out of it like Michael Schofield always seemed to. But now wasn't the time for backing down. I had to blag like my life depended on it.

'Okay, I will pay the fine at the police station.' The intonation in my voice seemed to be obeying my false bravado, each sentence seeming more assured than the last. 'If you and the other officers lead the way, we will follow you?'

'Alex, don't you think we should just…'

'It's okay Liv, I think we should go to the station. Trust me, I've read about situations like this before.' My mind was working overtime, how I imagined an engineer's mind would work, assessing all possible outcomes and angles, weighing up the risk reward coefficient.

The lead police officer sneered and turned towards his uniformed companions, allowing me a brief respite from his steely glare. I glanced over to my friends and tried to give them a look of confidence, the face of a man with a plan. Matty knew me well enough to know when I was making things up as I went along, but he met my look with a resigned acceptance that he would be willing to do what it took to get out of there. Olivia

181

nodded back at me, willing to place her trust in me yet again. But it was Grace who's look intrigued me the most. It was not a face of fear and worry that I had perhaps expected of a 19 year old girl in a crisis, but a cunning arch of the eyebrow and a tilt of the head in the direction of our ticket out of there.

Talk about a saving grace.

Chapter 34

I swore loudly as the front wheel of my bike narrowly missed the headlight of an oncoming lorry, the rush of hot air hitting me with nearly enough force to knock me off course. Shit. I had to keep it together.

An open road once promised so much. An expanse of endless opportunities now seemed like the only option we had left. An option we had taken with both hands. It had been easier than anticipated, giving the police officers the slip. With Grace and I taking the lead, our compliance with their supposed demands was made all the more convincing with Olivia's *fake* tears as we were led back towards the highway, our motorbikes in tow.

Much to the lead officer's frustration, we had insisted that he should follow through with his threats and take us to the nearest station to deal with our supposed crimes. It appeared that our willingness to abide by the *law* had spooked a number of the would-be officers, three of which had abandoned their posts and resumed the hunt for some more subservient offenders. The remaining two officials had stuck to their guns, albeit with a reluctant edge to their demeanor.

But that had been enough. The momentary lapse in their intimidation strategy was all that we required in order to give the green light to our dastardly deed. How were they to know that underneath our shivering, sodden disposition was a scheme very much underway. Free of the handcuffs that had earlier bound us, we made sure to give nothing away as we mounted our noble steeds back out on the roadside, faces plastered with apologetic acceptance. But as the keys turned in the ignition, our true intentions were made clear.

The smoky blast of four Honda SH automatic motorbikes shooting off in unison must've looked like the roadrunner from the Looney Tunes, constantly out of reach of the pair of coyote's dressed in blue. But the cartoon's scripted safety was not yet secured in the grand scheme of things. Whether we deserved it or not, we were on the run from the police.

A loud crack perforated my ears as I urged the bike forward, the hazy outline of a road in front of me becoming less and less defined as we took yet another left bend of the Hai Van Pass. Was it an exhaust? Were they shooting at us?!

I don't think the reality of the situation had quite dawned on me as I twisted the accelerator, matching the speed of the three bikes ahead of me, Matty, Grace and Olivia putting Clarkson and Richard Hammond to shame. The closest I'd come to running from the police had been a runner from the "Lucky Wok" in Sale at the age of 14, the outcome of which didn't fill me with hope. A red faced boy caught soy sauce handed.

But here we were. 120 km/h and not even a peking duck roll to enjoy. It was difficult to gauge whether or not we were gaining ground in our escape, the black night shrouding all but a hurtling set of beaming lights every time a vehicle noisily rattled past us, spraying water from the road. All I knew is we had to keep the pedal to the metal and push through the fear until we were sure of our safety.

But then I heard it. The groaning whine of a siren ripped my safe haven reality to shreds with a heinous moan, the police hot on our tail. The effect was palpable. Each one of our party of four seemed to find the little thing inside of us that had previously held back from really testing our bike's capabilities. Full throttle. I'd certainly come a long way from the nervous stop start moped journeys in the mountains of Pai.

But our newfound momentum made no difference. The hounds were gaining on us. The wail of authority grew with each passing second. How would we explain this? It was one thing getting caught without a helmet or fabled motorbike license, but now we had actually fled from arresting officers. We would likely be in real trouble. Trouble perhaps even money couldn't get us out of…

The Hai Van Pass was supposed to be a highlight of the trip. It was supposed to be unmissable, a rite of passage that we would never forget. Well, it certainly had one of the assurances. Tied up in a neat little handcuff shaped bow.

The sirens grew louder. They can't have been more than 50 yards behind us. We were caught, soon to be back in chains. I pictured the phonecalls home, my mum sobbing through the phone as they informed her I'd become a Vietnamese vigilante. My brother would probably brag about it to his stupid friends. I would become the punchline of a meathead's joke in a dead end pub in Sale. Not the place I imagined finding myself, that's for sure.

Defeated, I released my clenched fist from the accelerator, waving the proverbial white flag of my surrender as the siren became unbearable to the naked ear. I was done for. Toast. *Finito*. But the siren didn't seem to accept my defeat. It blared louder than ever as it approached, not five metres from my peripheries.

Panic. Fear. Dread. Were they going to knock me off the road? The t-shirt and shorts combo probably wouldn't do a good job of breaking my fall. Maybe this was it. First Brown Shoes, now me. I braced the muscles in my body preparing for the worst, mentally consigning myself to the inevitable. But it never came.

The whirlwind of blue and red hurtled past like a scuffle in the Manchester derby, screaming obscenities in a wild uproar. Without stopping. Through the corner of my squinted eye I managed to dissect the rain and darkness for long enough to steal a look at the passenger side door. An unmistakable red cross. It was an ambulance.

Never had I been so happy to see a mighty St George's cross. The pride of England. Three lions on the shirt. Football's coming home and so were we! Pass me a fucking pint.

Who knows if the police ever pursued us. They probably knew it was coming. It's not like we were particularly sneaky, masters of espionage taking them for fools. For all we knew, they'd probably just tired of standing in the rain and waved us off. No big deal. There'd be tomorrow's tourists to bribe.

But this was my truth.

The name's King, Alex King. International man of mystery. Vietnamese vigilante. The keeper of secrets.

Chapter 35

Hội An was the Pai of Vietnam. As quickly as our fortune had been stopped in its tracks, it had broken free of its shackles once again and let loose on the narrow streets of the city. With a mind of its own, the charm of the city's melting pot history was not left behind by the contemporary colourful shophouses, French colonial architecture, and vibrant bar and restaurant selection that lined the roads of the Old Town. Like the bioluminescent wonders of the sea in Ha Long Bay, Hội An came alive at night, a city of lanterns that captured the imagination no matter which way we turned.

But it was not merely the elegance of the place that dazzled the eye and enchanted the heart. From the moment we arrived we felt instantly at peace. In fairness anywhere would've felt relaxing compared to a fucking high speed chase but this place was definitely special. An almost intoxicating atmosphere engulfed every evening stroll down the river, each time we sat down to eat a Banh Mi, the people, the vibe, the very streets of the city seemed harmonious with one another, creating a smooth and stress-free ambiance. Just what we needed.

As we sat down for our first meal in Hội An, the owner of the restaurant had told us of a unique plant that grew exclusively in this part of the country, something to do with the soil I guessed, although I was most likely wrong. The more I thought of it, I started to believe in the idea, the poetry of something special being formed in exactly the right conditions, at exactly the right time. And I think that best describes how I felt in Hội An. Right place, right time.

The first couple of days we were under the strict supervision of the girls, who's enthusiasm seemed to have no bounds. Proper carpe diem shit. They were up at the crack of dawn, piling into our dorm with hands full of brochures, plans, and newfangled ideas at the ready for how we would spend our days. They dragged us on bike rides, forced us on hikes, fed us local delicacies, and yet still managed to go toe to toe with us at our one area of supposed expertise, getting tanked up at the hostel bars.

We spent every minute with Grace and Olivia, their blossoming friendship beginning to mirror our own in a remarkable way. Matty had taken a real shine to both of them, even enough to distract him from his increasingly impressive womanizing ways on a couple of occasions. We were learning so much about them, establishing bonds that transcended the limited time we had spent together.

The wonderful Grace Lewis had journeyed to Asia solo, squeezing every last drop out of her gap year experience, her infectious energy, and intrepid attitude proving a formidable combination. I found myself looking up to her in so many ways despite her fledgling age, an admiration that Matty and I professed wholeheartedly after six or seven beers. She was patient as well, perhaps a less celebrated trait of hers considering what was to come.

And Olivia? Where to begin with Olivia Cohen... Whether a mere account of her character traits and idiosyncrasies could do her justice without a sonnet or the penmanship of Billy Shakespeare himself. I liked to think she was similar to me in a lot of ways but that was most likely the musings of an egotist, desperately trying to highlight an affinity in our character in a bid to gain her affection. But what was undeniable was our developing closeness as the days went on, hours spent siphoned off in DMC's (deep meaningful chats) about everything and nothing, finding newfangled ways to impress one another, or so it seemed to me.

By the time the sun set on our third day in the city, the group was almost symbiotic, our daily shenanigans becoming a welcome routine. Slamming his fist down on the Sunflower Hostel bar with a mighty thud, Matty demanded "the usual" as we sat down for round three of Hội An's delights.

'Where to tonight, my friends?' I asked, adjusting the jazzy floral shirt I saved for special occasions, worn for the second night running.

'Good one!' Grace yelled, giggling with glee.

'Surely we're not going Tiger Tiger again…'

'Alex, you know we're going to end up there so why fight it? We had an unbelievable night there last night so no sense changing it!' Matty said.

'You had an unbelievable night you mean, where is Laura anyway?'

'It was pronounced L-a-y-r-a I think you'll find! I hate it when Brit's butcher the Argentinian language…'

'Matty, they speak Spanish in Argentina!' Olivia laughed, barely looking up from the pages of Matty and I's travel journal that she'd been perusing.

'Whatever… She left today anyway! Another night on the pull for me and Grace I imagine?' He put his arm around Grace in a brotherly embrace, to which she returned with affection.

'And Alex as well! I'm sure he wants his Argentina flag too?' she said, looking expectantly towards me.

Matty and I fell silent, speaking volumes in itself. In truth, I hadn't had much luck with girls since I'd met Olivia. But I guess it's pretty difficult to catch a fish if you're just sitting gormlessly on the beach staring at a chippy.

Olivia broke the silence. 'Oh I barely gave Alex much of a chance, I was chewing his ear off all night about what he wants to do when he gets back to England. He's a budding writer I'll have you find!'

189

'Alex that's amazing!'

I made a pfft noise, attempting to satirise the ambition.

'Anyway, tonight is the night!' Matty interrupted, sensing that I had become a little uncomfortable. 'We can all get amongst it and Olivia can wingman!'

She smiled and cast a fleeting glance in my direction. I looked down, avoiding her gaze which prompted her to respond. 'Sounds good to me, I'm a great wingwoman!'

We continued on in customary fashion, beer, wine, and gin mixers the only friends to attempt to join in. Fortunately, my dad had sent over a truckload of beer money to Matty's account whilst the situation with my bank was being resolved. This particular night, I made sure to put that money to good use, throwing back anything that was put in front of me in what could be described as a bit of a frenzy. As we set off to go out, I remember feeling a little unsteady on my feet. Nothing I couldn't handle of course.

The familiar route to Tiger Tiger was always entertaining, each narrow street offering up a fable of its own, the whimsical lantern light illuminating the local people's faces as they bid us friendly smiles along the way. The bar/club combination was located on the bank of the river, enticing travellers in with a mish-mash of old school hip hop and chart classics. As we entered we laughed again at the sign that read, "Welcome To Tiger Tiger Bar, Don't Be A Pussy!"

The night out began much like it had the two nights prior, drinks flowed as we made fun of people dancing stupidly near us, before getting up to join them minutes later. I found that I couldn't take my eyes off Olivia that night, her midnight hair swinging to the beat of a surprisingly well mixed Notorious B.I.G remix, her tanned skin creating a perfect contrast with a white loose-hanging dress. She looked amazing and I wanted to tell her. Fortunately for me, she had just set off in my direction, wiggling her way across the dance floor like a lantern's flame.

190

'Alex! Alex!' I loved how she said my name, so simple, so well pronounced.

'Hello, Liv.'

'Are you having fun?'

'Loving it yeah, how about you?' Must not slur words.

'It's okay yeah, can't really talk much in here, can we? It's pretty loud!'

'Oh I know, we could go somewhere? I mean... if you wanted to?'

'Yeah definitely, I wanted to pick up where we left off last night, I really wanted...'

Before she could finish, a pop-up stranger sprung out of nowhere holding two liquor shots in front of my face. It took my eyes a few seconds to readjust before revealing the outline of an attractive looking girl grinning at me.

'Oh no thank you, we've got drinks already!' I managed, trying to avert her gaze and focus back on what Olivia wanted to tell me.

'No silly! I don't work here, I got these for me and you!' She spoke with what I deduced to be an Australian accent, although her voice was so loud it could really have been anything. I mustn't have disguised my confused displeasure very effectively as she quickly followed up. 'Oh c'mon handsome, I don't bite!'

Now I don't know what red-blooded male on this earth could resist a free drink at the hands of an attractive blonde Australian, especially a single man who'd just redefined the term "one too many". I grinned back, my goofy disposition somehow spurring the mystery girl on further. We took the shots in the manner

Australians allegedly take them, arms linked and down in one. By the time I'd regained control of my facial spasms caused by the strength of the liquor, Olivia had disappeared from my peripheral vision.

But I had little time to think about her whereabouts. The Australian girl had commenced with a strange but pretty spectacular dance routine pressed up against my body. There were limbs, there was sweat, I'm pretty sure there was a kiss? The grasp on my conscious actions began to slip away at the hands of the liquor, leaving me helpless in the arms of this mystery stranger.

I can't say I remember much more from the evening aside from that, instead relying on the account of the girl in question the following day, who claimed she had dragged me back to the hostel shortly after, fortunately, the same one we were staying at. According to her, we'd been exchanging glances all evening over pre-drinks but that was news to me, most likely finding herself in the eye line of a few of my Olivia-provoked daydreams.

As I stumbled back to my dorm, avoiding the free breakfast bar like the plague, I wondered what had happened with the rest of the evening, the fear of missing out higher than ever. It was the first night I'd spent with the girls and not drunkenly escorted them home, the first night my attention had been divided.

I assumed my most casual face, took a deep breath, and strolled into my dorm room to find Matty pulling on his favourite NBA jersey. As his head emerged, I saw his eyes instantly fix on me with a look of foreboding wickedness, concluded with the craftiest of grins.

'Oh, mate. Have I got some news for you…'

Chapter 36

The Crazy House in Dalat felt like it belonged in a fairy tale. The convulsing cement branches that intersected the compound appeared to double as bridges between four gigantic tree houses, warping the mind with Salvador Dali-esque out of the box artwork in a playful, yet almost ominous result.

But there was one thing that overshadowed the expressionist architecture in the afternoon that Matty, Grace, Olivia and I rocked up, a fact that had plagued me since that fateful morning in Hội An. Like the crazy structural principles of the tourist attraction we were visiting, my head was still all over the place from the news Matty had bestowed on me after returning to our dorm.

'She's into you mate!' he had said, a giddy child on Christmas morning. 'When you went home with that girl last night she got well upset and ended up telling Grace and I that she felt really guilty about being jealous, but she couldn't help it.'

She was into me. I still couldn't believe it. It was what I'd wanted more than anything else, from the drunken daydreams in the hot springs of Pai to our chance rendezvous on the beach of Ha Long Bay, each section of our story felt like crossing stepping stones through a river, taking one leap of faith to the next, never able to see the other side. I had imagined her returning my feelings in a thousand different scenarios, each one having the same fairy tale ending, but now I'd actually found out, the far side of the river somehow looked more shrouded than ever.

I guess that was partly down to the fact that we hadn't actually spoken about it ourselves. The remaining days in Hội An were some of the busiest we'd had, taking part in cooking courses, visiting temples, beaches, viewpoints, and what seemed like an endless carousel of shopping meant that we had our hands very much full. The evenings were spent a little differently than we had

193

gotten used to, collapsing in bed exhausted most nights from the daily grind.

It was this lack of communication between us that prompted our eventual departure from the city, at my incessant requests to move onto pastures new. I thought we needed to shake things up a little, create a new normal, a normal in which Olivia and I could finally talk things through. We decided to head straight for Dalat, a mountainous city in the south of Vietnam, known for its cooler climates and waterfall abundance.

I'd organised for a carrier bus to take us and our motorbikes the length of the journey, to save us from another draining day-long trek and potential bribe at the hands of the police. But by the time we'd arrived in the city, the chilly air stung our tired faces, all energy sapped from us by the night bus twists and turns. We arrived at the "Family Hostel" around 11 a.m. to find hordes of backpackers busily chatting away in the communal dining area, the devil's alarm clock.

Thankfully, Matty had remembered a recommendation from one of his past conquests that gave us a quick exit strategy from the advancing would-be friends, a guesthouse/museum combo that was supposed to be crazy by name but quite relaxing by nature. With a drop of the bags, a check of the map, and a rev of our engines we had arrived at our destination around 15 minutes later.

'I wonder if you can actually stay here?' asked Grace chirpily as she entered the third ridiculously painted room. Even with a couple of hours of sleep, you couldn't stop her enthusiasm seeping through.

'I fuckin' hope so, we might actually get a bit of shut-eye,' Matty said.

'Aw, I think that Family Hostel is pretty nice, it will be great when everyone wakes up a little!'

194

'Grace is right, as usual!' Olivia said, albeit with a little less conviction than we were used to.

'Yeah, we just need to put a brave face on today. Why don't we play a game?' I asked, sensing a bit of an opportunity to lift the mood. 'This place would be unreal for hide and seek.'

'Yes, Alex!' Grace shouted, her gleeful words echoing around the cavernous walls of the sculpted ocean cave we appeared to be standing within.

'Sack that,' Matty said bluntly.

'Yeah, I don't think I've got the energy…'

'Oh come on guys. We'll play as teams? Then we won't get lost!' Grace said.

'Great plan Grace, we'll both have to pair up with one of these two killjoys so they don't sulk too much.'

'Okay, blondes vs brunettes?'

'Deal.'

I grabbed Olivia round the shoulder and pulled her close, nudging my head into the side of hers to try and cheer her up. I felt her shoulders soften and relax, which I took as a good sign to press ahead with the plan.

'Okay, we're going to hide first so you two stay here for about five minutes?'

'Fine, but only because this octopus-shaped sofa looks fucking comfy!' Matty said, collapsing wearily onto the outstretched tentacles.

Olivia and I quickly turned and made our way to the seahorse surrounded hole in the back wall of the room, taking the barnacle

195

staircase two rungs at a time. Once we'd emerged from the hole, we found ourselves in a garden of gigantic mushrooms, with a company of rude gnomes and nosey fairies eavesdropping on our conversation.

'You okay, Liv?' I asked.

'Yeah, I'm just tired. I'll wake up in a little bit.' She smiled up at me through resting lips, before allowing her head to drop a little as we strolled on.

I realised that this was the first time we'd been alone together since I'd found out the big news. I knew it wasn't exactly the ideal time to bring it up, but we were such a tight-knit quartet and I didn't know when this opportunity would arise again.

'Hey, I wanted to talk to you about what happened the other night? I just realised I haven't had the chance to speak to you about everything since then...'

'What do you mean, what happened?' she asked.

I paused. 'I mean, erm, you know when I went back with that girl and everything? Matty said you were upset later that night?'

I watched her carefully as her eyebrows knit slightly, clearly mulling over what to say next. It felt like a long time before she eventually spoke, with a harsher tone than I expected. 'Alex, I don't know what Matty has told you but I wasn't upset you went home with that girl.'

Like a police baton to the ribs, I winced at her words. 'Ah, okay fair enough!' I managed through gritted teeth. 'Sorry for bringing it up.'

We walked in silence for a while, traversing the tricky terrain inside the apparent cave walls until Olivia stopped sharply, cutting me off from the toadstool forest ahead. 'Alex! I'm a little upset that you've brought it up because now we have to talk about

196

it. And you obviously know that it's the one thing I can't talk about with you!'

'Can't talk about what? You haven't told me anything!'

'Did you ever stop and wonder why that is? Alex, you're not stupid. You don't need me to spell out why I got upset, regardless of what Matty told you…'

'Maybe I do need that!'

'Well, unlucky, it's not happening.'

She looked at me unflinchingly, her eyes ablaze. But I wasn't having it. She couldn't just leave me in the dark. I summoned up a deep breath, bracing myself to spill out the weeks of torture I'd felt second-guessing myself and our confusing relationship, ready to confess it all in a grand triumphant last stand amongst the whimsical sculptured forest we stood in. But by the time I'd mustered the energy to take her on, the fire in her eyes had gone out, replaced with a rippling pool of stars.

'Alex… I'm sorry… I know we need to talk. I'm just trying to process it all myself and I've had no sleep and I'm confused… and… and…'

She couldn't finish, breaking down in front of me, all my frustration melting away. This was the first time I'd ever seen her be vulnerable, or even show any other emotion than positive for that matter. My own emotion proved equally difficult to process as inexplicable affection took over my body, feeling unable to stop myself grabbing her into a tight embrace. Her tears had the same intoxicating effect as her laugh, the quiet muffled whimpers felt like listening to the saddest song in the world. It left me helpless. Utterly helpless.

I scrambled around my weary mind to find the right thing to say, incapable of finding anything substantial for what felt like a long time. I wanted to comfort her, reassure her that everything would be okay. But how would I know that it would? Each day we spent together seemed to be posing more questions than it answered and I didn't have the words to make it seem like everything would be alright. We ended up simply standing silently in that embrace until she eventually broke free and quietly swept her tears away. The tension was only broken when a happy voice called out from a little way behind us.

'There you are! You two aren't very good at hiding are you?' Grace shouted. 'You need to come with us anyway, we've found a stepping stone bridge to the next treehouse!'

Chapter 37

There are countless cliches about the travelling experience, ranging from the widely professed act of finding oneself to the incessant and gradual categorization of places as being "too touristy" to visit. Most backpackers we'd met dismiss these cliches as mere conjecture, taking the stringent view that the stereotypes don't apply to them as they sing Oasis' "Wonderwall" at the top of their voices for the twelfth time around a communal bonfire on the beach.

I liked to think we weren't too suspect of falling into the worn-out, hackneyed mold of the typical traveller, but if you were a fly on the wall on our first night in the Family Hostel in Dalat, you'd likely take a very different point of view.

'One more time! Everybody!'

Matty strummed the tired strings of the hostel guitar with a practised hand, launching himself into the now-familiar introductory chords of the song he'd written a few hours earlier. Like any rockstar worth his salt, a crowd of adoring females cooed along with him as he played, eyes glued to the hair he'd just managed to tie up into a bun. I felt my foot tapping along involuntarily as I perched on a table on the far side of the common room, watching Olivia and Grace sway happily from side to side.

Forget the cliche, it was pretty great to see my best friend in his element. I was ashamed to admit it had been the first time I'd listened to him play in our 15+ years of friendship, typically sidestepping the topic when it'd been brought up in the past due to a lack of shared interest on my part. And despite my frustration at his hair reaching the hallowed milestone faster than mine, I had to admit he was pretty fucking good.

Aside from those captivated by the performance of Matty Cobain, the rest of the hostel crowd were generally in great spirits.

Drinks were tallying up, friendships were forming and the overall consensus of everyone who'd joined us was to stick two fingers up at the ongoing thunderstorm and have a boozy night in. We'd bucked the trend of our recent hostel stays and decided to immerse ourselves in the action of the biggest group we could find, snowballing into a pretty cool party at the grace of the pouring rain.

I leaned over to Grace and tapped her lightly on the shoulder. 'He's pretty fucking good isn't he?' I asked, raising my voice above the noise.

'Alex, he's amazing! You must be very proud!'

'So must you! He's your best friend too!' She grinned an enormous grin and tapped Olivia to get her attention. 'Look how proud Alex is, it's adorable…'

I instructed my foot to stop tapping immediately and rolled my eyes as fast as I could, doing my best Turner impression as she turned towards me. She accidentally laughed to the tune of the song as she saw through my false bravado and leaned over to speak.

'Alex, don't pretend you're not buzzing on my account. I love that you and Matty big each other up so much, it's a really attractive quality.'

My feet began to tap with the vigor of a well-drilled marching band and before I knew it I was on my feet, unsuccessfully trying to whistle through my fingers. It was probably the beers talking but the day had really seemed to have turned around since our tiff in the Crazy House that morning, brushing any and all unresolved feelings under the carpet like unrequited lovers do best.

The night to follow passed by like the plot of a movie, with so many different genres I didn't know where to start. The thunderstorm outside would have you believe it was a tempestuous thriller but the sing-song serenades of funky folk music suggested otherwise, perhaps a coming of age classic of some sort. Action was covered by one of the drinking game installments, inciting rows over who was best looking between a group of Irish girls, spiralling into comedy as they insisted on a hostel wide vote. Thankfully horror was left off the table but there was a close shave with science fiction as someone clearly used mild telekinesis to hit every shot to eliminate me in the beer pong tournament. It was a cross-genre hybrid of a night, blending every theme and element thrown at it into a timeless, Academy Award-worthy classic. But there was one genre missing.

You guessed it. Romance. The big R. The emotional tension that comes with a believable plot and a happy-ever-after ending was certainly missing from my night thus far, aside from the endless flirtation with the bottom of the beer bottles I had so effortlessly knocked back. As the night had gone on, the division between our merry quartet had become wider and more pronounced, constantly finding myself stuck in conversation with Tom, Dick, or Harry about whether Manchester United were going to sack their manager sooner rather than later.

One particular chat I was having was of such low quality, scraping the bottom of the conversational barrel for whether they wanted to buy a Mercedes or a BMW with their parents' money, I had to double-take more than once to check it wasn't fucking Toby chatting on at me. In any case, I'd had enough. I made my way through the pockets of conversation and Matty's third encore into the makeshift smoking area at the front of the common room. I was happy to find I was alone out there as I sparked up another cigarette.

'Alex?'

The protagonist emerged from the light and laughter of the hostel common room, creating another dazzling silhouette as she slowly came to join my side. The sloped cover that stuck out above us created what felt like watery walls as the rain pelted down all around us, aside from a small car-sized rectangle of respite that we huddled beneath.

'Hey Liv, you okay?'

'Yes thank you, aside from this freezing blizzard, I'm feeling pretty good to be honest!' She shivered a little as she stood beside me, a faint smell of liquor rested within her usual lightly perfumed aroma.

'Come here ya dope!' I said, opening my arm out to warm her up.

'Okay, thanks.'

I grabbed her tightly around the shoulders and offered her my cigarette, which she took and faintly dragged a couple of times, before passing it back.

'We really should quit those things. I never thought I'd start again out here, but it's just too tempting.'

'Oh don't I know it.'

We stood in silence for a while, passing the cigarette between us and watching the rain tumble down. I felt her breathing shallowly under my embrace, prompting me to turn my head towards her. She was staring up at me, lighting fire under water.

'Alex, I think I'm ready to talk to you about what happened in Hội An.' She spoke with a hushed, almost strained tone of voice, as if every word was requiring her full attention to get out.

'Oh really? It hadn't crossed my mind to be perfectly honest.'

She sniggered, despite herself, letting out a spoiler of a laugh. 'Take me seriously you goof, I'm ready to actually talk if you want to!'

I smiled, trying to covertly create a little distance between her body against mine to avoid my bastard of a heartbeat chatting all kinds of shit. 'Fire away, Liv. What happened?'

She took a deep breath without taking her eyes off me and began to speak. 'Since we met in Ha Long Bay, or in the hot springs in Pai in your creepy case, I feel like we've been literally inseparable, like the best of friends.'

I rolled my eyes accidentally but her glare made them stop.

'Wait! Let me finish before you start judging, okay?'

'Okay, I'm sorry. Continue…'

'So because we've been so close, I've found myself getting increasingly drawn to you on nights out, especially as the drunken Olivia is a little less responsible than the poised, elegant sober me. Anyway, when that girl, who was stunning by the way, came over and got with you, it came as a bit of shock that I felt so protective and weird about it. I don't know if it was because you haven't really shown interest in getting with people since I've known you or whatever, but anyway, I got a little upset and stupidly ended up telling Matty about it when we walked home. In the morning, I was mortified as I knew he would tell you and we would end up in this situation.'

'And what situation is that?'

'You know what situation!'

'Enlighten me Olivia, you said you were ready to talk!'

She sighed heavily. 'That you know I like you Alex. As in like you, like you.'

'Oh, that situation.'

'Yes, Alex! But you know better than anyone that I love my boyfriend. We've been together for so long and my ties to him run so deep that I cannot ruin that by entertaining the idea of you and I. No matter my feelings for you, it simply cannot happen.'

I expected the words to hit me like a roundhouse kick, but I couldn't escape the overwhelming feeling of relief. Pure, unadulterated relief that she had finally admitted there were feelings between us. I had spent weeks battling to keep the feelings at bay for the good of the group, to pacify Matty and Grace and save them from the inevitable parting of ways that my admission would bring about. But I didn't have to pretend anymore.

Even though I knew nothing could happen, at least I could finally admit my feelings to her. To myself.

'I know Olivia. I never want to make you feel like you have to act on anything between us. You know I respect the fact you're with your boyfriend and I haven't tried anything with you because of that. I really like you too Olivia, of course, I do. But like you said, I love you as a friend more than anything, and even if I want something more, I can make peace with the fact that at least you feel the same.'

She looked up at me for a few long seconds with her mesmerising eyes, telling me all the things that her words could not. 'Well then, Manchester. Sounds like we've got an extended arrangement.'

'Sounds like it. Couple of friends who like to share a few laughs and a few cuddles as I remember it?'

'Is that how I worded it? Fucking hell pass me a ciggie, I'm dying of cringe.'

I chuckled and passed across my packet of cigarettes, feeling a breath of fresh air reside between us. It felt as though all of the pressure that had been building between us for the last few weeks had been relieved in one fell swoop, leaving me with an improved sense of clarity, a newfound path to the other side of the river.

'Liv, I thought you said you were quitting those things?'

'Ah well, I was never one to resist temptation,' she said with a wink.

Chapter 38

After canyoning down waterfalls in Dalat, quad biking across the sand dunes of Mui Ne, discovering an aptitude for Vietnamese cooking on my third course in as many weeks, and the endless hours spent roaming through the jungle backdrop of the country on my now trusty Honda SH, it would be fair to say the domineering sight of Ho Chi Minh City's overarching skyline was like the wave of a distant relative I'd come to visit.

The country's business and financial hub was a sleek goliath, swapping beach bars for rooftop terraces and street vendors for skyscrapers, the pagodas, and ornate temples celebrated the rich history of the city that was laden with western modernisation down every busy and bustling street.

And it was in this city that the final decision to travel together as a four to Cambodia was made. Personally, I had no reservations about sticking together for pretty obvious reasons. But I was surprised to find no resistance amongst my companions when sharing the sentiment. Each one of them had justifiable cause to doubt the suitability of the group dynamic going forward, especially now the situation with Olivia and I was out in the open.

I'd spoken to Matty first, pulling him to one side at the Hangout Hostel in downtown Ho Chi Minh to discuss our long term plan of action. I felt that he was well within his rights to suggest parting ways with the girls, considering I had all but abandoned our two-man crusade to woo wandering women as a dynamic duo.

'Mate, I've done better with girls since you stopped trying to help if I'm perfectly honest,' he had said, quite frankly I may add. 'Plus, I love our girls, they make us actually get up and do shit instead of just getting fucked all the time. Also, I don't think this you and Olivia thing is quite over with just yet. I've never seen ya so buzzing over a girl, it's nice brother.'

With Matty's vote in the bag, Grace was next in line to give her blessing, albeit in very different circumstances. Her motives were revealed during an intense but amusing negotiation with a market trader on our second evening in the city.

'Okay, my good sir. I completely see your point of view that these flip flops are worth 150,000. They are extremely well made and I applaud your enterprise for having stocked them in the first place. However, I have a secret motive behind the purchase that I hope will reduce the price to around 100,000 as this is all I can afford. This is my friend Alex and he's been wearing the worst sandals imaginable for far too long. If I'm going to travel to Cambodia by his side, buying your incredible flip flops for him is my one stipulation.'

She spoke with candid grace and of course managed to haggle down the bemused trader, ending up alluring him into a chuckled laugh as she expressed her gratitude with an excited cuddle. This was the first time she'd openly conveyed to me her desire to travel on with us, a decision I appreciated more than she knew. She had more of a reason than any of us to want to part ways, considering the situation with Olivia and I had created a dynamic that she hadn't exactly signed up for.

With Matty and Grace on board, that left only Olivia to give the green light to our continued adventure. I had planned to speak to her on my own, to put forward a comprehensive and well thought out argument to convince her it was the right course of action given the circumstances. But in the end, I hadn't needed to. It was her who approached me as we retired to our respective private rooms on the third night of our stay.

'Alex?'

'Olivia.'

'Can we talk?'

'Yeah, you want to come in here?' I indicated over to my room and padded barefoot along the hostel corridor, the bright overhead light illuminating her stripped-back features.

'Sure.'

I pushed open the heavy wooden door of my private room, the creak of the fixtures sending out a word of warning as it swung closed behind us. I propped a few pillows up against the headboard of my single bed and offered it to her, slapping on my most courteous face.

'What a gentleman. Come on, there's room for both of us in there. Sit!'

I lay down next to her in the place where magic usually happened and rested my head on the crown of pillows, allowing my arm to casually place itself around her dainty shoulders.

'So? What did you want to talk about?'

'Can you dim these lights? It feels like I'm under interrogation.'

I laughed as I flicked the main light in the room off from the switchboard next to me, plunging us into darkness. I then pretended to struggle to find the lamp that was right next to it, entertaining the glimmer of hope that the absence of light would leave our judgement blinded.

'Turn the lamp on then, idiot.'

The lamp's blessing offered a dim, suggestive ambiance in the room, creating what I believed to be a slightly steamy tension between us.

'Okay, I'm just going to blurt this out because I've been a little nervous about bringing it up. I know we haven't spoken much about what the next move will be so I just wanted to tell you that I really think we should carry on travelling together. All four of us I mean, of course. I know Grace wants to, and Matty and I have spoken about it a few times as well. I'm having the time of my life with you three and it'd be a shame to end things here so… prematurely. Do you agree?'

I felt myself edge a little closer to her without really meaning to. 'I couldn't agree more, Liv.'

'Good.'

'Good.'

I stared at her in the ambient light, her beautiful eyes staring back with fierce intensity. It wasn't the first time I felt like she would kiss me but on this occasion, we were barely six inches away from it becoming reality. I felt the room heat up as our face-off exchanged passionate, silent counters back and forth, solar flares bouncing between us. For the first time, it was I who came out victorious as she broke her gaze.

'You going to check flights then?' she said, stumbling over her delivery.

I sighed and reached for my phone in my pocket, cloudy headed from desire and not wanting the teasing face to face to end. I winced at the bright light that emitted from my phone, expecting the background of Matty, Grace, Olivia, and I to greet my eyes. But an email notification cropped up instead, the contents of which spilled out across the illuminated page.

Halifax Banking

We have identified the fraudulent activity that caused your account suspension. If the below transaction was issued by yourself, please contact us immediately:

07 Aug 15 - CALEB ANDERSON - 07AUG15 -£10,000.00 - BANK TRANSFER

I was stunned. I blinked a couple of times, adjusting my eyes to what was surely a mistake, something I must've misread. But there it was. Clear as day. An online banking transaction of ten grand had been made from my account directly to my friend Caleb.

I bolted up with a start, causing Olivia to fall away from my embrace and into the adjacent wall.

'Fucking hell, Alex?'

I couldn't think straight, I didn't know how to process what I had just found out. It didn't make sense. I was convinced that my purchase of the motorbikes in Hue was the cause of the account suspension? Who had authorised this money to send to Caleb?

'I'm… I'm sorry Liv. I just have to go sort something out… Stay here okay?' I mumbled, leaving her confused and alone in my room as I shot into the corridor, slamming the door behind me.

What time was it in England? 5 p.m.? I roughly scrolled the contacts of my phone to find the number for Caleb and slammed the dial button, with zero thought cast to what the hell I would say.

RING RING, RING RING, RING RING, RING...

Welcome to the O2 messaging service.

I tried again and again, to no avail. I racked my brains trying to think of how this could've happened. Had I drunkenly commissioned the transactions in one of my hazy nights out? But it couldn't be that. I would surely remember.

The only other person with access to my account was my brother, Steve. But he wouldn't send Caleb money from my account? I scrolled from the C's to the S's with the speed of an overnight bus driver. Anger, fear, and worry made up a tornado of emotions running through my head as I dialled.

RING RING, RING RING, RING...

'Hello little brother, you missing me already, you little melt?' came the voice of Steve.

'Hi, listen, weird question but you haven't sent any money from my account have you?' I realised my voice sounded accusatory, but needs must.

'Chill out inspector. No, of course I haven't. Why would I?'

Fuck sake. How had this happened? 'Ah, fair. I don't know, it's weird, did Dad tell you that my account got suspended a couple of weeks back?'

'Oh yeah, I assumed you'd just be paying off ladyboys or something...' he sniggered. Nothing had changed at home then.

'Good one.'

'Init. How are ya anyway?'

'Stressed mate. Look I've gotta go, I've gotta ring the bank or Dad or something.'

'Oh, nice catching up with you too.'

'Sorry bro, just gotta sort this fraud stuff.'

'Sound, no worries. Oh yeah, before you go... Get your mate Caleb to ask you himself for your sort code and account number next time? He rang me out of the blue asking for your details and I can't be arsed with all your mates ringing me, I've got better things to be doing. See ya kid!'

BEEP BEEP BEEP

And he was gone.

I leant back against the corridor wall and slumped down to the floor, holding my phone in both hands, slowly bringing it up to my head. Torrential thoughts, questions, and worries bombarded me as I got my head around what my brother had just said. How had he hoodwinked Steve into giving him my details? How had he known my password? Was he in deep with the wrong people yet again?

From the rolling pinnacle of the next wave of the trip I had felt a freedom like no other, finding solace in the hearts of my closest companions and the promise that we would be journeying on further into another land of discovery, ready to take on whatever Cambodia had to throw at us. I had found a girl who seemed to tread the tightrope between friendship and something more with an acrobat's confidence, veering from one side to the other as and when she pleased, leaving each day an unpredictable stone unturned. I believed I was on the way to something truly great. But this was a curveball I didn't see coming.

My friend Caleb, who I had given a £15,000 handout to as if it was nothing before we came away, had likely been pushed to the point of desperation at the hands of his gambling addiction, and I had done nothing to help him aside from absentmindedly throw him a bone with no thought of what would become of it.

If I had learned anything since coming away to travel, it was that wealth only got you so far. I had all the riches in the world yet had still seen the horrifying crash of my best mate Brown Shoes, embroiled myself in a love story that risked complete disaster and now I had most likely pushed my friend to the brink of thievery because of my ignorance.

I vowed then, on the floor of the Hangout Hostel in Ho Chi Minh City, that I would stop avoiding the negatives in my life.

I would do better. Be better. And that vow would begin with Caleb.

Part 4

Chapter 39

After only a few days in Cambodia, it became clear to me that things had changed.

Since I'd journeyed to this side of the world, I had felt free of the clutches of time constraints, each day offering up a new adventure that took precedence over fleeting thoughts to the past or future in a way I'd never thought possible, redefining my perspective on living in the present. Sure, I still cast cursory thoughts to what was forthcoming, wondering what would happen between Olivia and I, when I would next see my family and who I would become once my travels were over, but the uncertainty over these segments of thought seemed like a puzzle I didn't need to solve right away.

But since I'd spoken to Caleb about the money, I struggled to completely regain my focus on what was going on around me, not finding it easy to be truly present in the days spent with my companions. The conversation hadn't exactly been an easy one, having to endure the affliction of his current predicament in excruciating detail, hearing the emotion in his voice as he apologised for taking the money, ensuring me it was a last resort in what sounded like a vicious cycle of gambling and borrowing.

But I'd listened. I'd heard his story, properly listening for the first time. I tried to picture myself in his shoes, the daily suffering at the hands of addiction. We'd spoken for a good few hours over the phone, toing and froing between a multitude of different emotions until I made a decision on what to do next.

I'd offered him the chance to come out to meet us, to join the travelling pack in mind, body and spirit. In truth, I'd wanted to show him this way of living, to help him understand the mental limitations we'd all been trapped into growing up in the United Kingdom.

It was hard not to sound like a pompous idiot if I'm honest, assuring him that if he came to meet me I'd show him a new way of life. But in my head, I believed if he experienced anything like I had over the past two months, he would at least see how little my wealth came into play, how finances were barely discussed in conversation and gain an insight into how people lived in a completely different culture. On the whole, the local people we'd encountered seemed as happy as anyone in the world, going about their daily rituals in a serene and contented existence, despite many of them living in what I would've previously described as poverty. If I could show him that, help him see the world how I was beginning to see it, then at least I would have done all I could to help out my friend.

Caleb being Caleb, he'd ripped the living shit out of me for the hippy dippy bullshit. And perhaps he was right to do so, I did sound like a bit of a cliche. As sad as some of the conversation was, it was great to hear his voice, listen to his ridiculous stories and his nonsensical ramblings of life back at home. Naturally, he'd jumped at the chance to meet us and to my surprise he'd not even needed me to pay. Funnily enough, he'd won big on one of the wagers he'd placed with my *loan* and he was only too quick to pay back the money he'd taken. Lady luck, meet Caleb Anderson.

So that was that. He was due to fly out and meet us in a couple of weeks time to see out the rest of Cambodia and likely beyond. And I was happy. It was a strange kind of happy, one that harbored mixed feelings about what was to come. In hearing Caleb's story, I felt as though I'd taken on a bit of his baggage. It wasn't too dissimilar from how he had taken my money, as a final last resort. In doing so, I felt less ignorant to the toils of the world I'd left at home, less disconnected with the social politics of pre-existing friendships and felt more empathy for those other than myself and those immediately around me. I guess it made me feel as though I had responsibilities that extended beyond myself, for one of the first times in my life. Like I said, a strange kind of happy.

So as we journeyed on through the first few days in Cambodia, I continued to have crazy and exciting experiences, armed with my best friends at my side and the opportunities endless. On the surface, nothing had changed. But with the impending arrival of another huge character to add to the mix, the situation between Olivia and I, and the gradually increasing intensity of the barrage of my conscience, I felt like the once dense travelling fog had lifted slightly, unveiling the crystal clear clarity of responsibility.

Chapter 40

'How on earth have we ended up in this situation? Last thing I remember, we'd agreed on staying friends and now look at us! Look at the state of this place! It looks like cupid's thrown up all over the room...'

Although exaggerating slightly, she did have a point. The satin pillows could've numbered in the hundreds and there was more lace on show than the shoe tying world championship finals. The freshly scattered rose petals that lined the entrance to the suite didn't exactly spell out 'just friends' in fragrant little letters, instead insinuating that multiple high-octane romantic activities were due to take place within.

It wasn't *entirely* my fault that we'd ended up in this situation, alone in a private room with ensuite hot tub and flat screen tv, the varnished wood walls chock-a-block full with suggestive paintings and a rather suspect wall hanging of a supposed Cambodian fertility goddess. It really was a happy accident that they'd only had private rooms left. And it wasn't *my* fault that Matty and Grace had both pulled on the same night, four days into our visit of Phnom Penh, Cambodia's bustling capital city. It really was our moral obligation to bestow the two single rooms initially booked for Matty and myself to accommodate for Grace's wild escapades. All in the name of fairness I'd say.

'Ah well old chum, looks like we're in here for the night. Unless you want to go and try yanking that guy's sweaty body off Grace next door...'

'Okay! Okay! I think that's quite enough detail thank you.'

She drunkenly kicked off her brown leather sandals, each shoe travelling in different directions and skidding off the tiled floor. I watched her sit down on the king size bed, the cogs in her half cut mind evidently whirring away in a bid to find justifiable cause for staying with me in this apparent honeymoon suite. She looked adorable when she was burrowed away in thought, even if that thought process was likely assessing the best ways to get rid of me.

'Liv, don't look so stressed. I can be quite a fun roommate given half the chance. Also, look what I managed to smuggle back from the sky bar…' I paused for a few seconds, teasing the mystery surprise with exaggerated dramatic effect, before revealing my grand trick, pulling an innocuous bottle of red wine from the rucksack on the floor. My rabbit out of the hat maneuver had its desired effect as my audience's eyes lit up, swinging her legs round into a much more welcoming cross legged pose on the crisp white linen sheets.

'Okay, I've decided to let you stay with me just this once.'

'Just this once?'

'Yes Alex! But if you're staying I have some conditions…' She signalled at the space next to her on the bed and indicated that the wine and I should sit down. As I approached the bed, she took the bottle from my hand and slowly twisted the cap off, before taking a pretty sizable swig.

'The conditions aren't that you get sole custody of the wine are they?' I asked, grabbing the bottle back and returning fire with a gulp of my own.

She smiled wickedly. 'No, you're not that lucky, I'm keeping well in control of my inhibitions tonight thank you very much.'

I sat down next to her in the bed, shuffling along to the headboard and allowed myself to lean back into a half-sitting, half-horizontal pose, praying to the gods of chirpsing that it was a flattering posture. 'Okay fine then, what are these conditions Olivia?'

'Before I tell you, can you tell me why you're sitting like a nude model waiting to be drawn?'

'Stop thinking about me naked, you psycho!' Nailed it.

'Pfffft, you wish.'

'Conditions Liv!'

'Oh yeah, okay. So, I'll allow you to stay in here on three conditions. Number one. Don't you dare snore, I've heard some suspect noises in the dorms we've shared and it better not have been you, okay?'

I took another steady sip of the rouge, having a private word with my sinuses to keep it in check for the night ahead. 'No drama, I'm a silent sleeper.'

'Gimme that,' she said, pulling the wine out of my hand and mirroring my actions like an adult game of copycat. 'Okay, I'll take your word for it. Anyway, stipulation number two. Under no circumstances do you bring up the whole Caleb situation. I love ya Alex, but you haven't stopped harping on about how excited you are that he's coming out in a couple of weeks. I get it, he's your best mate and you're buzzing that he's booked his flights, but let me make my own mind up on him, deal?'

I winced a little at the mention of Caleb. But I couldn't let myself get distracted by it, I was in the end zone and I wasn't going to let anything ruin it for me. 'Deal. Number three?'

'Number three? Are you sure you're ready?'

'Olivia, this is my serious face. I'm ready.'

'Okay, here we go.' She mimicked my dramatic pause from earlier, pulling it off much better than I did. 'Condition number three is the most important of all. If you can agree to this, then prepare yourself for the most comfortable, relaxing, rejuvenating sleep of your life.'

'I'm waiting…'

'Okay, okay! Condition number three is the adherence to the six inch rule.'

'The what sorry?'

'The six inch rule.'

I looked at her, a smirk appearing slowly across my face. 'Wow, that's certainly presumptuous… Have you got a tape measure or how are we doing this?'

She doubled over onto the bed and fell back into my shoulder, cushioning her fall in a perfectly executed take. Her intoxicating laugh filled the room as she giggled in my arms, a slight red tint making itself known within her cheeks.

'No you freak! Get your head out of the gutter! That's not what the six inch rule means!'

As per usual, I couldn't help laughing along with her. 'How am I supposed to know? You've lured me into a honeymoon suite and all of a sudden we're talking about how size matters…'

'Alex! You're being outrageous! No, no, no. The six inch rule is the distance you have to stay away from me at all times when we're in bed together. That way I can keep an eye on you. I don't want to be waking up in the night as an involuntary small spoon or with any inappropriate brushing or grazing of each other's… erm…'

'Okay, okay, don't hurt yourself Liv. I get it. Six inch rule? I like it. Sounds like we agree, so when does this kick in? As it looks suspiciously like you're the one trying to cuddle me right now.'

She jumped up, taking the bottle with her and swigged another mighty gulp. 'From right now of course! I'm glad you agree, Alex. You do get why I have to set these rules don't you?'

'Yes, Liv.'

'Good! Okay, sleep time, big day tomorrow!' she cried, finishing off the last of the wine and clattering the empty bottle onto the bedside table. 'Now, don't go hogging the covers.'

I weighed up trying to argue, debating whether I could somehow manipulate the situation so we could stay up a little longer, or possibly make use of that hot tub? Although that was probably pushing it…

I stood up and pulled off my Brooklyn Brewery printed t-shirt, throwing it onto the pile of belongings we'd made upon arrival. Heading over to the light switch, I looked back towards the bed to see Olivia had relieved herself of her clothes and burrowed deep under the sheets. I flicked off the lamps, plunging the suite into the mysterious nature of the dark, rendering all units of measurement surely redundant?

It took until I entered the bed to realise that my heart rate had quickened, the amalgamating effects of cheap red wine, pillow talk and midnight's bounty taking their toll. I crawled into the Olivia-less side of the goliath mattress, all of a sudden feeling very lonely and ambitious, a hazardous combination. Erratic thoughts entered my mind, the angel on my shoulder was nowhere to be seen thus leaving the devil's sole perspective.

It's not the six metre rule, you pussy…

I edged towards her one millimeter at a time, plotting my path with military precision, each unit of distance I gained was wildly celebrated with an internal high five. I cast a glance to 'my' side of the bed, an empty shell, a discarded skin that I had shed, where cowards were banished to sleep. I laughed silently at the alternate dimension Alex who would quietly accept defeat, as I charged on into the breach with my head held high, inching closer and closer to salvation, the taboo realm of 15cm or less. I was on the cusp, on the precipice of nirvana...

'ALEX! Six inch rule!'

Chapter 41

While Phnom Penh had been quite the conversation with culture, it became clear on the first night in Sihanoukville that we had arrived in a very different place. Our temple hopping tendencies of the first few days in Cambodia were going to have to be put on hold in this new city, for it demanded a different currency entirely.

'Welcome to Sinville!' cried the hostel rep, crushing his cigarette butt with apparent disregard for the stained bartop he was posing on, hollering at the top of his voice to ensure it was heard amongst the ear-splitting jungle bass music that was clattering around the room.

"Sinville" certainly captured the place well, a city that gave the islands of Thailand a run for their money. The Cambodian beachside town provided a new backdrop, but an all too familiar plot slowly revealed itself as the fluorescent buckets of debauchery bid us a recognizable handle held hello.

Matty and I were buzzing. I wish I could say we were past all this nonsense, but the dirty music, disorderly patrons and boisterous backpacker binge drinking had certainly slowed down in recent weeks and I'd be lying to suggest it wasn't exciting to be back amongst it. I believed there was no place better to get away from my pestering thoughts and the uncertainty between Olivia and I than a big stinking rave.

And rave we did. Against the better judgement of the girls, we'd joined the hostel-wide bar crawl to the strip of the nearby Otres Beach, infamous for its wild parties and scandalous reputation. The bar crawl consisted of some of the most questionable miscreants we'd met on our travels, scary groups of bickering Brits, scantily clad local women who must've been in their 40's, noisy hooligans from Russia and a smattering of bewildered stragglers that we joined the ranks of.

We made our way to the beach in a hostel shuttle bus, crashing head first into wild drinking games and singing at the tops of our voices. It was juvenile but I was enjoying it, losing my inhibitions to the raucousness of the night, slowly shrouding my mind from the allures of the rest of the world.

The party was something else entirely. It was the grungiest night I'd seen since coming away, reminiscent of the Leeds basement house parties in my second year of university but with a few palm trees dotted around. Fortunately, I liked grungy. It didn't take long for the four of us to take to the centre of the beach dance floor, debuting questionable dance moves and bopping along to the heavy techno music. The lights, the fires, the colours swirled around as we two-stepped like our lives depended on it, throwing caution to the winds of rebellion.

It was only when I received a sharp tap on the shoulder that I fell out of the trance of a jungle remix that I swore I'd heard before.

'Alex!'

'Hi Liv!'

'Let's go for a chat!'

'Now? Okay, one sec, I swear I know this song!'

'Alex! I need to talk to you!'

I peeled my eyes to dissect the fluorescent spotlights bouncing around my peripheral vision. She did seem to be laughing and a chat with Olivia did sound marginally better than the tune that was playing, so I relented and allowed her to drag me out of the sweaty congregation of backpackers that lined the sandy shore. We zigzagged through the beachside liquor salesmen and neon paint artists that heckled our every move, tiptoeing around a couple who were getting well acquainted in the sand.

Eventually, she led me to a grassy hill that sat up above the action, the echo of the music now allowing for uninterrupted chat.

'Hey, how unreal is it here?! I feel like we've not been to a party this mad in ages…' I felt my heart rate slowing a little as I wiped the sweat from my forehead, adjusting to the cooler temperature outside of the party.

'I know, it's pretty crazy! But it feels like we can't really talk in there, I'm missing your stupid wisecracks a little bit.' She looked at me with glistening eyes, the reflection of the party making them dance on their own.

'Yeah, I can imagine that must be tough.' I winked at her for some reason, but came away without deserved retribution.

'Oh, extremely tough…'

'So what did you want to talk about?' I asked.

'Oh nothing specific, you've just been on a mad one all night so thought you might've needed a breather!'

'It's not just me on a mad one, have you not seen Matty and Grace? I thought Grace was going to take off earlier with those dance moves!' I laughed.

She giggled quietly, tucking the dark strands of hair behind her ear. 'Yeah, we're all pretty boozy actually. I'm feeling super guilty to be having this much fun with you if I'm honest.'

'You shouldn't feel guilty for having fun Olivia, it's not like we're even doing anything wrong, we're just having a sick night with the others!' I looked at her with a confused smile, the intro of the next song calling me back to the fold.

'I know, I know. I don't feel guilty for what we're doing, I just feel guilty for how I'm feeling. That's all,' she said, avoiding

226

my eye. I hadn't seen her act like this before, a shy demeanor replacing her usual fierce and confident aura.

I laughed softly and turned to put my arm around her, facing away from the ongoing party. 'Go on then, what are you feeling that's making you guilty?'

She shrugged me off playfully, but settled into my embrace, resting her head on my shoulder, the smell of shampoo and cigarettes filling my nose. We sat there for a while, not saying anything, swaying back and forth to the distant sounds of the party of a lifetime.

'Alex, do you think it's odd how we don't talk about my boyfriend?'

'Erm… Not particularly no…'

She paused. 'Well, do you not want to know anything about him? Or what he looks like for that matter?'

'Na, not at all to be honest.'

'Why not?' she asked, a little bit of impatience in her voice.

I paused in turn. 'Honestly? Because it makes this whole situation a lot easier if I pretend he doesn't exist.'

I felt her body tense up a little as she processed what to say next. This was new ground for Olivia and I, a conversation that we'd put off, or should I say avoided since we had met.

'I wish I could do that sometimes…' she said, almost muttering her words.

'You and me both, Liv.'

She looked up at me with a disapproving look, but softened into a cheeky smile when we made eye contact. 'Alex, I do fucking fancy you you know?'

I laughed, a wide grin spreading across my face. 'Oh I know, the feeling is more than mutual...'

'Don't get too cocky now.'

'I'll try my best, but no promises!'

'Yeah, it's crazy, I'd say you're bang on my type to be honest. I fancy you way more than I fancy my boyfriend,' she said, looking away into the distance.

'What can I say, ey? I grew this face myself...' I laughed, awaiting a giggle in return. But it never came. Her body had become rigid and she quickly shrugged out of my arms.

'Liv? What's up?'

She stood up with a start, brushing the sand off her denim shorts, each grain being cast down to the ground in anguish. 'Oh, nothing. Nothing.'

'Liv, there obviously is something?'

'Genuinely it is nothing, I just shouldn't be saying shit like that to you, it's not fair on either of us and it's definitely not fair on my boyfriend. Oh shit. Look, let's just go shall we?' She looked flustered, annoyed even as she led me down the other side of the hill towards the road.

'Go?! We've only been here an hour?' I pulled my hand back a little, but she held on until we reached a stop.

'Alex! I'm just not feeling it, will you come back with me or not? I can pay for a taxi or something...'

'But what about Matty and Grace? And the party sounds like it's going to be…'

'You stay if you want, Alex. I really really don't mind, I just think I've had a bit too much to drink and I don't really want to go back in there. But honestly, stay. I want you to.'

I looked at her for a second, trying to read her face and decipher what was really going on. She looked worked up and a little upset, her small frame shaking a little as she stood. How could I say no to that face.

'No, it's fine. Let's go.'

'Are you sure? If you want to stay, you should stay, Alex!'

'No, it's crap in there anyway… Grace and Matty will probably both pull anyway, knowing the form they're on!' I forced a laugh and made my way over to her side, throwing my arm around her once again. 'Let's just go back to the hostel, get a good night's sleep and be primed and ready for a big day tomorrow.'

And go home early, we did.

Chapter 42

Koh Rong is Cambodia's largest and most idyllic island. Locals and travellers alike had sewn yarns of how the lapping crystal waves tickled the rolling white beaches with the intimacy of a married couples first kiss. The island was supposedly about the back to basics approach to living, with little to no grand hotels, a notable absence of roads or cars and what proved to be more than enough to deter a main bulk of the travelling masses, absolutely no wifi.

Before we'd arrived on the island I'd been sceptical at best, expecting a scene somewhat similar to the port of Koh Phi Phi, another supposed untouched paradise that had been promised, yet delivered something else entirely. But it has to be said, Koh Rong looked like the business.

As our narrow wooden boat approached the picturesque beach, we were baffled to not be met with the expected humdrum of repetitive electronic music, or a haggling crowd of salesmen imploring us to take their taxi or go to the 'best bar in town.' The only signs of life on the beach were a few laid back shops and restaurant huts sitting comfortably along the treeline to a dazzling jungle backdrop, as well as a couple of groups of people in two's and three's floating casually along the shore. We tentatively stepped off the boat with nothing but our senses and the word of mouth to guide us.

'Wow, doesn't it look amazing guys?!' exclaimed Grace, defying the weight of her rucksack with lamb like skips forward, the sea water splashing up from her playful steps.

'Yeah I'm pleasantly surprised to be fair, I was expecting another Phi Phi and I wasn't quite prepared for that after Otres Beach the other day…' Matty's voice hadn't been the same since that night, the victim of a seven am bender.

'Yeah this looks perfect,' said Olivia, giving me a lighthearted bump as she walked beside me through the shallows.

And she wasn't wrong, I thought as we made our way out of the water and onto the cloudlike sand, dropping our bags to the floor and shaking off our sea legs from the 45 minute journey.

'Where to then?' asked Matty.

'Dunno, shall we ask around or do either of you two girls have a recommendation?'

'We did speak to those Irish girls the other night and they said there's a pretty good hostel not far from the main beach, which I guess is where we are?' said Grace, sitting down on the sand.

'I was thinking we could get a private beach bungalow, the four of us!' said Olivia.

'I'm game for that, my head's battered so I can't really be arsed with a hostel right now…'

'Yeah Matty needs his beauty sleep so we can get a fresh little beachside place. Let's head that way, away from the bars is probably our best bet!' I was more than keen to get a place to ourselves considering the way things had been going with Olivia and I, the more time I could get alone with her the better. It wasn't exactly that I held much hope that something would happen between us, but our time alone was exhilarating to me, cautiously tiptoeing between what was appropriate and what wasn't, each glance or sentence exchanged holding a thousand different meanings.

After a brief rest stop, drinking in our glorious surroundings like the first beer of the day, we set off along the beach at a happy trot, reminiscing and forecasting in equal measure. The sun was high in the sky, offering a pleasant heat when paired with the generous sea breeze, making for a near perfect environment for the four of us to enjoy. It wasn't long before we came to a bit of a clearing, a multitude of pathways leading up into the jungle. A weathered signpost jutted out of the sand inoffensively, detailing exactly what we were looking for.

The Paradise Bungalows were exactly what they said on the tin. A vast wooden framework made up the foundation of the hut, standing tall above the jungle floor. A grand and lofty staircase rolled up the side of the structure, leading to an impressive patio / balcony combination, complete with a hammock swinging in the midday breeze. But it was the interior that really decided that the place was for us, offering a cosy, authentic spectacle of a room, partitioned slightly by tall bamboo walls between two enormous four poster beds.

I'd expected our regular rigmarole of pretending the girls were in one room and Matty and I the other, paying no attention to the agreement thereafter. This had been the case in the last few places we'd stayed but it seemed even these rules were now being broken.

'Alex and I are in this one!' chirped Olivia, throwing her bag down onto the bed. 'We need to keep the early risers together!'

'Sounds good to me, this one is nearest the toilet which I'm going to need full use of this afternoon.' Matty slung his backpack to the floor and starfished out on the far side of the room.

'Hmmm, okay then,' said Grace, quietly.

I cast her a brief glance, trying to catch her eye but she had turned away, wandering over to the rainfall shower that was fixed out in the open air bathroom.

Over the past couple of weeks, our group had developed somewhat of an unspoken ritual when we arrived in new places. Grace would without fail head out to the shop for supplies, taking the opportunity to explore a little on her own before returning with a smorgasbord of beer, snacks and other miscellaneous items she'd picked up on her trip. Matty, a man of simple tendencies, either fell asleep or christened the toilet, whichever primal urge took hold of him first. That left Olivia and I, who usually opted for making the most of our limited time alone, diving head first into flirty chats or coy exchanges over what we wish we could do if our situation was different. It was a delicate ecosystem but it worked for us.

And this day was no different. Grace wasted no time in embarking on her mini solo adventure, hopping out the door armed with a list of things to check out. Matty was already snoring away, hopefully shaking off the final effects of that 'party of a lifetime' on Otres Beach.

'Liv, I can't believe what you said last night about us not working back at home. Don't think I've let you off the hook that easily…'

'Alex, you can't honestly think we would. I thought we'd already covered this!'

'You've covered it, I disagree.'

She sighed playfully, making her way out onto the balcony and staring out across the beautiful vista of the ocean. 'Look, we're very different people Alex. You're a party boy and a lazy bastard half the time. The only reason you're having such a sick time travelling is because I'm forcing you to do half the stuff!' She giggled as she mocked me, lying down outstretched across the rope hammock.

'You've got this idea of me that I don't want to do anything but go out and booze but in reality, I've done everything you've asked me to do. Never once have I sacked it off for being too hungover or whatever.'

'But that's precisely my point, Alex. I'm asking you. Half the time forcing you!'

'I think we'd work pretty well.'

'I know you do, Alex.'

'And to be fair, half the time I think you'd agree with me. The other night you were chatting on saying how much I'd get on with your friends and family!' I struggled to keep my voice down to prevent waking up Matty, but she had this catalyst effect on me when we were together.

'Yes, which you would. You know I think the world of you. I just think I'm a bit too *busy* for you. I like hiking and exploring and cooking and all my girly stuff. You like footy and beer and chilling. It doesn't mean I don't fancy you, I just don't think we'd work.'

'You underestimate me, Liv.'

'I really don't Alex! I love who you are, I don't want you to change for anyone, let alone to suit me. I know you've had an unreal time with Grace and I showing you the ropes, dragging you along to things that you and Matty would never be caught dead doing, but I think once we've parted ways, you'll go back to doing what you do best.'

'And what's that?' I asked, laughing before her response as I knew what was coming.

'Being a top boozer. Enjoying yourself. Getting with a million girls!'

'Liv…'

She laughed, patting the tiny space next to her on the single hammock, shuffling over slightly to make room. I slumped down quickly and tangled us together as the ropes took our weight, laughing furiously as we tried to unweave our knotted limbs. We tussled for a while, reaching a tired stalemate pushed together, peas in a pod.

'Do you realise that this is the main reason I'm finding it so hard to process my feelings for you?'

'Why? Because we're stuck in this hammock?'

'No you goof. Because I'm so sure we wouldn't work together, it doesn't make sense why I like you so much and can't stay away from you. You know better than anyone how decisive I usually am. But with you? I've got no idea what I want. And it's getting worse and worse every day.'

I took this in slowly, trying to maintain as serious a face I could whilst squished up against the side of the hammock. Did she really think we wouldn't work? I truly believed that over the month we'd spent together I'd found someone who was perfect for me. Someone who made me want to do better things, see better places. Someone who made me want to be a better man. But did she really think we weren't suited? Or was it just a coping mechanism that she told herself to protect from further hurt? It felt like she was refusing to see past the guy she'd met, or the guy I was back at home, ignoring the progress I believed I was making and all the things I was trying to change for her.

'Ah well. At least you fancy me!' I exclaimed, plastering on my most light hearted face.

She laughed, my drug of choice, giving me the sweet sensation it had done all those lifetimes ago in the hot springs of Pai. The laugh that made it all worth it, all the heartache, the dishonesty, the single minded desire to make it happen again and again.

Chapter 43

If we entertain one of the ongoing schools of thought that have ebbed and flowed throughout this journey, there have been moments, adventures, situations and experiences that have stood out as perhaps more striking than others. From the day I won my fortune to the moment I stepped on the plane, it seemed like my life was playing out in fast forward. But after the Muay Thai fight in Phi Phi spiralling into time spent under the sea, being treated to a mini Songkran festival, all the way to friendships found and lost in Pai, these significant moments became more and more regular, travelling blood beginning to flow through my veins. Onto Vietnam where the game changed entirely, Olivia and Grace stealing the show, adapting to new and bold ways of approaching life as we journeyed on. Fear, fantasy, ambition and elation don't scratch the surface of what I had been through.

Koh Rong offered up the next in a long line of these pivotal moments, one that would signal the end of one episode and the beginning of another. Perhaps not in the way one would expect, considering the intangible differences from one day to the next, but introspectively the day stands out as one of those key junctures in my life.

If I hadn't been privy to countless other examples of near panoramic perfection, the scene itself would likely be enough to catch the eye in a highlights reel of my life. 'Adventure Adam's Boat Tours' may not sound like the most authentic hidden gem in Cambodia, but what the tour lacked in naming conventions it made up for in its comprehensive and exciting itinerary. We hit the waves early doors to the sound of the Beatles on the overhead speakers to set the mood.

Then came the sun which naturally didn't let us down, providing a fine feeling within the small group we'd assembled. We arrived at our first stop, introducing ourselves to the locals in Sok San Village. With a little help from my friends I managed to help articulate the difference between a high five and a fist bump with the local children, before we came together holding hands, dancing round the village square. Just a day in the life I guess.

When back on the boat, things took a turn for the better as we cracked open the first beers of the day and embarked on an ocean floating, drink guzzling, in-joke vortex of fun. As had been the case on each of the mantra stimulating expeditions of the trip so far, the boat party spiralled back onto the main land like a roulette wheel reluctant to stop. Fortunately for us the spin landed on the nearby Bong's Guesthouse, apparently world renown for its outrageous live music sets and the promise of Cambodian cocktails that had the power to turn enemies into friends with one or two careful sips.

When the bartenders got wind of Matty's musical prowess from our incessant chants to take to the stage, the dye had been cast for what was to come. It didn't take much persuasion from the screams of the gradually growing crowd to coax him on stage and before we knew it we were embroiled in an intimate concert of Manchester's most well known music. Oasis to Courteeners, Blur and the Roses were gracious gifts given to the ever increasing capacity of the guesthouse.

'Alex, get up there and sing with them!' shouted Grace, following a particularly funky rendition of F.E.A.R sung by the Cambodian Ian Brown, complete with his feigned moody indifference to the crowd.

'Pffft, imagine the day I grow the balls to get on stage! It's not even karaoke, this is a full on band!'

'Matty's up there!'

'Matty may as well be a professional singer!'

'Alex, we're getting up whether you like it or not!' interrupted Olivia, pulling me off the sofa that Grace and I were sat on, to a rapturous applause from Matty's fans. She led myself and Grace in tow as she beelined for the stage, spurred on by Matty on the microphone shouting a slurred but comprehensive introduction.

Before I knew it, I was being thrust centre stage, side by side with Matty, Grace and Olivia, with the backing of the Bong Guesthouse resident band as our only source of support. The drums started. Then the familiar guitar riff. My friends huddled round the microphone in a tight knit formation, leaving a gap just big enough for me. Throwing caution to the wind, I jumped in, cast my arms around them and let myself go.

'I NEED TO BE MYSELF!'

'I CAN'T BE NO-ONE ELSE!'

'I'M FEELIN' SUPERSONIC, GIVE ME GIN & TONIC!'

'YOU CAN HAVE IT ALL, BUT HOW MUCH DO YOU WANT IT?'

The crowd, the lights, the intoxication of beer, nerves and growing confidence screamed out to me alongside the countless faces cheering up at us on stage. I don't know how, but I knew it was time. I reached for the hair tie on my wrist and expertly manipulated the sweat covered strands that bounced around my face, pulling them effortlessly into a neat bun at the back. I had reached the promised land.

But the night was far from over. From one amazing incident to the next we stomped on into the night, not knowing when to quit like a Las Vegas gambler on a never ending winning streak. We'd bid a fond farewell to the band after our energetic cover of Oasis brought the house down, only for them to tell us to meet them later at a nearby local's favourite, Police Beach, a well disguised gem of the island.

Without sounding too boorish, Police Beach was fucking mint. It had everything you'd want from a final destination on such a crazy, memorable day. The low key house music that built in slow rhythmic waves like the scene just outside the entrance of the bar, adding an upbeat relaxing ambience to an already stimulating occasion. Every person we met was charming and inoffensive, simply enjoying the evening to the fullest, introducing themselves pleasantly like the passing cool breeze on our first day on the island.

And we were all together. The four of us. Kindred spirits, breaking off in tangents of one's, two's, three's and four's whenever the mood demanded in a harmonious and effortless fashion. As the sun began to rise, we took the well trodden route back to the bungalow with full and goofy smiles on our faces, nostalgic about a day that we were still living.

A day that could not be written, so complete with far-flung and whimsical scenarios, each so specific in their relative merit that I couldn't begin to describe them in full. It was the small things, the jokes, the chats, the smiles and the attitude that bound the day together, but the big things, the Beatles boat trip, the welcoming village tour, my debut as a rock star and heaven's afterparty that made up the juicy and memorable centre.

And at the end of it all, a day of all days, I got into bed with the girl I had fallen in love with. I can't say when it happened for sure. For all I knew it was from the first moment I saw her. I just knew in that moment, there was no doubt in mind, looking at her face in the dappled light provided by the sunrise, peeping through the miniature gaps in the wooden walls around us. She looked so beautiful.

'What a day,' I whispered, putting my head on the pillow next to hers. Our mirrored bodies were covered by a thin bed sheet and the four poster bed was surrounded, engulfed within an insect repellent blanket, multiple barriers keeping out the rest of the world, leaving us in a world of our own.

'What a day indeed.'

'It was good to spend a full night with them two as well, I feel like we've been a bit too stuck in our own bubble recently…'

'Yeah, I guess. I do feel for Grace because she knows I'm only torturing myself and I don't think she approves very much,' she said, lowering her voice even further and edging a little closer in the bed.

'I know, I know. She's probably right. We *are* torturing ourselves.'

'I can't help it Alex. I'm sorry but days like today make it a thousand times worse. Seeing you with those children in the village today, my heart melted. Then I have to deal with you walking out of the sea like fucking James Bond. On top of that you get up and butcher Oasis with all of us even though I know you didn't want to. Then you want to know the cherry on the cake? Your hair looks fucking unreal tied up for fucks sake. Don't get cocky but it's been fucking hard to stop myself jumping all over you today.'

'Liv, you're saying these things like it's just you struggling. Do you realise that all these things you're starting to feel, I've been living through them for nearly two months. Seeing your face light up whenever you talk about the people you love, your genuine passion to see, learn and do anything and everything you lay eyes on. It's infectious Liv. You seem to think that I'm this guy who's doing things because you force me to do them. I'm doing them because you make me want to! You make me want to be a better person. Someone right for you.'

We both fell silent for a few seconds, staring at each other in our four poster den. The heat that existed between us had been kept at bay on her part for the entire time I'd known her, typically doused by an icy downpour of mocking or a cheap joke to diffuse the tension whenever things got too real. But her face was unbreaking, unflinching, just like the moment I'd met her in Ha Long Bay. Her gaslight blue eyes were ablaze, fanning the flame

240

of our desire. I moved closer, obliterating the six inch rule from the history books.

'Alex.'

'Liv.'

'I…'

'I know…'

And I kissed her.

Chapter 44

At that very moment, an enormous size 13 Nike Air Max trainer crunched the gravel of the runway at Phnom Penh International Airport, creating an echo that dwarfed the ear-shattering roar of the plane's propellers. The big man had arrived.

Okay, the likelihood of Caleb's arrival coinciding with the exact moment of my first kiss with Olivia sounds pretty far fetched, but in the interest of dramatic effect let's roll with it.

My first kiss with Olivia? If I was to speak poetically, I'd describe it as the allure of a fresh cup of coffee brought to you in the morning by the one you love, breathing in the delicious rejuvenating aroma to the deepest part of your soul, tentatively dipping your grateful lips to the surface of the brew to be met with the burning molten lava of Mount Doom as your reward.

Her impressive strength came in handy when pushing me all the way to the far side of the bed, before wiping her mouth and stifling every curse word under the sun so not to wake our two friends. She then proceeded to instigate the ever-effective, age old classic, silent treatment until we both dropped off into a frustrated slumber.

Fumbled apologies the following day from both parties meant that no lasting damage was done to the friendship, even managing to keep the whole charade private from Matty and Grace. We even joked about it a couple of days later, slipping back into old routines of flirtation and temptation, same old story, same old result.

Our stay on Koh Rong was the tropical island paradise that most people sign up for when heading to Asia, full of the dazzling white sandy beaches and crystal clear surf that populate the cover of most travel magazines the world over. But it was time to go back to the capital, to greet our now not-so-distant friend and welcome him into the fold. I'd be lying to suggest I knew how he would slot into the group dynamic, but one thing I did know for certain was a guy that big in size and character would make a pretty significant splash.

As we arrived at the port in Sihanoukville, the return to modern day civilisation was defined by the orchestra of text tones and notifications that echoed around the boat, wifi connection welcoming us back with open arms. Scanning through the Whatsapp, Facebook, Snapchat and text barrage I found a message from Caleb sent a day earlier that read as follows:

'Yes lad! Arrived in Pon Pem, fuckin weird place this, literally nowhere at the airport was doing a fry up so had beef noodles for breakfast. I'm at some place called Mad Monkey hostel now. What time u gettin here? I'm bored as fuck.'

Location secured, all that stood between us and our friend was a five hour bus journey. It was times like these that made me regret selling our bikes back in Ho Chi Minh City, nothing clearing the head like a rigorous motorbike ride across the highways of Asia. Alas, we trundled to the nearby bus station and secured tickets for the impending departure.

My own internal confliction aside, the mood in the group was pretty content as we took our seats at the back of the surprisingly modern and spacious bus. Air conditioning flowed freely down the aisles and each of us were blessed with ample leg room, a rare treat for those well travelled.

'And here we have it. The end of an era!' said Matty, throwing his arms around the girls beside him.

'Oh shut up Matty!' laughed Olivia, shrugging him off. 'You two are making such a big deal about Caleb joining our group. He sounds hilarious to me so it should be a welcome addition!'

'Yeah, he's your best friend!' pressed Grace.

243

'Yeah he is hilarious, I actually can't wait to see him but it'll definitely shake things up a lot. He's quite the difference maker.' I tried to picture Caleb as part of our group on the bus, rendering the four seats across the back row no longer sufficient, the leg room no longer ample.

'Yeah, I'm obviously excited as well. I'm just going to miss it being us four vs the world you know? We've been travelling as a four for so long, it's obviously going to be weird with another person, no matter who it is!'

A brief silence fell over the group as we pondered what Matty had said, the imminent arrival spelling the end of our travelling quartet. The creeping feeling of dawning reality was impossible to ignore now, with longer term thinking continuing to burst the bubble of acting in the moment. Would Caleb's arrival lead to the eventual separation of ourselves from the girls? Had my love story come to an unceremonious end? Questions without answers, problems without solutions, the curious channels of thought were becoming all too regular as time went on.

The journey felt like a long one, more so than any of the others I'd been subject to in the months preceding. Whilst I fought off the pangs of anxiety, I did my best to keep up with the excited chattering of the group, planning our next adventures and playing silly car games. It was only when we'd reached our destination and disembarked from the bus that Olivia pulled me to one side as we searched for our rucksacks in the storage hold.

'Hey, are you okay? You were weirdly quiet the whole way here.'

I felt the heat rise in my face, frustrated at myself for not being able to mask my feelings. 'Yeah, I'm fine! It's difficult to get a word in at the best of times with you lot!' I laughed a stupid laugh and turned away to hide my tells.

'Very true. Look Alex, if there's anything you want to talk about, or anything you want to tell me, I'm here okay?' She grabbed my shoulder and made me look at her, the sun's blaze the third degree.

'Liv, I'm fine honestly!'

'Okay, well good.'

I plastered on my biggest smile and gave her a little jab under her arm, where I knew she was ticklish. The plan worked to perfection, achieving a giggle and welcome break from the inquisition.

It had been just shy of three weeks since we'd last trod the streets of the Cambodian capital city. Those three weeks had been spent flirting with the coastline of the country and far removed from hectic city life. But with the rumble of the bus' engine as it shot off from the curb, the metropolis sprung back to life around us.

The howls of the street dogs were dwarfed by the creaking fixtures of a nearby wagon rolling past, filled to the rafters with super seismic watermelons. Hundreds of motorbikes zipped around in every direction to the tune of a nearby temple blaring out an unknown prayer at the highest volume imaginable. The sleepy shores of Koh Rong were consigned to last night's dreams.

The Mad Monkey hostel was only a five minute walk away from the central station, so we set off without a moment to spare. The time had come to welcome our friend into our new way of life, show him what all the fuss was about, give him a taste of 'travelling' in a figurative sense as well as the literal journeying from A to B.

'What are we going to do if he's not there? It's like four o'clock now, he might've already gone out with some people from the hostel?' asked Grace.

'Fat chance of that. He'll be in bed waiting for us most likely. You have to remember, he's new to this whole travelling thing!' said Matty.

'Oh check you out, top traveller…' said Olivia. 'I thought he was supposed to have the best first impressions of all time?'

'Yeah, he does but I remember our first day in Asia, we fucking shit ourselves when trying to talk to people. We barely made a proper friend until you two came along!' We turned out onto the main road in central Phnom Penh, scanning the many supermarkets, restaurants and bars that lined the high street. A familiar black and white face protruded out the side of a tall imposing building in the distance, recognisable as the Mad Monkey logo, infamous around Asia.

Our pace quickened, anticipation building as we took the streets at a trot, zigzagging between the local shopkeepers, city dwellers and travellers who dotted the pavement. On our final approach, I took a deep breath and braced myself for the inevitable dive into the next chapter of our travels, reunited with Caleb Anderson once again.

A welcome embrace of cool air greeted us as we plunged into the hostel entrance, the happy hour buzz spilling out of the nearby bar area parallel to the reception lobby. My eyes were peeled for the obvious, a six foot seven man being easy to spot in any crowded place. But I couldn't see him. I checked the reception. Nothing. I scanned the bar. Nothing. But I should've guessed. It wasn't just his height that set him apart from the travelling norm. It was his volume.

'Yesss laadssss!'

Was it a bird? Was it a plane? Was it the eruption of Mount Vesuvius? All decibel barriers were left in tatters as the entire hostel and it's surrounding 15 kilometer radius turned to see what the commotion was. And there it was. Submerged to his thighs in the deep end of the hostel swimming pool, holding an unashamed pink cocktail like a trophy, donning the most vibrant swim shorts ever dared to be put through mass production, grin the size of a beached whale, stood our mate, Caleb.

Matty and I let out a roar of our own as we charged the swimming pool, abandoning all 'too cool for school' notions in our wake. He met us in a slimy hug on the artificial grass that decorated the outdoor area, his booming laughter drawing all eyes towards us.

'Yes mate!' we chimed, breaking free of his soaking wet arms. 'What the fuck are you saying?'

'Fucking unreal to see you is what I'm sayin!' His voice was even louder than I remembered, especially when drunk, which he evidently was. 'Oh and as if this isn't enough, I've got a fuckin top surprise for you two!'

'What?' I asked, unsure of what he could mean.

'I think you need to come see my new best mate…'

As the girls joined our side, Caleb opened his body out to reveal the rest of the busy pool area. Amongst the pool top beer pong, rows of girls and boys lined the side of the water, travellers of all shapes, sizes, age and colour could be seen. I looked at Caleb with bewilderment, only to see his enormous outstretched arm pointing at a group sat at the far side of the pool. Amongst a sea of unknown smiles, a tanned face locked eyes with me, his hand pulling off an effortless salute. Against all odds, beating the bookies, it was the one that got away in Koh Phi Phi all those months ago.

It was Ryan.

Chapter 45

Two for the price of one. Two birds with one stone. Buy one get one free. However you spun it, it was clear we had gotten a lot more than we bargained for stepping into the Mad Monkey Hostel that late August afternoon.

Not only had we finally met up with our friend from home, but had now been treated to an appearance from the nomadic Ryan, a guy we'd given up hope of bumping into long ago. The celebrations were comparable to those that took place in the garden of 23 Jester Street on the day of my jackpot win, wild eyed disbelief the face of the day, rushed and erratic plans overlapping with doey eyed nostalgia of times gone by.

It was difficult to introduce Olivia and Grace with the emphasis they deserved amidst the ungovernable madness that took place in the first few hours, each of them struggling to get a word in with a drunk Caleb, Ryan and a shell-shocked Matty Alex combo to contend with. It was only when we'd retired from the pool to the neighboring bar, sitting on a four person table with two chairs pushed into the corners, that we managed to regain some form of rationale to the conversation.

'So girls, I'm terribly sorry about our behaviour the last hour or so. I feel like we've been caught up in our own little world reminiscing. Alex mentioned you've just been to Koh Rong?' enquired Ryan, his Canadian accent as charming as I remembered.

'Oh don't be silly, you'd be surprised how much these two have blabbered on about meeting you in Phi Phi. I actually thought you were a figment of their imagination at one point, the mystical Ryan who taught them what travelling was all about.' Olivia put her arm around me as she spoke, which initially surprised me. I saw Matty raise his eyebrows across the table, before Caleb interjected.

'I bet these two were absolutely *buzzing* off you to be fair. All that "live for the moment" bullshit is right up their street!'

Cringing at the audacity of his words, I looked to Ryan to see his reaction. To my surprise, he was laughing harder than ever, nodding his head maniacally. 'Yeah they lapped it right up, putty in my hands.' He gave a cool wink to Matty before clearing his throat and raising his glass above the table. 'Anyway, enough of this talk. I just want to say, listen Caleb you're going to love this, my travels in Asia have consisted of six countries, four seas, eight islands, three flights and over a hundred beers and I couldn't be happier to be sitting here with you five people. Salut!'

We all pushed our glasses together in unison, from the petit arms of Grace all the way up to the overarching limbs of Caleb. Looking around the group as we each took a swig from our respective drinks, it appeared as though my worries of how the dynamic would work as a six were misplaced, a happy harmony seemingly settling over the evening.

'So, how did you two get chatting anyway? Did you realise straight away that Caleb knew Matty and Alex?' asked Grace, giggling at the face of Matty as he struggled to finish the end of his beer.

Caleb was quick to answer. 'I dunno how it even got brought up actually, we were chatting for ages today before we twigged. I think I mentioned Brown Shoes first actually and realistically how many people go by that name?'

'Yeah it was Brown Shoes that jogged the memory. I can't believe he had to go home, that crash sounds crazy!'

'It was mental mate, I thought our travels were over when he went down!' I said.

'Have you two still been riding motorbikes? I'm shitting it to try now I've spoken to Brown Shoes at home. He was saying you were all drunk driving and shit, fucking crazy bastards!'

'They didn't want to at first!' said Olivia, squeezing my arm under the table. 'It wasn't until Grace and I convinced them to get back on the horse that they changed their mind! Then Alex found this ridiculously cheap rental deal in Hue and got us these amazing motorbikes for the rest of the time in Vietnam! I still have no idea how you got them so cheap...'

I looked over at Caleb as he eyed me up suspiciously, shaking my head slightly to avoid a line of questioning that I didn't want to answer. With the need to change the subject, I posed another question to the group.

'What's the plan tonight then?'

'Huge night out obviously!' shouted Caleb.

'Hear hear!' quipped Matty.

'You won't hear any complaining from me!' said Ryan.

'Actually, Grace and I want to go to the Cambodian killing fields thing tomorrow morning. It sounds like something we shouldn't miss really. Plus all we've been doing recently is partying!' I felt her grip tighten on my arm.

'Yeah you should definitely go, it's crazy interesting!' said Ryan. 'I went the other day and would definitely recommend it.'

'Sack that,' said Matty, getting a big laugh out of Caleb. 'I've had enough Asian culture for the time being. It's Caleb's first night and we need to have a big one in celebration!'

'Definitely!' bellowed Caleb.

'Alex? Are you coming tomorrow or you going to go party with these lot?' asked Olivia, with the attention of the group now turning to me.

I paused, avoiding eye contact with everyone at the table. It was a strange dilemma I faced. On the one hand, I had been striving to prove to Olivia that I was a changed man, a man who turned down a party for the chance to soak up the culture and experience new things. Plus I was a history grad, this should've been my bread and butter. But on the other hand, it was Caleb's first night and I'd be admonished for not joining the boys on a boozy one.

'I… I did want to go to the killing fields at some point to be honest,' I said, stammering a little. 'We can go on that bar crawl tomorrow instead?' I looked up expectantly, to find looks of mild confusion across the faces of the boys.

'Yeah, we can go out both nights!' said Caleb triumphantly, his most well thought out plan to date.

'Alex c'mon mate?' said Matty.

I felt Olivia release my arm under the table, turning towards Grace to begin a separate chat. I guess in a moment of panic that she may have thought less of me, I strengthened my resolve.

'Na, I'll sit this one out. I'm gonna go with the girls and then we can catch up with you lot tomorrow.'

A few rolled eyes and taunts from the boys and I was eventually off the hook. We sat and talked, laughing and joking, putting the world to rights, before Grace, Olivia and I retired to the dorm rooms a few hours later, preparing for the early start the following day. I'd had a brilliant time catching up with Caleb and Ryan, leaving me in a buoyant mood about what was to come. But the mood didn't last for long.

As we finished brushing our teeth in the communal bathroom, I pulled Olivia to one side in the hall. 'Hey, sorry about all that earlier, you know what Matty's like, ey!'

She sighed, looking at me with repressed annoyance. 'I don't know what you're talking about Alex! If you wanted to go with the boys, you should've just gone!'

'What?' I asked incredulously. 'I thought you'd be happy I'm coming with you?'

'I am. It's just… I don't know. I just think you should do what you want to do. Oh forget it. Ignore me. I'm just knackered so let's talk in the morning.' She quickly kissed me on the cheek, before turning away and walking off.

Not for the first time and not for the last, I stood watching her go, confused and very much in love.

Chapter 46

Travel writing typically consists of an in-depth exploration of the do's and don'ts within a bustling city, an authentic village, an idyllic island or such like. It is advised to exclude personal mishaps where possible, keeping the narrative on track with interesting facts and accounts of the place, bringing to life the very things that make it so special, unlike anywhere else in the world.

In certain places it can be difficult to capture the true essence of what makes it so unique, a buzz that emanates around the streets of a city lives beyond the realms of the written word, a sensation that makes you feel something different, taking you along for the exclusive ride.

Of all the places I'd journeyed, in Asia and beyond, no such place construes this notion as romantically as Angkor Wat, the city of temples. I shouldn't have been surprised to be honest, it was one of the seven man made wonders of the world for crying out loud.

Before we delve too deeply into the awe inspiring details, the story of the morning we'd arrived proved to be a little easier to tell. Billed as the 'greatest sunrise you'll ever witness' by the Hideout hostel rep in Krong Siem Reap, our party of six had performed a minor miracle in rallying for the 4am wake up call. Managing to prise Caleb from his bed before lunchtime was a feat in itself, so the plaudits had to go to Grace for her patient persistence.

Siem Reap was a resort town within the north western province of Cambodia, not too dissimilar from many of the other places we'd visited in the country thus far. But the city was Angkor Wat mad, every shop you entered had fridge magnets, mugs and other miscellaneous items plastered with emblems, logos and photos of the famous ruins.

The short 15 minute journey to the ruins was like taking a trip in the world's slowest time machine, made clear by the flickering neon signs of Tiger beer that jutted out of every bar on the main strip gradually giving way to the stripped back local eateries at the edge of town. As we trundled on in our trusty taxi, the quaint buildings faded away into the darkness of dawn, replaced by wooden fences as the only stopgap between us and the dense jungle thicket. With five minutes left of the journey, innocuous rock formations grew larger and larger with each passing yawn from our collective, soon transitioning into formations of stone that boggled the eye. It was only when our taxi came to an abrupt skidding halt that each member of our group had their eyes truly opened.

'Caleb, I've finally found a door you won't have to duck under to go in!' I said, loud enough for the group to hear, pointing in the distance. An intimidating stone archway stood menacingly above everything around us, announcing itself to the pockets of gathered tourists as the entrance to the ruins.

Rubbing his eyes, he squinted up at the stone beast and let out a thunderous yawn. 'Pretty fuckin' big that innit.' As I said, beyond the realms of comprehension for some.

The sensory delights of the vast stone complex became more endulgent with every echoed step inside the ruins, dispelling any tiredness in our ranks. The network of rock formations spanned wider and further than the eye could see, suggesting our decision to take on the wonder without a tour guide was a little short-sighted itself. But guide or no guide, it didn't take twenty twenty vision to be drawn into the sight of the Angkor Wat, the prize temple and namesake of the Angkor park.

Slap bang in the middle of the Cambodian flag, the Angkor Wat temple's mighty three pronged presence was clear for everyone to see, providing a striking sight for even the most cynical of eyes. I had a testament to that by seeing Caleb's jaw physically drop the moment he laid eyes on the beauty.

The bizarre inescapable truth about the attraction was that every tourist in the park wanted an Instagram worthy shot of the sunrise over the temple. This meant that hundreds of people had squeezed into one section of grass in front of a nearby lake, each one taking up an amusing display of either prone, crouched or tiptoed positions. We attempted to infiltrate the floundering gaggle of photographers, feeling like a flash mob could break out at any moment, but gave up on a second time of trying. Instead, we opted for the more accessible hillside to settle for the moment of sunrise.

And when it came, it was beautiful. It wasn't beautiful in the obvious sense of the word, but more in a monumental, fascinating and privileged to see it kind of way. I'm ashamed to admit that when the sun rose to the optimum point behind the temple, as a thousand cameras clicked and captured the moment, the dazzling silhouette reminded me of my first night with Olivia in Ha Long Bay, bioluminescent light surrounding another wonder of the world. Pathetic I know.

As breathtaking moments tend to, the sunrise at Angkor Wat set the tone for the remainder of the day, each one of our party seemingly rejuvenated with a newfound sense of appreciation for the history and architectural intricacy of the site. By mid morning Matty was reciting the many achievements of the Khmer Empire from the back of a brochure he'd found in one of the ruins, speaking with vigour about the 162 hectares that the park covered and how he intended to explore it all.

But it wasn't until we travelled to the nearby Bayon Temple that I truly appreciated what a marvel we were blessed to have visited. The Bayon Temple was best known for the serene faces that have been carved into its towers, depicting some form of idols celebrated by the Buddhist monks who still walked amongst the grounds. We spent hours traversing the twists and turns, admiration overtaking amusement for a brief moment of our travels.

Matty and I had split off from the remainder of the group, lost in conversation about all the temples we'd missed out on in Thailand, whereby we happened across a cross legged man, dressed in crimson robes, hollering in an indistinguishable tongue. We stopped to admire the sight and before we knew it we had silently fallen into a daze, entranced by the repetitive routine of vowel sounds and glottal stops. After a while, I managed to avert my eyes from the unusual performance and noticed a small ceramic dish at the foot of his person, full to the brim with red string bracelets, next to a sign that stood independently nearby.

'$5 FOR YOUR FORTUNE' read the scrawled words, a proposition I found quite remarkable considering the man's appearance and gibberish song suggested English wouldn't be his first language. I decided to put my skepticism to one side and reached out to take a bracelet from the dish, dropping the $5 note into the now outstretched hand of the wouldbe monk.

The moment the note touched his weathered hand, the hypnotic chants came to an immediate halt and the man slowly creaked his face towards me, arching a bushy grey eyebrow above his wild unruly stare.

'Yes. *Yes*. I tell your fortune *very* easily. You seek something beyond what you already have. You will know it when you see it. It will know you when it sees you. If you want to be found, stop hiding!'

He barked the words with a degree of petulance in his voice, looking like a bad tempered child despite his haggard features. He looked away from me immediately and returned to his peculiar chant, this time with more melodramatic volume than before. Before I could react, Matty let out an audible, exaggerated snort.

'This guy is hilarious!'

'Yeah I didn't understand a word of that,' I said, turning back towards where we had left our friends.

'I understood it just fine. He's just politely mugged you of a fiver!'

Chapter 47

The most frustrating endings come when you least expect them. Or at least that's what I thought as the credits rolled down the screen after we'd sat through 'No Country for Old Men' in the hostel cinema room.

'Well that was fucking terrible!' said Caleb, loud enough for the group at the back of the room to cover their ears, scorned for their movie choice.

'Yeah, that ending was awful. Literally came out of nowhere!' said Ryan, hoisting himself out of the beanbag at the front of the room.

We'd agreed to stay in and watch a movie together following the early morning at Angkor Wat, but as with any commitment that turns out to be a let down, a bitter taste was left in the mouth after what started out as a brilliant day. We spoke amongst ourselves in a disgruntled manner for a good ten minutes before Olivia eventually sparked into life.

'Look you grumpy bastards, let's not let a stupid movie ruin our day! You've been talking for about half an hour and I've not heard one positive thing said! So I've come up with a plan to get you off your arses and back into better spirits! Understand?'

Like school children in detention, even the mighty Caleb was silenced. We each nodded our heads and kept quiet in fear of another scolding. Wow, she looked fit when she was angry.

'Okay, good! So here's the plan... Grace and I are going to go on *another* shop run and buy you boys a shit load of beers, cider for you Caleb obviously. You boys are going to go back to the dorms, get your swim shorts on and meet us at the pool in ten minutes. We're going to stop feeling sorry for ourselves, remember how amazing today was and have a big fat pool party!

Spread the word!' She eyed us up and down, before turning on the other groups of people gathered in the common area. 'That means you lot too! This is not optional!'

Without another word, I watched her and Grace stride off giggling like madmen towards the hostel rep behind reception. In a few animated movements it appeared as though they'd not only convinced him that the party was happening, but also employed him as party co-host. His laid back demeanor was replaced by that of a spider in shock as he frantically tried to do three jobs at once, spreading the word over the hostel tannoy, rummaging through the army of inflatables that resided behind the counter and adjusting his anime character hairdo in sync.

'Fucking hell boys, looks like we've been told,' I said, standing up from the table.

'Yeah, she's fucking scary when she wants to be. Good luck with that Alex mate!' said Caleb.

'Aw, she's harmless. I'm just happy she's getting us beers!' laughed Ryan, visibly struggling to drag Caleb up from the floor.

'You reckon tonight's the night then Alex? You two were getting awfully close again at Angkor Wat today!' Matty nudged me suggestively and the others laughed in turn.

'Fuck knows. It's been getting ridiculously heated between us recently so I'm hoping something happens soon, one way or another I'd rather just know where I stand I think.'

'As if, you've absolutely loved it regardless of nothing happening, you're about as smitten as can be!' he laughed, causing the other two to join in on the act.

'Yeah mate, from what I've seen you're happy enough being the side chick!' bellowed Caleb.

'You've gotta make a move bro! She's obviously into you, she's probably just waiting for you to initiate.' Ryan patted me on the back in reassurance but I remained silent. The boys didn't know about our 'kiss' in Koh Rong, and had no idea how I was feeling. But Ryan did have a point. Over a week had passed since Koh Rong and the vibe between us was more intense than ever. Maybe it was my opportunity to go for it one final time?

If grand gestures required grand stages to make them succeed, then that pool party was doing me a fucking massive favour. We'd been to a handful of pool parties thus far, but whatever the girls had said to that hostel rep had certainly worked. Seemingly every backpacker worth his salt had clicked attend on the night's invitation, revellers drawn in from hostels far and wide. Matty and Ryan had taken it upon themselves to DJ back to back, ignoring the countless queued playlists of psy trance remixes and opting for a tasteful, yet ambitious selection of dance floor ragers, prompting sing-a-longs and a perfect solution of nostalgia and shouted questions of 'what the fuck's this tune boys?'

Outside of the antics of the poolside party, Caleb and Grace had taken residence in the common area that lay parallel, instigating a drinking game so complex and all absorbing I won't begin to try and explain what was going on. All I knew is that they'd captured the attention of nearly every attractive person at the party, a man very much in his element at a laughing Grace's side, gambling seemingly the last thing on his mind.

And you guessed it. That left Olivia and I. How predictable. With more twists and turns than the mountainous roads of Pai, more ups and downs than the waves of Ha Long Bay, we carried on adding to our story across the entirety of the party, laughing, joking, cuddling, teasing, delving deeper and deeper into each other's defining chapters.

'You want to go upstairs?' she asked, pushing the midnight hair from off her face, splashing me with the illuminated water.

'Upstairs? Yeah of course.'

'Let's go to your room.'

We stepped out of the pool, dodging the dancing backpackers that dotted around the water's edge like the limestone cliffs of Koh Phi Phi. She took my hand and dragged me up the stairs of the hostel, leaving a trail of water from our dripping bodies. We arrived at the door to my private room and she patiently waited as I rummaged in my soaking wet pockets for the key, looking me up and down as I struggled.

'C'mon Alex, we haven't got all night…'

'Look who wants to start moving faster…'

'Fair point.' She laughed loudly, making it all the more difficult to concentrate. Was this finally going to happen?

I maneuvered the key out of my shorts and into the lock, turning it with emphatic, decisive intent. The door swung open and she skipped inside, leaving me to follow in her wake, pushing the door closed behind us, alone in our own little world, like so many places before it.

She stood in front of me, the dim light of the room enabling for a vivid picture of her beauty. Her dark hair sat effortlessly across her shoulders, droplets of water reluctant to fall from each strand. Her body was shivering a little, but stood confidently revealing her dainty bikini and impossible figure. I looked at her eyes, simultaneously telling me to come forward, yet stay back, luring me in and casting me out.

'Okay. Before I say anything, I just want to ask you something,' she said.

'Okay.' My heart began to beat like the resident band in Bong's Guesthouse, the introductory drum patterns before I was due to sing.

'Is there anything you want to tell me? Anything at all?'

I paused, unsure of myself. 'You know I'm not going to say it Liv, what's the point?'

'If you want to say something, you should say it. This is what I've wanted from you all along.'

'If I say it, you better say it back.'

'I always say how I feel, you know that.'

I took a deep breath, reaching to the bottom of my emotions before I spoke. 'Fine then. Liv, if you must know, I think I've fallen in love with you.'

She looked at me in silence for what felt longer than all the journey's I'd been on combined. I couldn't read what she was thinking, what she was going to say next was a complete mystery to me. All I could do was look into her gaslight blue eyes, raging fire within them.

She sighed a deep, endless sigh. 'I love you too Alex. That's why this is so sad.'

Confused hysteria took over my basic motor functions, catching my breath in what came out like a cough / burp cocktail. 'What? What's sad about that?!' I spluttered.

'I'm not talking to you about it now. But I wrote something in your travel journal that will explain it. I ripped the page out and hid it in one of the pockets of your rucksack until I wanted you to know. So here. Take it.'

She bent down next to my bed and unzipped the inconspicuous pocket on one of the straps of my bag, revealing a neatly folded piece of paper. She slowly walked over to me and placed it in my hand, before stepping back. The motion of handing me the small piece of paper was extraordinarily similar to being handed the scratchcard that got me here in the first place, sending my mind into overdrive.

'Don't read it now. Well you can do what you like, of course. But I'll ask you to wait until I've gone to read it. I don't want to be here when you do, it's too embarrassing.'

'What is it?' I asked, unable to articulate the storm of emotions that refused to subside.

'Just read it.' She hesitated for a second, before stepping back towards me and planting a long, lasting kiss on my cheek. She was freezing cold but the heat between us soon changed that, her face resting so close to my own. So close, yet somehow so far. She broke free of the kiss, sniffed and smiled softly, before walking past me, opening the door and slipping away.

I stood very still for a long time, the puddle of water that formed around me gradually started to stream across the white tiled floor, sliding down the nearby drain. I looked at the piece of paper in my hand, it's contents a mystery.

I wished for good news. She had told me that she loved me after all. She may well have been unable to muster the courage to tell me her true feelings in person, unable to act upon her feelings of love.

But I feared bad news. Whilst she had told me that she loved me, she had also indicated there was sorrow behind it. The contents of this page could well be the final dagger to the heart that ended whatever it was that we had nurtured between us.

A wish and a fear, perhaps a combination of the two. I wouldn't know until I read the words she had written, finally facing up to the possibility of either outcome head on, exercising avoidance no more. I had sworn to change and change I had. Gathering my thoughts, feelings and emotions, I unfurled the corners of the paper with cautious unknowing, each expanded crease revealing the true nature of the real story of Olivia and I.

Alex,

Where to begin?

In true Alex and Olivia fashion, we may as well take a trip down memory lane. It all started when I saw a boy across the hot springs of Pai who in truth looked like a bit of an oaf, showing off in front of his army of friends, blabbering on in a silly Manchester accent, giving me cheeky smiles across the water in the least subtle way possible. Little did I know back then that he'd follow me across country lines and all the way to the beaches of Ha Long Bay. What a stalker!

I was shocked when I saw him sulking in the sand and thought I better nip it in the bud before he chases me again, having no idea I'd just happened upon someone so unbelievably special. 'Just two friends, sharing a few laughs, having a few cuddles in the sea of Ha Long Bay' I'd said, but look how that's turned out...

Nevertheless, when Grace and Matty agreed to put up with us as travelling companions, I believed we could just be the best of friends, putting all feelings aside for the good of the group. That lasted all of ten minutes. Before I knew it, we were deeper than I ever intended, real feelings had taken over and I was conflicted of what to do next.

Then I found something out which changed everything.

Classic me being nosey, having to know absolutely everything. I don't know if you will remember but at the hostel bar in Hội An I was poking around in your travel journal (Matty & Alex's Adventure Journal - LOL!) browsing what you two had written about your travels thus far. I think I just wanted to get an insight into what was going on in your head if I'm honest, you're very difficult to read! But instead I found the story about your travels in Thailand, more importantly how you got to Thailand in the first place. Does a £20 million jackpot sound familiar?

I'm sure you had your reasons for not telling me. I respect that you wanted to keep something like that a secret. If anything, finding out helped me understand why you were so shifty whenever we mentioned money, or when paying for stuff. But you know better than anyone, honesty is my biggest thing. It's what I liked about you from the moment I met you. So I've been waiting, patiently, for you to open up about this part of your life, for no other reason than to prove I could trust you. I couldn't give myself to you fully whilst I knew you were keeping the secret from me, so no matter how hard it was to resist temptation, I made a promise to myself that I wouldn't let things go any further unless you trusted me with your secret. If you're reading this, it means you've decided against it.

I imagine you'll call me a hypocrite about being honest, acting the way I have whilst having a boyfriend. And you'd be correct. That's why after I have left you boys, I'm flying home to tell him everything. I think it will be the end of him and I, and maybe that's for the best. I don't know what will happen. It's broken me having to do this to him. And to you. I haven't been feeling very good about myself for a while.

But as horrible as it has been for both of us, keeping you at an arm's length all these months made me realise something, something I didn't pick up on straight away. I was holding you back. I saw the change in you, a change that I realised was on my behalf. I didn't like it Alex. Yes, I loved what you were doing for me, but I never wanted you to change. It made me realise that we were never meant to be. We would never work in the real world.

And that's why I'm leaving. If I've given you this letter, I've done everything I could to help you open up, to be honest to me and to yourself. But please don't be sad. Our story has been an amazing one, probably the love story of my life (WHAT A MELT).

So now you know, Manchester.

I did love you. I do love you.

Olivia

PS I guess the six inch rule didn't work out…

Part 5

Chapter 48

If there is no burden heavier than that of a secret, maybe you should just give up and spill the beans.

That's the kind of advice that is only blessed upon you by the gift of hindsight. A wonderful thing? You could've fooled me.

Although, it is sometimes difficult to see the true outcome of a decision without allowing a certain period of time to pass. Some call it a chain reaction. Others a domino effect. It has many names, all of which gave me a glimmer of hope that my story had not yet reached its end.

The first ripple of a stone thrown into water is rarely the last. I noticed this as I waited for the tram at Sale metrolink station, kicking out a rock and sending it scattering into a nearby puddle. The rain pelted down in unrelenting fashion, almost as though it had been waiting for me to arrive. The grey clouds, thick winter coats and grumpy faces meant only one thing. I was home.

A hero's welcome had to be put on hold, with no faces of adulation waiting for me at the arrivals lounge of terminal one. My brother's flat warming party was later that evening and my cunning plan was in place to steal the limelight, surprising my entire family with an unannounced arrival.

It was not without a heavy heart that I'd prized myself away from the shores of south east Asia, but a decision I deemed necessary with everything that had happened. After Olivia left, things just didn't make as much sense anymore. I had given it my best shot to forget her. But there's only so much soul searching you can do when beer, banter and bikinis are being forced down your neck by your excitable travelling companions.

The familiar electronic beep of the tram's imminent arrival echoed overhead as I hoisted my backpack over my shoulders and stepped out from under the shelter. I must have looked quite a sight to the pockets of huddled Mancunians, swim shorts, flip flops and a rain mac not a typical ensemble sported on the streets of Sale. But given the circumstances I didn't have much of a choice. I was already running a few hours late following my flight delay and I didn't exactly have the time or clothing for an outfit change.

The tram arrived. Late of course. As I stepped through the automatic doors I was hit with a feeling of nostalgia, a blanket smell of damp clothes, cigarette smoke and remnants of spilled lager greeted the senses as I drew the eye of a few sneering strangers. The days of grinning shopkeepers and jubilant waiters felt a long way away as I took my seat amongst the disgruntled onlookers that populated the busy front carriage.

I recited my speech in my head as the tram rattled past Dane Road and Stretford, two stations I'd spent time dawdling around as a child. I couldn't exactly tell my family I'd come home because I missed a girl, so I'd rehearsed a spiel about missing them instead, Steve's flat warming party being too convenient an opportunity to miss out on.

And while she wasn't the only reason I'd come home from my travels, I knew I'd be lying to myself to pretend it wasn't a pivotal factor in the decision. Once Olivia had left, Grace soon followed suit, continuing on solo as she had always intended. That left myself and the boys, the new family of four. I have to admit, I never thought I'd see the day that my mantra for life would pass its expiration date, but there's only so much beer, sun and chatting shit a guy can take.

I sighed as I looked out of the window, the drops of rain running across the surface of the glass at a million miles per hour. In the reflection, I saw a group of three teenage guys sitting across from me, gathered around one of their phones, roaring with laughter at whatever video was playing. I smiled, imagining Ryan,

Caleb and Matty carrying on where I had left off, each one of them still immersed in their own tale, living their own stories. It was a welcome thought.

The robotic voice of the overhead announcement called out that we'd soon be arriving at Castlefield station. The city side suburb of Manchester was the place my brother had bought his new 'bachelor pad' as he so eloquently described it. I stood up, shaking the remnants of rainwater that had gathered on the hood of my coat, before making my way to the door. I felt a mix of nerves and excitement building inside of me, having not seen my family in over five months. I could've done with a lucky Chang.

As I stepped out into the rain, pulling my coat up high against my chin, an irrational thought crept over me, an icy drip running down my spine. What if she was here? After all, it was chance that led to each one of our previous encounters. What if the dice had rolled again, leaving Olivia standing at this very tram stop, waiting to head into town? It was hardly inconceivable that she could be, being that it was her hometown as well. I looked around erratically as I padded forward, my flip flops adding extra meaning to their name as the onomatopoeic sounds drew even more attention to me.

The sad fact is I had barely heard from her since she'd returned home. I was in the dark as to where she was, what she was doing, who she was doing it with. The last communication we'd had was a brief conversation over text whereby she'd implored me to 'stop worrying' and made me promise to 'have fun.' Relatively easy requests to adhere to on the surface, but in practise not so much. After a month of partying in Bali, I'd done the exact opposite. I'd packed my travelling in.

The icy wind had no intention of letting the rain have all the fun as it whipped around the tram station, sending bits of newspaper, crisp packets and discarded tickets flying in every conceivable direction. Battling my own demons as well as the elements proved quite the task as I struggled to keep my eyes on the pavement in front of me, not wanting to risk catching the eye of friend or foe. I pulled my phone from out of the inside pocket of my coat, hoisting the zipped walls over my head to cover it from the rain.

Unlimited 3G coverage was a friend I'd sorely missed. A few swipes of the thumb and my route was determined, a short five minute walk to my brother's new address. I hurried down the station steps, avoiding people's umbrellas in a bizarre zig zag fashion, making sure to keep my head down. I don't really know why I was so scared to see her, but now didn't feel like the time or the place. The more I thought about it, I didn't know when it would be the time or place again.

My maps directed me to an imposing building just off the main road leading into town, the industrial brickwork of Manchester's architecture leaving nothing to the imagination. A subtle entrance almost evaded my eyes, its sleek glass doorway providing a stark contrast to the rugged archway that it sat beneath. A dim light blessed the keypad as I punched in my brother's flat number, my heart pounding.

BEEP BEEP BEEP BEEP

The door clicked open without a word on the intercom as I quickly took refuge from the October night. The interior of the building was neat and modern, tiled floors, matte wallpaper, an understated light offering a swanky ambience to the lobby.

I darted towards the lift as I saw the door starting to slide shut, catching it just before it closed. I briefly caught sight of myself in the mirror as I pushed the button for the penthouse. I had to admit, I looked pretty ridiculous. A navy blue raincoat zipped up to my nose covered up my shivering, yet immensely tanned face. My hair had sprung out in dripping ringlets that had wormed their way out of my bun. My shorts were creating a puddle where I stood. I laughed out loud as I looked in the mirror, wondering what a sight I'd be for my unsuspecting family. It felt good to laugh. To be excited.

271

I reached the top floor and stepped out into the hall, a solitary doorway meeting my gaze. Number 1224. My brother's apartment. The sound of DB Boulevard's Point of View, one of my mum's favourite songs, thumped from behind the door.

I checked the handle. It was unlocked. I pushed open the door, drew in a deep breath and walked in.

'Surprise!'

Chapter 49

What a night.

You can take the man out of Manchester but never Manchester out of the man, or however the saying goes.

Whether it was the wild eruption of noise as I first entered the foray, or the irish jig of my Grandma as she celebrated with a fifth glass of prosecco, Steve's flat warming party was a night I'd not soon forget. My mum, dad and brother's faces were a sight to behold as I'd splashed into the party, making me regret not filming the moment for future ammunition and the inevitable haul of Facebook likes.

My dad was first to snap back to reality, shaking off the shock from his face and replacing it with a look of feigned amusement, clearly pretending that he'd known all along. Like father, like son I'd say. Steve was next, breaking into booming laughter and immediately charging through his gathered guests for a guillotine-like embrace. But it was my mum who inevitably took the cake, mustering up her bravest and most supportive smile, before promptly passing out.

Typically, the night had gone past in the blink of a teary eye and I was left with just the memories and a headache in my party bag when I woke up the next morning. As I scrambled for my phone within the confines of the giant sofa bed in my brother's apartment, I noticed that it wasn't the morning at all. I squinted at the oversized clock that loomed over the electric fireplace, the time reading 4pm.

Where was everyone? The lounge was a lot bigger than I remembered without drunken family members resting their arses on every surface, with only the half finished bottles of liquor remaining. Like a beach clean up crew, I scanned my surroundings with a turned up nose, eventually spotting my phone

273

lodged underneath a novelty vinyl player that I'm confident nobody knew how to use.

The transition from horizontal to vertical confirmed my worst fears, the hangovers were back with a bang. I groaned as I padded over the footprint covered laminate floor, reaching over to grab my phone. Expecting a message of explanation as to where my brother was, I was shocked to see a barrage of notifications that proved too many to count. It didn't take much scrolling to get to the bottom of the mystery, discovering that I had drunkenly posted a story or seven on my Instagram profile, showcasing a wild homecoming charade.

'You're home?!' said one perplexed onlooker, the simplest of my inquisitions.

'When did you get back you prick?!' lambasted Turner, followed by three angry faces.

Countless messages from bewildered friends tumbled down my phone screen, each one quizzing me as to why I had kept my return under wraps. But it was one message that caught the eye more than its counterparts, a diamond in the rough. Three guesses who that was from…

'Alex! I can't believe you didn't tell me you were coming home?! What happened to Bali? Is Matty home too? Your family looked so happy in those stories, I bet your mum is super excited you're finally back! Do you want to get a drink this weekend? We probably should catch up, I already have a million things to tell ya! Let me know xxx'

Being the master of reading into things too much, I allowed a smile to craftily creep across my dehydrated mouth, the cogs of opportunity beginning to spin against my will. The use of my first name on a message? Very intimate. The reference to my mum? Intentionally personal. *Three* kisses? It was on.

I slumped back down onto the commodious couch and summoned up the highest form of social cognition I could muster in preparation for a reply. It had to maintain the perfect balance between keen and disinterested, excited yet breezy, a "take it or leave it" work of art.

'Hi Liv, I completely forgot to message you, soz! Yeah a drink sounds good, providing you've sacked off that douche of a boyfriend and are ready to start the rest of our lives together?'

I hungrily looked at the send icon, forecasting the look on her face when she saw such an outrageously forward message. Probably a look of complete disgust. I watched the words disappear on my phone as I backspaced, the possibilities that the message would bring evaporating just as quickly. Time for round two.

'Yeah sure, you free later?' Nailed it.

Like all good plans, the details fell into place like the pieces of a jigsaw, which coincidentally was the name of the bar we had decided to meet at 7pm. I'd intentionally chosen it as part of a twofold ploy, showing off my knowledge of Manchester's bar scene as well as being conveniently located within a five minute walk so as to avoid walking in looking like a victim of Songkran.

The next couple of hours could be likened to backstage at an Oasis reunion gig in Heaton Park, sprinting around my brothers flat in hurricane-like fashion, trying on every piece of clothing I could get my hands on from his walk-in wardrobe, most of which seemed unworn. He'd certainly taken to wealth like a duck to water.

I finally settled on an ensemble that I believed was built for success. A crisp beige Ralph Lauren shirt that fit nicely, overlapping some skinny Levi jeans that felt alien on my shorts-accustomed legs. What was even more bizarre was the feeling when strapping on a heavy pair of Dr. Martens, weighing down my every step. To complete the look, I slung a quilted jacket

275

around my shoulders, that particular brand too expensive to even recognise.

Thankfully, my brother had left a scrawled note on the mantelpiece that indicated he had gone out to meet some friends, with some basic instructions of how to lock up. Looking back at the state of his room following my one man fashion show, I couldn't imagine he'd be too trusting again in the near future. But there was bigger fish to fry than concerning myself with any other menial tasks that I probably should've been doing that day.

It was time for the reunion.

Chapter 50

It was 7.38pm by the time I arrived at Jigsaw.

The seemingly elementary instructions of how to lock the apartment door were left redundant the moment I stepped outside, facing up to a three-tiered mechanism that would surely baffle even the most accomplished engineers.

It took three missed calls, two angry texts and a voice note of expletives before I eventually got hold of my brother who spilled the beans on how to *actually* lock up. But this episode of senselessness had cost me dear, my second attempt at a first impression ruined by tardiness, the one trait I usually championed the most.

But all that repressed frustration melted away the moment I pushed through the steel framed glass doors to see Olivia Cohen sitting in a two person booth at the far side of the bar. Apt didn't even cover it.

Accustomed to seeing her in a lot less clothes on the beaches of south east Asia, I can't say I was shocked to see that she pulled off winter attire in a similarly effortless fashion, a black skin tight jumper shaped around her shoulders like it didn't want to let go. She looked up from her phone and caught my eye on a double take, her face curling into a repressed smile, a smile I hadn't seen in over a month.

As I approached across the dimly lit room, the lyrics to the infamous "Bigmouth Strikes Again" by The Smiths served their purpose as I fell under their spell.

'What time do you call this?' I asked, peering down at an imaginary watch on my wrist and tapping it.

'Alex, you're half an hour late! I was about to clear off!' she exclaimed, furrowing her eyebrows into an expression I knew well, the old fake annoyed trick.

I swung into the booth in what I hoped would translate into a cool manoeuvre, only to knock the table and spill a little of the beer she had ordered for me. 'I'm sorry, I'm sorry, long story but my brother's flat wouldn't lock so I had to wait until…'

'Save it, Manchester!' she interrupted. 'That beer has been sitting there for half an hour so I hope you enjoy a flat pint.'

I laughed as I caught her eye, causing her to break the subterfuge and reveal her dazzling smile underneath some ruby red lipstick. I struggled to think of a time I'd seen her with a full face of make-up, studying the intricacies of her face like an explorer plotting his route on a map of unchartered territory.

'Are you just going to stare at me?'

'Sorry!' I laughed. 'It feels like it has been a million years since I've seen you so I'm just checking you still look the same. You do look stunning, Liv…'

Her smile faltered slightly as she received the compliment, but only momentarily as she grinned back at me. 'You don't look so bad yourself Alex, what is that you're wearing? It looks like Gucci has thrown up on you!'

'Ah well, the cat is out of the bag now! I may as well lean into the wealthy wave, ey?' I watched her closely as she broke eye contact for a second time, seemingly a little uncomfortable with the joke.

'I guess you may as well, yeah!' she managed, pushing a dark strand of hair behind her ear and scanning around the bar. 'What is this place anyway? One of the edgy Manc bars that you bring all the girls?'

I pulled a face of disbelief. 'Me? Never... I've been back for about 24 hours so give me a chance Liv!'

'I bet you'll be quite the ladies man now you're back home, all those adventures and life experiences that I dragged you along to. You're going to be quite the catch!'

It was my turn to stifle a wince, looking at her with a quizzical expression. 'Do you reckon yeah? If I'm being perfectly honest that is the last thing on my mind...'

A silence hung in the air as we shared a look across the checkerboard table, the candlelight wavering between us, an invisible barrier that had suddenly appeared. Without warning, the moment was cut off by the abrupt arrival of a roughly shaven waiter, wielding a torn notepad and trusty biro like a sword and shield.

'Any drinks guys or you good?' His voice was unmistakably Mancunian, the northern twang taking hold of every word.

Olivia was first to react, offering up a sweet smile before she ordered a single vodka and coke.

'I'll take a double gin and tonic when you're ready mate, cheers.' We both sat silently as he wrote down our orders slowly, eying up Olivia over the end of his notepad with zero subtlety. Once he had left, I formulated a joke in an attempt to lighten the mood but it was Olivia who spoke first.

'Look Alex, I just want to say, it is amazing to see you. But I really can't understand something. Why have you come home? When I left you guys, you were about to head off to Indonesia and barely a month later you're back on your own! What happened?'

I tried to hide the bafflement from my face, probably to no avail. Did she really have to ask me that? The last time I had properly spoken to her we had confessed that we had fallen in love and then she had upped and left without so much as a proper goodbye.

I forced an unconvincing laugh. 'Well, I thought you would have pieced together yourself to be honest...' When she didn't respond I pressed on. 'But in the interest of complete honesty, I came back because it just wasn't the same without you.'

She looked at me with a growing intensity developing between us. I had expected at least half an hour to pass and preferably six or seven drinks before we got to this kind of talk. She broke the silence with a heavy sigh, gripping the edge of the table tightly before she spoke.

'Alex!' she said sharply, the fake annoyance having made way for the real deal.

'What?' I asked incredulously. 'What did you expect me to say? Last time we spoke we admitted we loved each other and you expected me to just carry on as if nothing had happened?'

'We were travelling, Alex! It was a different world!'

'What? So you didn't mean it?'

She rolled her eyes, clearly unhappy with the direction of the conversation. 'Look Alex, shall we not do this now?'

I had spent over a month thinking about how this conversation would go, what I would do and say, none of which was going to plan of course. I needed to hear her side of the story and find out what had been running through her mind in the time we had spent apart. But perhaps pushing it wasn't the best avenue to success.

I took a deep breath and forced my face into a smile. 'Agreed, I've literally just got here, we can talk about all that stuff later. Tell me what you've been up to!'

As she began to speak, the waiter came swooping in to deliver our drinks, clattering mine to the table as he delicately placed Olivia's on a folded over piece of tissue. 'Here you go, love.'

I felt a pang of jealousy attempt a hostile takeover of my mind, but I quickly dispelled it as she flashed a look at me, probably wondering why hot steam was blowing out of my ears. The waiter lingered for another elongated moment before turning away, grumbling his way back to the bar.

'Cheers anyway!' said Olivia, holding her drink up in front of her. 'Like I said, it's amazing to see you. Who would've thought it, me and you back in Manchester?'

I clinked her glass and offered a warm smile. 'Just two friends, having a few laughs and cuddles in their hometown, ey?'

'Exactly, our journey has finally come full circle!'

I took a sizeable gulp of my drink, the bitter taste taking residence in the far corners of my mouth. Swallowing hard, I planned out my next line of enquiry. The strategy wasn't exactly complicated, a guy sitting across from a girl, trying to win her over.

And that's what I did. With every amusing story told I managed to ease the tension. With every memory shared, she softened in disposition and settled into the night. A smile, a nudge, a wink and a flirt and before I knew it we were back where we had started, riding the waves of laughter, back and forth, to and fro, an endless tide.

I have to admit, my sole prerogative did become blurred as time passed in the evening, the need to find out her feelings obscured by the gratification I felt just to see her, to spend time with the girl I had missed. It felt good to revisit our shared memories, to discuss the amazing Grace and her next steps of a solo adventure, how many girls Matty had wooed in Bali, how much we missed our travelling quartet. But as last call was announced by the clang of a brass bell, the pressure of questions unanswered began to mount once more.

'I feel like we've been reminiscing all night and haven't even covered what your plan is now...' I began, fighting off the gin's hold of my articulation. I waited a second for her to reply, before hitting a long ball and going route one. 'Oh yeah I forgot to ask as well, what happened with you and your boyfriend when you told him about us?'

I braced myself as she processed the question, expecting her to freeze up, sigh or even storm off. But instead, she looked up at me from the remnants of her drink, swilling it around slowly in the glass. A sad smile rested across her face, a solemn look in her eye.

'We broke up Alex,' she said softly.

To be honest, I have no idea what look flashed across my face but whatever composition it made up, caused an instant howl of laughter from Olivia.

'Try not to look too upset!' she managed, feigning a look of annoyance again.

But I could barely hear her over the booming melody of Hall and Oates 1980's classic "You Make My Dreams Come True" playing on full volume inside my head. She was single. I was single. If I still maintained the ability to do simple arithmetic, there was only one outcome, providing I played my cards right.

'I am really sorry Liv, that must have been really hard,' I said, wondering how quickly I could change the topic.

'It was actually. But it was the right decision so I'm actually okay about it now.'

'I'm glad.'

A long pause hung between us as we looked across into each other's eyes.

'Sooo...'

'So indeed! I mean, I guess the million dollar question is... Where does that leave *us*?'

Looking back, I probably should've worded that a little better, given everything that had happened. But that's exactly what it was, a question that had been brought about by a millionaire's fortune being bestowed upon a 21 year old post grad with not a penny to his name. Everything that had happened had been a product of implausible odds, triggering one improbable outcome to the next, a journey mapped out across multiple countries, twists and turns at every junction, resulting in a simple question from a boy to a girl. Where does that leave us?

'I think I know where you think it leaves us!' she said, raising her eyebrows in a suggestive fashion. 'But really, Alex? Have you not figured it out yourself yet?'

'Figured out what?'

She grabbed my hand across the table and squeezed it as hard as she could. 'That we're so much better suited as *friends*! Think about it! Every happy memory we have talked about tonight was spent together as friends, in the sea in Ha Long Bay, in Dalat stood in the rain, even Koh Rong until that stupid kiss it was perfect! Sure, I fancy the pants off you and we flirted nonstop but at the very core of it, we are simply just amazing, amazing friends.'

She paused, taking a breath and watched me as I processed her words. Casting my mind back I scanned over the overlapping and vivid memories that I had of my time with Olivia, each one slowly taking shape in the way that she described, a new perspective warping the patchwork of my experiences. Against the tide of my desires, all of the fondest memories from my travelling experience had happened in the exact way that she described, by the side of a friend.

'Look, Alex. I do love you. And for a time I thought I would go against my better judgement and try and make a go of something more. But the more I went over it in my head, the more I began to realise that we were always at our best when Matty and Grace were with us. It was the dynamic we had as a four that felt the most natural, like it fit into place or something... Anyway, trust me when I say, there is someone out there who is much better suited to you than I am. Someone who can keep up with your crazy party boy antics. Someone who doesn't drag you out of bed at 6am for a hike. Someone who doesn't have any doubt that you're the man for them. And I think we both know that girl isn't me...'

"An epiphany (from the ancient Greek ἐπιφάνεια, epiphaneia, "manifestation, striking appearance") is an experience of sudden and striking realisation. A comprehension or perception of reality by means of a sudden intuitive realisation."

When was the next flight back to Bali?

Chapter 51

I met her on the 3rd February 2016.

Or should I say I re-met her. I looked upon her face with fresh eyes, eyes that had seen foreign lands, eyes that had gained wisdom amongst the shores of different cultures, eyes that had come to terms with the ways of the world.

'Why are you staring at me like that, you weirdo?' she asked, taking a sip from the preposterously large gin and tonic that she held almost protectively, a mother bear and her cub.

It was my chance to impress her, to use all my learnings to charm the girl who got away. Back then, I wielded naivety and simple mindedness as my weapons of choice. Now I had a vast array of tools to choose from, strings to my bow she would never expect. I could offer her things that her colleagues wouldn't be able to learn in the mere pages of a book, or at her snooty lectures, the undisputed wealth of life experience.

'You used to like it when I stared at you like that!' I said, assuming my deepest and most exotic intonation of voice, making sure to be loud enough to drown out the dull murmur of the surrounding crowd, but not so loud that I drew the attention of one the many circling hordes of thirsty bachelors at the House Bar in Altrincham, South Manchester. It was a delicate balance.

Her devilish blue eyes narrowed, but the whisper of a smile was all I needed to press on with my play for her affection. I'd been speaking to her for about five minutes, yet I'd not felt this alive for months. There was something about the look in her eye, the look of possibility, that at any minute she could do the unexpected, throw herself at me or throw a drink over me, both an equal chance, 50/50. After what had happened to me over the past year, I liked those odds.

'In Asia, I learned a little saying about forgiveness. Do you want to hear it?' I asked, tactfully tucking a strand of hair behind my ear and back into its now familiar bun.

Now, I'd seen her eyes roll before. Countless times. But somehow, her pair of celestial gems had perfected the manoeuvre to nonsensical levels. With the ingenuity of the inventors of the wheel, it was like watching it spin for the very first time. She manipulated the dismissing facial composition of the most heralded portraits in the art world with effortless charm. Her eyes wielded the 'suck you in and spit you back out' dynamics of a hole on the world's hardest mini golf course. Mesmerising didn't begin to cover it.

'No, I don't think I would like to hear it, thanks Alex! You know, you don't need to worry about forgiveness, it was a long time ago. I'm sure you'll find this difficult to believe but I have just about gotten over it.' Her voice was poetry to my ears, the sarcasm in her words a sweet poison I could not get enough of.

'That's sad to hear, I held quiet hopes that you might still be into me after all this time!'

'You always were a dreamer. At least you've sorted out your hair, I saw a few pictures on your Instagram that had me seriously worried for a second.'

'Oh, I didn't realise you'd been stalking my Instagram! I would've made more of an effort to look good if I'd known I had you as my audience...'

Then she laughed. I hadn't heard her laugh for what felt like an age. It was like a sink unblocker for the soul. When she laughed, it didn't matter if anyone else was laughing. When she giggled, it made me feel like we were the only two people in the world. A snigger, a chuckle or a howl, it didn't matter to me, as long as she would continue to bless me with the sweet sound of that laughter.

'I forgot how cute your laugh is,' I said, sheepishly.

'Shut up, you cringe. Now are we going to get another drink or not? I've been standing here for five minutes and you've not even tried to get me drunk yet. What kind of seduction technique is this?' She flashed a smile with her brilliant white teeth, her lips juicier than a ripe papaya fruit in the islands of Thailand. And she even spoke my language. Drink first, ask questions later. Who would've thought it?

We made our way to the bar, dissecting the pockets of drunken Mancunians that lined the busy outdoor area. I was at my vigilant best, carefully manipulating her slim frame past the wandering eyes of the northern chancers that would do anything to be in my position, the best girl in the bar on my arm.

As we pushed through the crowd, I caught eyes with Matty who had peeled off from the group I had arrived with. Still flexing his Indonesian tan, his crafty grin struck a stark contrast as he formed an 'okay' symbol with his non-drink wielding hand. I watched as he tapped the shoulder of an already giggling Grace, indicating over at me across the bar and whispering something in her ear. The giggle soon transformed into a howl as she fought against herself to come and say hello to the girl on my arm. I think the look on my face did the trick as she graciously accepted defeat, her beaming smile brighter than any of the spotlights in the bar.

But there was one smile that I hadn't accounted for. A wordless whisper of a smile that spoke a thousand words but none at all. It had a "told you so" rhetoric, yet held sincerity and encouragement in equal measure, willing me on with a symbolic seal of approval. Behind the smile stood Olivia, making up my beloved travelling quartet, enjoying our second reunion in as many weeks. I grinned back, accepting that this was a significant moment for myself and for the group, finally free of the self imposed shackles that held back a true harmony existing between us.

Turning back to the task at hand, we finally arrived at the bar, pressing up against each other at the far end of the counter. I wondered how I'd been so short sighted in times gone past, how I'd allowed such a girl to slip out of my grasp. I always imagined I'd end up with some foreign backpacker after I'd headed away on my travels, someone who epitomized everything I was trying to be, a free spirit consumed by wanderlust, someone who made me want to strive to be a different person, opening my eyes to things I'd never experienced.

But there was something about her I could never put my finger on. Something felt more right about her than any of the girls I'd met who fit the bill. It was so easy with her, not in the avoidance of great effort kind of way, but through the flow of rewarding conversation, our unique dynamic, the way her eyes met mine in a look of intrigue and caution in equal measure, a perfect balance that made every word, every glance so exciting.

How inconceivable that the thing I'd been looking for was right in front of me this entire time. The unlimited possibilities that were bestowed upon me at the hands of my jackpot had given me the platform to travel to the ends of the earth to find, or rather to chase happiness, yet right now staring at this girl at a bar I'd been to a hundred times, I felt closer to it than I had on any of the foreign soils I had crossed.

'Oi mate, I said what can I get ya?'

I shook my head, dismissing the wild drunken daydreams as a little more than a fool's hope and ordered two large gin and tonics with no further motive than to share a drink with the girl smiling up at me. My ex girlfriend, my namesake. Alex Perry.

Whatever would come of it, would come of it, I assured myself as we headed back out into the night. The buzz and energy of the smoking area had been taken up a notch since we journeyed inside, with little to no room available to chat. I scanned the crowds of smoking Sally's and footy chat, peeling my eyes in hope rather than expectation. It was times like these where Caleb would come in handy, towering above all others, but I doubted I'd be seeing him anytime soon considering he was still travelling with Ryan. Funny how things work out. Low and behold, a solitary two person table materialized at the very far reaches of the veranda.

We took a seat opposite one another, sharing a look of promise as we pushed our glasses together in cheers of this happy coincidence, a serendipitous meeting, our chance encounter in the streets of south Manchester. As we toasted the night ahead, I noticed the thin red bracelet that was loosely wrapped around my left wrist, triggering a flashback to the strange man in the Bayon Temple at Angkor Watt, his words tapping a finger on the glass of my mind:

'Yes. *Yes.* I tell your fortune *very* easily. You seek something beyond what you already have. You will know it when you see it. It will know you when it sees you. If you want to be found, stop hiding my friend!'

I couldn't help but laugh. A lunatics ramblings might just have been smart words after all. Perhaps, just perhaps the best $5 I'd spent since winning my fortune.

It was time to stop hiding in the hope of becoming something I wasn't, trying to pretend to be anything but myself. And maybe I did know it when I saw it, gazing across the table from me, more beautiful, more mysterious, more intriguing than anything I had seen on my travels. Maybe this was in fact my true ace in the pocket, an ace I'd forgotten I'd hidden up my sleeve.

'So, what are we saying about going on a date then? I think I need to prove to you that I deserve a second chance!' I smiled at her with a cheeky and assuring grin, conveying that I had come full circle and was ready to start being the right man for her.

She smiled back, matching me with a look of untold possibility. She paused briefly before she spoke those oh so predictable words.

'Actually, I have a new boyfriend, Alex.'

Chapter 52

'Do I think the money changed you?' asked Alex, swilling the remnants of her fourth sangria around the bottom of a tall glass.

'Yeah exactly. Do you really think I've changed much since we first went out? Do you think I've become arrogant or anything?' I asked, somewhat fishing for a compliment.

She pulled a face that I'd become somewhat accustomed to over the past year we'd been dating, a face that was designed for a sole purpose, to stop me chatting shit. 'Alex, you've always been a cocky bastard. Money or not, I don't think anything will ever change that…'

I stifled a laugh as I lay back on the cushioned daybed, stretching out in starfish fashion, willing my limbs into submission. Whether it was the midday blaze getting to my head or the liquid bounty of the all inclusive hotel wetting the proverbial whistle, I struggled to think of a time I'd felt more relaxed than in that moment.

Alex and I were five days into a no expense spared trip to Marrakech, an adventure we'd planned to commemorate our six month anniversary since going "Facebook official" or whatever you want to call it. I would say it had been a whirlwind romance but I think the seven year sabbatical between our first attempt at a relationship and my gradual step by step quest to win her back probably skewed the narrative.

'I'm being serious though…' I said, playfully pinching her under the ribs, breaking our touch barrier for the millionth time. 'My travelling lot and I were having this debate in town the other day. Liv was saying she'd been surprised that I hadn't bought a place of my own or any fancy cars since being home from travelling, and Matty said I was even more of a stinge now than before, the joker…'

'He's got that right. You could've bankrolled our own private island but we have to settle for this five star Moroccan dump instead. I'm with Matty.'

'Yep, suppose he does have a point. I really need to learn to push the boat out. Is that necklace a bit too heavy as well? I could always take it back?'

'I bought this myself!' she exclaimed, sitting bolt upright in indignation, knitting her eyebrow into a disapproving, yet adorable look.

I burst out laughing and threw my arm around her, pulling her close. 'Oh, now I have your attention do I?'

'Cheeky shit!' she said, failing to hold back her beautiful smile.

Much of the past year had been spent in similar fashion to this, embroiled in a "can't kid a kidder" kidding contest across all corners of the globe, although mostly confined to the familiar streets of our little slice of perpetually drizzling paradise, Manchester.

Alex yawned dramatically as she rested her head upon my shoulder sleepily. 'Okay, do you want my honest opinion as to whether you've changed or the version that will stroke your ego?'

'Why don't we try both?'

'Okay, let's start with the alternate reality version and we can go from there. I'll let you decide which answer you'd like to see as the truth, deal?'

I smiled down at her and squeezed her against me, dumbfounded at my luck once more. 'Deal.'

'Okay, but don't get too giddy because you're about to get a very rare compliment from me.'

The steady breeze that had blessed us all afternoon with it's welcome touch seemed to drop slightly as I felt a prickle of heat from the unfiltered sun dance across my face. I shielded my eyes and looked down at Alex who was grinning expectantly.

'Wow, I've not even started yet and you're already blushing. I love it.'

'Get on with it then!' I challenged, kissing her forehead lightly.

'Fine. To answer your question, I don't think many people have had the *pleasure* of knowing you in such clearly defined stints of "before" and "after" as I have so I believe I'm pretty well placed to tell you that I don't think the money has really had much of a bearing on you at all. I honestly believe that we would have ended up right where we are now with or without the money because your ridiculous attitude to life is where your luck really comes from. I think you still would've gone travelling, still would have made amazing friends like Olivia and Grace and *still* would have somehow found your way to end up by my side, exactly where you belong. It just might have taken you a bit longer to get there, that's all. So no, the money hasn't really changed much in my opinion.'

Her words looped around my mind in intrinsic patterns, triggering internal questions of whether such an outlying, tangible event like hitting the jackpot on a scratchcard had actually changed the course of my life or if Alex may actually have a point. I wondered whether my story would have been any different had the money never have come into my possession and I had trod a more orthodox path, saving up for travelling in a dead end job, hitting hostel after hostel, friendships coming and going as quickly as the passing of a breeze.

My tale of adventure, friendship, love and fortune was certainly not defined by the wealth I had gained but merely ran alongside it, posing the question whether it was directly relevant to anything that had happened, aside from the odd swanky hotel and obscure motorcycle purchase.

It had even been made clear to me that the real reason Olivia and I didn't work out had nothing to do with the concealed truth of my wealth, but the simple fact that we were never meant to be. So perhaps, it was just my attitude all along, a will for things to work out in the way they're supposed to, never wishing for anything more, never fearing anything less.

'Oi dozy, do you want to hear the honest version now?' asked Alex, nudging me back into focus.

'Sure,' I said, closing my eyes and taking a deep, lasting breath.

'Good. So in reality, the money has definitely changed you. Not a chance I would've taken you back without all the cash that comes as part of the deal. Shall I tell you what would've been a good idea?'

I let a wide and honest grin take over my face as I held her tight under my arm, feeling the jitter of her laugh shudder through our bodies. I looked at her face, trying to figure out what punchline she was going to opt for, studying each feature of her face like the wax covered coating of a scratch card, none of them revealing their secrets. 'Go on, tell me Alex.'

'You should have kept your money a secret until you won me back of your own accord, because I hear that's *always* worked out well for you in the past...'

I couldn't help but let a laugh escape my mouth as she rolled closer into my arms, her beauty smiling back at me like the unclouded treasure of a multi-million-pound jackpot.

Printed in Great Britain
by Amazon